THE
APOLOGY BOX
by
NAOMI ULSTED

THE
APOLOGY
BOX

by
NAOMI ULSTED

Published by Idle Time Press
USA/EUROPE
2021

IDLE TIME
— P R E S S —

Cover design by Ardi Wahyudi

Library of Congress Control Number: 2021914100

Publisher's Cataloging-In-Publication Data
Names: Ulsted, Naomi Kristine, author.
Title: The apology box / by Naomi Ulsted.
Description: Bellaire, Texas, USA : Idle Time Press, 2021. | Interest age level: 013 and up. | Summary: "When sixteen-year-old Tessa's small mountain community is ravaged by a forest fire, people come together to heal. Except Tessa, because she set the blaze ... An unlikely friendship, a painful discovery and a box full of letters may be the only chance Tessa has at redemption"-- Provided by publisher.
Identifiers: **ISBN 9781737262992** (paperback) | **ISBN 9781737262985** (ebook)
Subjects: LCSH: Teenage girls--Juvenile fiction. | Arson--Juvenile fiction. | City and town life--Juvenile fiction. | Letters--Juvenile fiction. | Shame--Juvenile fiction. | CYAC: Teenage girls--Fiction. | Arson--Fiction. | City and town life--Fiction. | Letters--Fiction. | Guilt--Fiction.
Classification: LCC PZ7.1.U33 Ap 2021 (print) | LCC PZ7.1.U33 (ebook) | DDC [Fic]--dc23

For Joy,
who has shown me so many
forms of friendship over the years

It snows in Casper County. Last winter, our first since moving from the city, the snow piled up to my knees. I cleared Mom's Nissan, scraping ice off in big chunks that disappeared into the white blanket of the parking lot. It was cold enough for me to wear the fleece neck warmer from my dad, the one covered in giant daisies. I hate daisies.

Flakes fall from the sky, landing like kisses in my hair and on my cheeks. I reach my hand out to catch them. But this time it isn't winter, and these flakes aren't snow.

THE SPARK

CHAPTER ONE

"Put your mask on," Mom reminded me as she opened the door to our apartment, referring to my N-95 breathing mask designed to protect my lungs from the ash. I stepped out the door. It didn't seem real, her car sitting in the parking lot covered in ash, like a twisted winter landscape. An aberration. Something that didn't fit. Like the story I'm about to tell you. Like me.

I breathed deeply, the mask dangling from my hand.

"You can't wear that hoodie in court," Mom said. "And why must I forever tell you to put on that mask?"

Mom seemed really put together in her best black slacks and silk blouse, but her voice pitched like it did when she was fraying in a thousand directions.

"Sorry. I don't have the right outfit for going to jail." I picked at the doorjamb as ash gathered on my shoes.

"Tessa, you will not go to jail."

My mother named me Tessa after the tesseract in *A Wrinkle in Time*. As she read the story, she had some kind of epiphany when the ant walked across the two ends of string, the 'wrinkle', and she realized there was an entire world of possibilities out there. She named me after possibility.

"Juvenile detention then," I mumbled.

"You're not going there either," she said, pressing her palms into her thighs, smoothing her already smooth slacks.

"You don't know what they do with arsonists."

We walked past my car, which was covered in grimy layers of ash. I hadn't driven it in a week. Partly because I wasn't working, at least not getting paid to work, so I couldn't afford gas. And partly because I only left the apartment these days if I absolutely had to. But mostly

I didn't drive because the word "bitch" had been scratched into the side of the car.

I climbed into the passenger seat of Mom's sedan. She poured water from a large bottle onto the windshield and it flowed in dirty rivulets along the door panel and down, just missing my shoes.

Mom started in on my hoodie as we wound our way out of the parking lot and headed toward the other side of town. "You can't look like a deviant."

"But I am a deviant."

"Knock it off Tessa. At least pull the hood back. Let me see your face. Did you put on makeup?"

I pushed my hood back and faced her, closing my eyes so she could see the heavy eyeliner. I would have put on blush too but, with my mask on, who would see it?

"Good," she said. Mom's makeup was perfect, as always. Even when she quit going to the salon and started coloring her own hair, she still looked pulled together. But today, she didn't seem to notice that a blotch of mascara the size of a small mole had smeared just below her left eye. "And take your hair out of that ponytail? Wear it down?"

I ignored her.

Two people in N-95 masks walked toward a restaurant. Normally, this time in August, restaurants were packed with hikers and backpackers, vacationers from Portland out to play in the Oregon woods for a few days or weeks. And why not, Portland is an easy two hours' drive. But nobody was coming out to play today. It was hard to see the forest because the air was so choked by smoke and ash.

Mom began drumming her fingers on the steering wheel, then adjusted her N-95. These masks. I hate these masks. They cover everything, and even though the eyes are the most expressive part of the face, the windows to the soul, without seeing the nose and mouth you can't be sure what a person is thinking. Which is probably why

I got hung up at the grocery store talking to Brent. Maybe if he wasn't wearing a mask, I'd have seen his lips curling in disgust as he lied to my face. Without the mask, I might have realized that he, like everyone else I ever hung out with, was done with me. Without the mask, I would have realized he was stalling, giving someone outside time to scratch "bitch" into the side of my car.

"Tessa, stop that," Mom said.

I realized I'd been scraping my cuticles and my thumb was bleeding. Mom put a hand over mine. I let it sit there for a second, just long enough to feel the innocence of being a little kid again, then pushed her hand away and wiped the blood on the side of my jeans.

"We're going to get through this," Mom said. "We're going to get back on track. You're not the only sixteen-year-old who's had problems."

I might not be the only sixteen-year-old in the world with problems, but I was pretty sure I was the only one who'd burned down a forest and scorched a bunch of people's livelihoods.

Mom sucked air in sharp gasps as we turned into the parking lot of the courthouse. A large group of people were standing around, some carrying signs. One of them said, 'Grown Up Sentences for Grown Up Crimes'. A woman wearing shorts and a t-shirt held a sign, 'Where's the Accountability?' A group of five or six people wearing North Face and L.L. Bean attire held signs in one hand and Starbucks cups in the other. I'm pretty sure they were from the city. Their signs read, 'Nature's Playground is Burning Down' and 'Arsonists Come in All Ages'. I was glad, for once, for masks. I didn't need to see the disgust on their faces, it was all over their signs.

"Can I put my hood back on now?" I asked.

Mom turned off the car engine but otherwise didn't move except to tighten her grip on the steering wheel.

The door of a Mazda a couple of parking spots over opened and my lawyer stepped out. Tanesha Carlisle was dressed for a courthouse kill, wearing spiked heels and a slim skirt and business jacket in navy blue. Even her mask was no nonsense. Her heels clicked as she walked calmly toward us, as if there were no angry demonstrators waving signs behind her.

She stood beside the car for a moment, then knocked on Mom's window. "You guys okay?" She wore her hair in a tight bun, a few shiny curls framing her face. "Hold on," she said and came around to my window. I rolled it down for her. "This isn't going to be easy," she said to me.

"She thinks she's going to juvenile detention," Mom said, eyeing the crowd.

"Ellen, I'm eighty-five percent sure we can talk the judge into releasing Tessa into your custody. Honestly, the juvenile detention facilities are overcrowded, there's no reason to throw a first-time offender in. Trust me, Tessa?"

I picked at my bloody cuticle. "Okay," I mumbled. Eighty-five percent wasn't a hundred, but it could be worse.

"We've got to go in now." Tanesha looked over her shoulder. "Tessa, listen. We're going to walk up those stairs, together, and I don't want you to say anything to anybody, or even look at anybody. Just keep focused on putting one foot in front of the other. I've got you on this, okay?"

"Can I keep my hood on?"

She nodded and walked around to Mom's window. Mom leaned over, squeezing my hand. "It'll be okay."

I wasn't stupid enough to think things would be okay. But I got out and stood next to the car, putting my hand on the warm hood for support.

A neon "open" sign in a Subway Sandwiches restaurant blinked through the gray air. There was a park on the other side of the courthouse with a splash pad for kids. It was empty and dry. Kids weren't allowed outside because of the poor air quality and ash.

After Mom and Tanesha had finished talking, the three of us strode in the courthouse's direction. The steps seemed more distant than Subway, though they weren't. The crowd, who moments ago had been lounging around with their signs, jumped to attention as they realized who we were. I kept my head down and my hood up. I could see the polished black shoes of police officers who had inserted themselves between us and the crowd. Tanesha walked in front, and Mom behind. As always, the mask made me feel like I wasn't getting enough air, but I was glad to be wearing it. No one could see my lips trembling.

Half-way up the stairs, I realized the crowd had stopped shouting and chanting. I peeked out from under my hood and saw dozens of eyes glaring at me. I missed a step and stumbled into Tanesha's back. Mom grabbed me from behind to steady me. She would have kept hold of me until we made it all the way inside, but I shook her off.

I heard a woman's voice, "As you can see, quite a crowd has gathered outside the Elmsville Courthouse where the sixteen-year-old accused of starting the Horseback Falls fire has just arrived for her day in court."

I kept my face down, watching my feet take each step, trying to follow Tanesha's lead. If I wanted to, I could shut out everything happening around me. Then it would be just me, walking stairs. No big deal. They could be any stairs, and a kid from my elementary school could have left behind the gum I was stepping over. Or maybe I was walking the stairs covered in rubber matting that led up to the locker room in the community center in our old Portland neighborhood. Yes, I was walking those stairs, on my way to the gym for a workout.

"You took my home." The crackly voice of an old woman yanked me back to reality. "Why would you do that?"

My feet stopped in front of her.

"Why?" she asked again.

"I didn't mean to." I defended myself as Tanesha grabbed my elbow and pulled me up the stairs.

"Almost there," she whispered.

The voices of the crowd rose in unison, as if they were a choir who'd been rehearsing for this moment their entire lives. "Justice. Justice. Justice."

My feet kept moving, and I kept my head down. Finally, Tanesha pushed open the double doors and, as they swung closed behind us, everything went silent. I pulled back my hoodie. A long and life-altering list of charges blurred together in my mind. Arson. Reckless endangerment. Reckless burning of public land. Second degree mischief. They could tack on more, like being the worst daughter ever or choosing super stupid friends, or just sucking at life in general. It didn't matter. This was the end of what used to be my life.

In some stories, when problems seem too big and the path ahead is hazy, a mysterious tesseract shows itself and a glimmer of the world's infinite possibilities magically appears. My story is not that kind of story. This is the story where a girl who's supposed to be a tesseract, screws up big time and discovers she's nothing but a stupid wrinkle.

CHAPTER TWO

I wasn't always a loser. Or maybe I was, but I was just super good at hiding it. In some ways, being a loser out in the world for everyone to see is really freeing. But it's not who I am, or who I used to be, before Elmsville and before the fire. Things really fell apart when Mom and I moved here from Portland.

I remember the drive, my cheek rested against the half-opened window. I'd closed my eyes, letting the wind blow through my hair. Our belongings, the small amount of furniture and supplies Mom took from our family home, were already in a pod in Elmsville. I was trying to clear my mind by pretending I wasn't in the car but riding the commuter train downtown to meet friends. It was June, and the air was warm and smelled of Douglas Fir trees, which made pretending almost impossible. Through my closed lids, the sunlight flashed through the trees in brilliant orange, fast bursts.

These woods weren't completely strange to me. For two summers I'd attended 'survivor' camp where guides drove us kids out of the city a couple times a week, teaching skills like knot tying and how to build our own shelter in the woods. I got pretty good at shelter building. After packing moss into the gaps between the branches of my teepee, I crawled into my sleeping bag and stroked the soft moss. No matter how hard I tried to fill all the gaps, I could always spot stars blinking at me where I'd forgotten to put moss. I slept well in my little shelter, like a bird in a nest she'd made all on her own.

But that was four or five years ago, and the woods felt strange to me now. Maybe because I wasn't a visiting summer camper anymore, I was moving here.

I had a headache because, for the eightieth time that day, I was thinking of all the things I should have said to my dad at the courthouse when he divorced my mom. I shoved the visor to the side to block the annoying flashes of sunlight and thoughts of my stupid dad and, well, everything else.

"Tessa," Mom said, "it's going to be all right. You'll see." She tapped her fingers on the steering wheel like she always did when she was stressed.

"I know," I said, but nothing seemed alright. Dad was back in Portland doing his thing, being charming and making money. I could see him every night of the week if I wanted to, on The Food Network. But I didn't want to. I wanted to be back with my friends, playing volleyball and celebrating the end of our freshman year.

I checked my phone. Not even one bar of service. I turned it over in my hand. It would be disappointing if I didn't have any messages when we finally came down from this mountain. Most of my friends would be heading out for volleyball practice about now, preparing for the next game. I wouldn't be there, obviously. I'd be in the sticks, in Elmsville, living in a cramped two-bedroom apartment with my mom and trying to figure out what to do all summer before starting tenth grade in a new school where I wouldn't know anyone and where they didn't even have an orchestra.

I looked at my mom and let her see me smile. The little lines that she'd always had on her forehead had deepened to full on creases and dark circles hung under her eyes. Sometimes late at night, after I'd uploaded my homework for the day and come out for a drink of water, I'd see her online, teaching herself Excel. She'd be muttering, "Sum of cell B3, colon, B19, slash, fifty percent sign."

Some of my friends' parents had divorced, and for them it seemed so tidy. Like they had one long conversation and decided it wasn't such a great thing to live together anymore. They probably sat across the table from one another, drinking tea and saying things like, "It'll be better for the kids." Then they'd stayed up late outlining how it was all going to work, having a drink or two to toast their new lives, then went to bed and got divorced in the morning.

Maybe it wasn't quite that simple, but it didn't drag on in court, with constant screaming and fighting followed by days of suffocating silence. It didn't bankrupt one parent, forcing her to move with her teenage daughter to some lame town out in the sticks.

"Should be there in about twenty minutes," Mom said. Her perky voice should have sounded reassuring, but it made me feel worse.

I'd already made things worse for myself by throwing my dad's new wife's phone into the toilet. I'm not sure why I did it, really. Maybe because her name was Tranquility, which kind of made me hate her from the first moment I met her. Or maybe because she was practically my age and reminded me of girls at my school who acted like they were perfect and made fun of less perfect kids on Instagram. Or maybe because that day, while Mom was being grilled by Dad's divorce lawyer about why she hadn't gotten a job or gone back to school since I was old enough to have a job of my own, Tranquility leaned into my dad and smoothed his tie as if she owned him. That really got me. During a break, when Tranquility left her phone sitting on the seat, I didn't even think. I snatched it without being noticed and slipped it into my pocket. I went straight to the bathroom and tossed it into the toilet bowl.

I know, stupid right? If I'd been thinking, I'd have put it in the tank so it wouldn't have been so easily found.

No one could prove it was me, but everyone knew. Tranquility pouted, Dad had angry words for Mom, and Mom scolded me all the way home.

As we drove out of the mountains, veering toward Elmsville and our new lives, I gritted my teeth and vowed not to make things that kind of worse. Well, what a joke that turned out to be.

In the beginning, Elmsville wasn't so bad. I mean, it wasn't awesome, like I would have ever chosen to leave all my friends and my comfy bedroom in Portland where I could step out of my window late at night and have the moon all to myself. But it could have been far worse. I mean, at least I was smart and had skills, the type of skills Tranquility would call "marketable."

For one thing, people have always said I was pretty. I know being pretty isn't a skill, but maintaining it is. I wash my face every night, patting it with a hot washcloth, then a cold one to close the pores. Then massage in moisturizer. Mom taught me this routine when I was thirteen and, most nights, we do it together before bed. My hair is long and wavy, and I can style it however, to look like all the other girls if I want. And I almost always know the right answer in class. I don't always say it; I mean, I'm not socially stupid. No one likes a kid who knows everything except when to shut up. I give out enough right answers to stay on teachers' good sides, but not so many that I piss everyone else off. Plus, I turn in my homework on time. Always.

You know those kids who lurk around the edges, and god forbid anyone say anything to them because they'll stammer and stumble and say something weird, or the ones who have terrible acne, or the ones who can never, and I mean never, get the right answer when the teacher calls on them? I'm not those kids. Although for the life of me, I can't figure out why because inside, I've always felt like one.

Did I say I'm good at sports? Well, I'm really good at volleyball. And everyone knows, if you're good at sports in a small town they don't care where you came from, or if your face is flawless, or your hair bounces and shines, you have an instant in. Back in Portland, I played in a community center league from the time I was ten, and when I was in ninth grade, I was the only freshman to make varsity. I expected to make varsity in Elmsville, and I did, but I never expected to be friends with someone like Cammie.

Cammie was thin, but strong, and beautiful. She had perfectly straight blond hair and her makeup was always on point. Cammie was the kind of girl who distracted boys. They would run into desks, drop their phones, or say stupid things as she floated past acting as if she hadn't noticed them. I was a month into tenth grade in

Elmsville when we became friends. Sort of. I mean, what passes for friendship in a brand-new high school, right?

Anyway, after practice one day, a bunch of us girls were changing in the locker room when a favorite song blared from someone's iPhone. I'd had a good game and was rocking to the music, pulling my boots up over my jeans. The zipper got stuck, as it often did, so I bent over and yanked on it. Cammie was standing against the locker next to me.

"Nice game out there," she said.

"Thanks," I said, still pulling on the zipper, but not really paying attention. The zipper released in a burst and my hand flew into the air and nearly smacked Cammie.

"You were a spiking maniac," she said, as if she hadn't noticed I'd almost spiked her face.

"Oh, thanks." I said, not sure what else to say. "We all had a good game."

Tan, another girl on the team, pulled a crop top over her tiny frame. "You guys, we should go get a coffee. I sooo need a mango dragon fruit tea. I'm obsessed with them."

"Tea's not coffee," Geri said, releasing her dark hair from its ponytail and brushing it out.

"It's way better! A venti cup of pink mango dragon fruit goodness," Tan replied. She covered herself in body spray that I immediately recognized from Bed, Bath and Beyond. The entire locker room suddenly smelled of coconuts.

Cammie finished applying her lipstick and rubbed her lips together. "I want a frappuccino." She tossed her lipstick into her bag. "Let's go." She and the other girls gathered their things while I pulled my hair up into a messy knot on top of my head.

"Come on, Tess," Cammie said, "Come with us."

I had exactly five dollars in my wallet. I knew that would be enough for a coffee, but did I want to go? I gathered up my stuff and followed them out of the locker room. And that's how I started hanging out with Cammie. Though, really it was Cammie, Tan, Geri and me. Volleyball got me in, and I quickly became an integral part of their group. We laughed at the same things; we rocked at volleyball; got coffees after practice and ran off campus for cheeseburgers during lunch. I quickly discovered I was like them in lots of ways, but I was different too.

For starters, I did my homework. And because my mom spent money we didn't have, for the one violin teacher in Elmsville to give me private lessons, I had to practice. And because their moms stayed home while their dads worked, or their moms worked jobs that provided 'supplemental' income, all those coffees and cheeseburgers weren't a problem for them. Also, their moms didn't sling drinks for a living down at the local bar.

A couple months after I started hanging out with Cammie and her friends, on a weeknight at nearly eleven o'clock as I was just finishing studying for a trig quiz, I heard Mom come through the apartment door. I listened for the familiar sounds of her keys going up on the hook, the drop of her high heels on the floor, one after the other as she pulled them from her swollen feet, and the sound of her tired body releasing a big sigh. Then I went out to the living room.

"Here, Mom, let me get you some soup," I said, heading for the crockpot. "How was your night? Was it busy?" I ladled soup into a bowl, putting in extra chunks of beef with the vegetables. This was the second soup I'd made this month. With Mom working swing shifts and my weeknight practice schedule, we ended up eating at weird times and not always together. With me cooking, at least we were eating something that didn't start out frozen or in a box.

"Not too bad," she said. "Pretty good tips. A group from the city were out for some winter backpacking, but it was too cold, so they hung out drinking all night."

I handed her the bowl of soup and poured a glass of wine and asked, "Did you talk to Jared?" Jared was the owner of Woods Hole.

12

Mom was super overqualified for a bar job serving drinks. Why? Because she had kept the books for Dad's food cart business for ten years, even when it started booming and he was running five carts while the pilot for his new show was in development. It was only when he signed the contract with The Food Network that Mom gave the accounting over to Dad's new team. She'd been rocking it all those years, but did The Food Network or Dad care? Of course not.

She'd built the business that made Dad all fancy and famous and moneyed, but on paper her resume was crap. She didn't have a degree either. So that's how she came to work at the bar, keeping her figure slim and her high heels on for tips. She'd be far better off running the books for Woods Hole, rather than running the drinks.

"Excellent soup, Tess," Mom said, pushing strands of hair away from her face. "I didn't talk to him. He left early and I was too busy before that."

I sat down at the kitchen table with a glass of water. "Mom," I said in a soft but firm voice, "you have to talk to him."

"I will," she assured me, then asked, "how was volleyball?"

"Good, I guess."

"What do you mean, you guess?"

"I mean, it was okay. I did okay." I was lying. Practice hadn't gone well at all. I'd missed some easy serves. I'd dug my fingers into my palms after the second miss and wiped the sweat off my face so roughly that I'd scratched my forehead with a jagged nail. Then, after Maddie missed a few easy shots, I lashed out at her. 'It was yours', I'd screamed after the fourth ball hit the floor between us. 'I thought you were on it" she screamed back. The next time it came our way I charged for it and rammed her from the side, knocking her flat. We argued after that about how sorry I was or wasn't. Coach Michelle pulled me aside after practice for a talk with a capital "T."

I was careful not to look into my mom's eyes. "Sometimes I just feel like I can't do anything right." This wasn't exactly what I wanted to say, but it was as close as I could get.

Mom rubbed her calf. "Maybe you just need more time on the court. Did you practice violin?"

"Yes, Mom. You know I did." I took a sip of water and put the glass down a little harder than I intended. "I don't know why you always ask."

From the time I was three years old, my entire day has been organized. I came along when it was fashionable to put your kid on a tight schedule and Mom was all in. When I was a baby, she scheduled everything: tummy time, nap time, play time, family time and even time for music. I know this because she wrote the schedule in my baby book. Apparently, it was successful because she kept me on a schedule throughout childhood. And that's why now, as a sophomore in high school, I keep myself on a tight schedule. School, volleyball, coffee with Cammie and friends, dinner, dishes, violin, homework.

Mom put down her empty bowl and took another drink of wine. I could barely keep my eyes open. I stood to go to bed.

Mom spoke, "Kyle at the bar told me his son got a full scholarship to Pacific last year."

"For what?"

"It was an academic scholarship. Some STEM thing. I don't even know what that means."

"Science, technology, engineering and math," I replied. "STEM is all the thing right now."

"Well, it's the thing for this kid. His ticket out of the dried-up timber industry. I think it would be good for you too." She stood and gave me a quick hug. "You'd better get to bed."

I should have gone to bed, but I didn't. Instead, I studied for another thirty minutes because, you know, universities don't give scholarships to underachievers. I took out a paperclip I kept in the back of my desk drawer and scratched it along my cuticles until they were raw and bloody. I don't know why this seemed to help, but as the metal dug into my skin, some of the pressure in my head disappeared. Afterwards, I went to bed because I had to get up at six in the morning to cram for another half an hour before leaving for school.

And that's how things went. I was on track for a scholarship which is what my mom wanted, and I guess what I wanted too. I was on track to be everything I was supposed to be until one day I did something stupid, and everything pretty much sucked after that.

CHAPTER THREE

The day I set the world on fire was a perfect summer day. Elmsville can be amazing in the summer. Unless the air, like now, is choked with ash. But in normal years, it's incredible.

In normal summers, tourists flooded downtown, buying up expensive boutique dresses, artisan jewelry and double-decker ice cream cones. They booked rafting trips and guided backpacking adventures and bought the latest hiking gear, hauling out their paddle boards and kayaks to the local lakes. When things were normal, getting a job was easy. Right after we'd arrived from Portland, I got a job at the grocery store in town working nearly full-time.

I put groceries into eco-friendly bags and gathered up carts the tourists had abandoned around the parking lot before heading back to their Airbnb or campsite. After work, I'd practice violin, go for a run, make dinner and, following Mom's list, I researched scholarship opportunities. The day I set the world on fire, for the first time in my life, I called in sick to work when I wasn't really sick.

CU in 20, read Cammie's text. I left my hair down so it would fall over my shoulders. I strapped on a pair of sparkly sandals and checked myself in the mirror, tugging my crop top down to cover the stomach bulge that seemed to be a trait Mom and I shared. We'd sometimes stand in front of the mirror, our tummies pouching out, Mom poking at mine with a laugh. I always brushed her hand away, but really it made me feel connected to her, even if most of the time I felt disconnected.

I studied myself in the mirror, then called the store.

"I don't feel good," I said, trying to sound sick, which wasn't too hard since my voice was shaking. "I've been throwing up," I added for good measure. I coughed and groaned. Maybe I was laying it on a little thick, but it must have worked because the manager told me to stay home and rest.

I had forty dollars in my wallet which would be enough for movies and coffee in Walton Springs, a town large enough to have a multi-plex theater. I hoped Cammie wouldn't decide we needed to go to the outlet stores because I didn't have money for that. Even though I made minimum wage at the store, there wasn't much left after paying volleyball fees and for my uniform and shoes and, well, whatever else I needed. Plus, I brought home groceries after my shift to keep our fridge stocked.

I peeked in on Mom. She was still asleep, her arms crossed over the covers. I dumped out yesterday's coffee from the pot and poured in water and fresh grounds. All Mom had to do was push a button.

On the drive over to Cammie's, I blared my favorite violinist to try and calm my nerves after the big lie I'd just told. You might be thinking, who blares a violinist, ever? Boring, right? But you should give her a try sometime. She's not the kind of violinist I am, playing Mozart and Bach while wearing a stiff, formal gown. She kicks ass. She plays a cover of AC/DC's "Back in Black" that's awesome. She's wild, talented, and sexy.

I felt a little queasy and caressed my stomach bulge. With my luck, I would get sick for real. But I reminded myself that people tell lies all the time. They call in sick to work, skip class to go with their friends to the lake or the mall, or like my mom, stay on the sofa all day. I was pretty sure those people didn't feel nauseous while doing it.

Even after Cammie, Tan and I were in Cammie's convertible Volkswagen beetle heading to Walton Springs, I felt a twinge of guilt in my stomach. Tan sat in front where I should have been, not because I felt sick, but because my legs were so much longer. I guess I got backseat because I was the newest member to their group. At least Geri's family was on vacation, which meant I could stretch out across both back seats, giving me a little more room. The top was down, and the wind whipped my hair all around, especially into my eyes. I tried to hold my hair back, but that became pointless.

In the front seats, Cammie and Tan were very chatty. Between the wind and the music, I could hardly hear what they were saying. I had to shove myself forward, straining my neck between the seats, if I wanted to be part of the conversation.

"I think it will be us, Benson, David Douglas and Sandy in the finals," Cammie said. She spoke quickly, gesturing wildly with her perfectly manicured hand while loosely gripping the wheel with the other. "If not Sandy, then Reynolds." They were talking about volleyball. The summer league had started, and we now had four practices a week.

"I don't know," Tan said. She extended a graceful arm out to ride the wind with her hand. "Those are good teams with a lot of money."

"When did Elmsville High last go to State?" I asked.

"This song is so dope." Cammie turned up the music, making any further conversation with me impossible. I sat back. My stomach bulge was sticking out and I swiftly tugged my top down to cover it. The on-again, off-again queasiness I'd felt since calling in sick surged its ugly head again. But it wasn't nausea I felt so much as a feeling of anxiousness I got sometimes when I'd stepped out of my comfort zone. When everything around me was wrong and if I dwelled on it for too long, I would vomit. The prickly feel of the seat cover on my legs, the sight of Cammie's perfectly straight blond hair blowing behind her instead of in her face, Tan's glossy pink nail polish. I closed my eyes, trying to will it all away by imagining I was with friends back in Portland.

Cammie turned down the music and said, "You guys, I need some boots for school. Let's hit the outlet mall first." Shopping was the last thing I wanted to do, but if Cammie needed boots, that's where we were headed.

Cammie dragged us through Old Navy, Ann Taylor, and every other mall store that carried some form of boot. She'd asked Tan and me for our opinions on every single shoe, but she always agreed with Tan's choices. My suggestions were pretty much ignored. I should have known then that I'd be relegated to the back seat forever.

And I was right. It was nearly 3:00 pm when we got back to the car. After I'd wiggled in, Tan and Cammie packed their shopping bags around my legs. If I was going to vomit, this would've been a good time to do it. They assured me we didn't have far to drive. Besides, they said, the early movies didn't start until 4:00 pm, so we had plenty of time to grab a coffee before show time. I was grateful when Cammie put the top down, at least my head had some space.

As we drove into the parking lot, I could see the line of people stretching out the door. Cammie sighed loudly and rolled her eyes. "Oh my God, are you serious?"

We went in anyway. The grunting of espresso machines and gurgling of milk being steamed and frothed, combined with shouts from the four or five people working behind the counter, filled the café even before all the people standing in line.

"What is the holdup? Must be training a new guy or something," Cammie said. The workers were hustling, wiping sweat from their foreheads as they handed over flavored coffee drinks and ice-cold brews. I looked at my phone. Mom would be starting her shift at Woods Hole about now, and she'd be thinking I was at work. I felt grateful she never called to check up on me.

There was a low, window rattling rumble from the street outside.

"Are you kidding me?" Cammie said. A familiar truck pulled up, one with a huge American flag waving broadly as if the President himself were at the steering wheel. It was Jackson's truck.

Jackson jumped out, his shaggy hair falling in his eyes. He wore his standard uniform of ripped jeans and t-shirt from a country music concert. I didn't have any classes with Jackson, since mine were all AP, but occasionally a bunch of us would climb into the bed of his truck and he'd run us down to Dairy Queen for lunch. On those days, eating my Blizzard under a massive American flag, I wondered if my old friends from Portland would even recognize me.

"Whoa, looks like we're not the only ones who skipped out for a vacay-day," Tan said.

I felt a little catch in my breath as Brent swung out of the passenger seat. Prickly heat stretched across my neck, and I put a hand up to cover it. Did Brent know I was supposed to be working today?

At the grocery store, I'd often see him in the back sorting watermelons into giant bins and throwing out bruised or damaged mangos and bananas. Last week while I was checking the schedule, something hit me between my shoulder blades. There was a grape lying at my heel. Brent was pretending with exaggerated care to be engrossed in stacking crates of grapes. When his back was turned, I chucked the grape at him, nailing him directly in the head. He turned to me, then lifted a watermelon as if to hurl it my way. We laughed and he leaned back against the watermelon crate. I watched his eyes roll over me. I blushed under his stare and found myself pulling at my shirt in case my stomach bulge was showing.

The boys swung open the doors, laughing. They strode in as if this were Elmsville and they knew everyone inside. I wondered what that kind of ease and confidence would feel like. Walking into new situations like you belonged. As if you were shiny and golden. On seeing us, they broke into even wider grins and shouldered their way through the crowd to us.

"Wassup?" Jackson asked, hanging a thumb through his belt loop. No one in Portland ever stood like that.

"Who let you girls out of town?" Brent asked, flashing a smile in my direction.

"As if anyone lets us do anything," Cammie countered. "What, are you guys following us or something?"

"As if," Jackson said. As if what? I wondered. But he didn't finish the sentence, using his crooked-toothed grin to complete the phrase.

I ordered an iced coffee, hoping the drink would cool my flaming red neck and cheeks. I wished my hair wasn't a windblown disaster. As I stood nervously tugging on my crop top, Brent shoved in next to me.

"I got hers," he told the cashier. "And I'll have a double frap with skim."

"You don't need to get mine," I said, reaching for my wallet.

"I know," Brent replied. "Maybe I want to."

Was I supposed to push money into his hand or just let him buy it? No boy had ever offered to buy me anything. I didn't know what to do. In my confusion, I blurted out, "Change that iced coffee to a double frap with skim milk, please."

Brent's arm brushed against mine. I smelled his sweat mingled with something like ivory soap.

Once we had our coffees, we went outside and leaned against Jackson's truck in the full sunshine. Jackson pulled the tailgate down and I hopped up. The metal was hot against my legs and I rolled the bottom of my cold frap up and down to cool them.

"So, what're you guys doing now?" Jackson asked.

"Chillin'," Cammie said.

"Out shopping, I knew it! That's what girls like to do, right?" Jackson was cute, but he was about as dumb as a box of rocks. Of course, I was feeling dumb myself to be sitting on the lava-hot tailgate of his truck in my shorts.

"Not all girls like to shop, you know," Tan said, as if we hadn't just spent four hours at the outlet mall.

"We're going to the movies," Cammie said, stretching her very tanned leg up onto the tailgate. I took a big gulp of my frap so I wouldn't have to talk.

"The movies?" Brent said, as if Cammie had directed them to spend the afternoon cleaning mold out of the refrigerator or doing push-ups. "Why would you waste a perfectly amazing afternoon inside a movie theater? You can do that ten months out of the flipping year. Come hiking with us."

I stretched my legs out to show my strappy sandals. "Sorry. Wrong shoes."

"Whatever," Brent replied. "It's not like we're hiking the Pacific Crest Trail. It's an easy hike." He swiped a finger along the curve of my ankle. "Nice shoes, by the way." I lifted my cup to hide my embarrassment.

"I don't know," Tan hesitated.

"Where are you guys going?" Cammie asked.

"Horseback Falls. About half a mile or so up the road. Come on," Brent pushed on. "It will be super easy. Just hang out for a while and then go see your movie. It'll be fun." He said the last part directly to me.

Cammie rested her back against the truck, letting the tanned patch of skin between her shirt and waistband widen. She was comfortable showing parts of herself I tried desperately to hide. A drop of perspiration slid down my side. Was I getting pit stains? Thinking about pit stains made me sweat even more, and I felt another drop. Just then Cammie shrugged. I knew it had been decided. We weren't going to the movies.

We left Cammie's car and Jackson's truck in the parking lot of Horseback Falls' trailhead and started up the dirt path that quickly disappeared into the forest.

"Whew, it's hot as heck out here," Jackson said, pulling his shirt over his head to reveal a very pale chest.

"Wow, like anyone needs to see that," Cammie said, putting up her hands as if her eyes were being blinded.

"Let the man be free," I said. I wasn't thrilled with his skinny, bare chest either, but something about Cammie and her superior opinions on every subject was grating on me.

"Well thank you Tess," Jackson flexed and stretched. He turned to Cammie and said, "You just wish you could have a piece of the ol' Jackster." He swung a backpack over his bare shoulders. Brent kept his t-shirt on, which I found a little disappointing.

The trail was only wide enough for two people to walk side by side. Cammie and Brent went first. Tan followed, then Jackson and me. Jackson was yammering on about his favorite YouTuber. Once again, I felt like the person relegated to the back seat.

"Yeah, so he did this vid on *Mortal Combat 3*. It was so badass."

"Oh, yeah?" I said, pretending to care. He had evidently interpreted my faked defense of his bare chest as meaning I liked it.

"Yeah, like it was raging. It had like five thousand likes."

As we walked the trail, dirt slipped between the gaps in my sandals and within minutes, my feet were filthy. Shriveled twigs snapped beneath my feet. It was well past 4:00 pm, and even under the shade of surrounding trees, it was way too warm for me. I'd finished my frap back in the car and wished now that I'd bought a bottle of water.

Cammie's high-pitched laugh pierced the dry forest air. We were too far back to hear what she and Brent were talking about. Tan glanced over her shoulder at us, flashed a look of pity, and then ran to catch up to Brent and Cammie. We rounded a corner and the edge of the trail beyond Jackson dropped off dramatically. As he rambled on and on about the intricate details of *Mortal Combat 3*, I imagined myself giving him a little shove, just enough that he thought he was going over the edge, but not enough to actually do it. Just to see the look on his face, just to get him to shut up.

We passed a couple making their way down the trail. They were dressed for hiking, wearing boots and backpacks, and using walking sticks. The woman glanced at my sandals as they passed. I was glad it was a weekday; the trail was less crowded. We still had to deal with people, since it was summer and the forests were never empty in the summer, but it wasn't rush hour traffic.

After what felt like a mile of drudgery, we reached a large fallen log. Jackson broke his monologue about first-person shooter games and called ahead to the others, "Hey, hold up!" He sat down on a stump. "Anyone coming?" he asked Brent.

Brent shook his head. I sat on the log and tugged at my sandal straps where dirt was clinging to two large blisters.

"What are you guys even doing?" Cammie asked.

"It's hot out here. We don't want to get dehydrated," Jackson said, opening his pack. He pulled out a 4 Loco.

"No way," Tan said. "You have booze in there?"

"Hell yeah," Brent said. "Come on, quick, before anyone comes by." Jackson handed him a can and he popped it open. Then Jackson held a 4 Loco out to Cammie. "How about one for the little lady?"

Cammie rolled her eyes. "Oh my God, you guys, seriously? 4 Loco is so ninth grade." But she took the can and opened it.

Jackson held a can out to me. Normally, I'd be getting off work right now. Heading out for a run or home to practice my scales. This hike wasn't part of my schedule, drinking a 4 Loco wasn't part of my schedule. I didn't even like 4 Loco.

"No, thanks," I said, pushing it back. "I prefer to hydrate with water. Or coffee, or whatever. But not that."

"Come on," Jackson implored. He wiggled the can back and forth in my face. "It's cold. Plus, it'll give you energy for the rest of the night."

"I doubt that."

"You never know," he replied, waggling his eyebrows toward me.

"Give it up," Cammie said. "She's not going to drink it. She's got to stay sober for homework and to practice her precious violin."

I didn't like that she was talking about me as if I wasn't there. And nothing she said sounded especially nice.

"Yeah," Tan chimed in. "It would be just like Tessa to have homework, even when there's no school!" She laughed, "Here, give it to me."

Jackson tossed the can to Tan.

"So, are we going to keep going or what?" Cammie said. To my relief, the conversation had turned away from my homework and my violin, but my feet wished we'd turned around and were walking back to the parking lot. Instead, Jackson ran ahead to walk closer to Tan and Cammie, while Brent fell back beside me. He took a drink of his 4 Loco.

"You can just share some of mine if you want." He held the can out to me. I took a small drink. Then another, but only because I was thirsty, not because I liked it.

"Did you have today off?" he asked. "Or did you call in sick?"

"I called in." I decided not to lie, but then said, "And I was sick, sort of, when I called. Don't say anything."

He laughed and wrapped his arm around me, pulling me toward him. A surge of warmth ran through me, not like the prickly heat of the late afternoon sun, but a soothing, comforting warmth. I wasn't sure if it was the 4 Loco or Brent's laugh that made me feel this way, but I liked it.

"That's my girl!" he said. "I knew you had a wild streak."

"Really?" I asked. I wondered how Brent could see something my super boring 'do-everything-you're-supposed-to-do' self had never seen.

"Oh yeah, you're serious, for sure. Like super smart and shit, but I knew there was some spark of crazy in you."

I smiled. I wasn't sure whether to say something that would confirm my craziness or try to convince him I was as boring as I seemed. I decided to say nothing, and we walked in silence until my stupid sandal hit a root and I stumbled. He caught my arm and, instead of doing a face plant on the trail, I fell into him.

"Shit." My sandal strap had broken completely in half.

"Here," Brent said. "Sit down." He sat beside me while I removed what was left of my sandal. "Ouch," Brent said, seeing the two blisters on the top of my foot that were raw, bleeding and covered with dirt.

"I'm okay," I shouted ahead to the others as I watched them round a corner and disappear. "Here," Brent took my foot, "let me check it out."

"Ugh no."

"It's just trail dirt." He squeezed my foot gently in a few places. "Feel okay?"

"It feels good," I said, as more of that soothing heat spread from my foot to the top of my head.

Brent moved closer to me, but I couldn't bring myself to look in his eyes. Instead, I stared at his chest as I leaned back into the underbrush, fern fronds scratching at the bare strip of skin on my lower back. Something amazing was about to happen. I could feel it.

Jackson's voice broke in. "You guys come on! We're almost at the viewpoint!"

Brent pulled away as Jackson headed back toward us. He stood and held out his hand. I grabbed it and he pulled me up.

"I can't go any farther," I said, pointing lamely at my broken shoe.

"It's just up here," Jackson said, pointing in the other direction. "We're not going past the viewpoint."

"Come on," Brent said. "Piggyback." He turned and gestured for me to jump on. I put his pack on my back and laughed. I reached for his shoulders and jumped, hoping my weight wouldn't crush him.

He grabbed my thighs and staggered forward, but quickly found his stride. It felt right to have my arms around his neck, which now that my face was so near, smelled more of soap than sweat.

When we reached the viewpoint, Cammie was stretched out on a bench with her ankles crossed. I envied her tennis shoes and wondered if this hike had been her plan all along. It would be just like her to tell me we were going to the movies when she'd had other plans. I didn't think she hated me, but she seemed to go out of her way to make me feel awkward. It was like she invited me along just to have someone to exclude.

"I didn't realize there were mule rides for sale today," she said, her eyes on me as Brent set me down near the railing.

The viewpoint overlooked forested hills stretching for miles in every direction. It was stunning at this time of day, vibrant splotches of green, blue, and brown bounced off the trees as the sun edged toward the other side of the mountain. A sign attached to the railing warned caution and respect for animals in the area: coyotes, bald eagles, hawks, and rabbits. I ran my finger across a picture of a mother fox with her pup.

I turned back to the group. I hadn't bothered to eat earlier, thinking I'd be into a giant tub of popcorn by now. I was starving. Why was no one else talking about food?

Two men hiking down the mountain stopped to take photos of the view. "You guys going all the way up?" one of them asked.

"No, sir, just enjoying the view," Brent replied smoothly. After another minute or two, they hiked on. When they were out of earshot, Brent reached into his pack and pulled out a bottle of tequila.

"That's what I'm talking about!" Jackson shouted.

"Oh my god, you guys are such delinquents," Cammie giggled.

Brent took the first drink, then whooped over the railing into the canyon. He handed me the bottle. I felt everyone's eyes on me, and I knew refusing it would mean instant and final rejection from this so-called group of friends, so I took a small taste. Everyone cheered. I rolled my eyes and handed the bottle to Tan.

The tequila was sharp and sour, and I wished there was something else, anything, to chase the nasty taste away. The next time the bottle came around, I passed it on without drinking.

"Just when I thought you were going to lighten up, Miss Serious," Cammie said.

I ignored her. We talked about our favorite bands. I'd seen a few concerts in Portland; more than they had since what band in their right mind would come to Elmsville? But then the talk turned to elementary school, which of course they'd all been in together. I fiddled with my broken sandal, trying to forget how hungry I was and hoping I could get by without saying anything. Brent had made no attempt to get close to me since I'd passed on the tequila bottle. Now he was play fighting with Cammie. When she bit him lightly on the arm, I stood up. "I have to pee," I said.

"Your toilet awaits, m' lady," Jackson flourished his arm toward the woods.

There wasn't much choice. It was the woods to the left or the woods to the right. I made my way into what looked like the most secluded area, trying to keep my broken sandal on my foot. The setting sun made it harder to see. I hoped some forest animal wouldn't bite me in the butt as I took care of my business.

When I emerged, Jackson was standing on the bench. He was still bare-chested, his pants sagging on his frame. He flexed his arms and let out a primal scream. I couldn't make out what he was holding in his hand.

"Oh my god," Tan shouted, "What are you even doing?"

He was holding a firecracker. It was a lightning rocket like those everybody sets off at Fourth of July parties.

"I got more, guys." He jumped down and pulled another from his backpack.

"Let's light these babies, up!" Brent said, rubbing his hands together like a little kid.

"You guys are such morons," Cammie said, as she slid in next to Brent. In one swift motion, she moved her shoulder under his arm and wrapped her hands around his waist. Then she smiled in my direction.

Jackson fished a lighter from his pocket. We all stood at the railing, lights from houses below twinkling up like stars poking through gaps in the moss of my handmade shelter from survivor camp.

"You guys dare me?" he said, grinning like a lunatic.

"Oh, come on," Tan said, slurring a little. "You wouldn't."

"We need fire!" Brent chanted. "We need fire!"

"You guys dare me?" he repeated.

"Oh, give me that," I said, and snatched the firecracker and lighter from Jackson.

Cammie leaned in front of Brent; his arm still draped over her. "Finally, Miss Boring to the rescue."

I flicked the lighter and watched its wavering flame leap onto the fuse of the firecracker. I heard shouts around me, "She did NOT just do that!" and "Shit, that thing's lit!" "What the hell?!"

The firecracker sparked brightly against the darkening sky, and I held it like a flare signaling to the world that yes, I had a bit of crazy in me. My so-called friends scattered as the fiery orange wick was about to engulf my hand. Panic exploded inside of me. I had no choice, I had to let it fly.

CHAPTER FOUR

After that, pretty much everything sucked. Horseback Falls burned for weeks, obliterating twenty-five hundred acres of forest. Nearly a thousand firefighters were deployed and even then, they couldn't save several houses that were reduced to piles of smoldering ash. Over nine hundred people were evacuated, and seventy-eight hikers had to be rescued. Mom and I evacuated too, along with the rest of Elmsville. We had nowhere to go and no money, so we ended up staying with Dad and Tranquility, which was humiliating for Mom. It was also a horrible three weeks for me. But nothing compared to what I've endured since being blamed for starting the biggest forest fire to burn this part of Casper County.

By the time we'd hiked out and driven back to town, there was no question the woods were on fire. Smoke choked our throats and ash began to fall from the sky. Apparently, we'd been identified almost immediately as the arsonists by the hikers who'd seen us along the trail and said we were up to no good. Cammie, Tan and Brent were charged with one count of first-degree mischief, and each handed a sentence of twenty-five hours of community service. During the initial hearing, they testified to their own innocence and refused to even acknowledge me. Not one accidental glance. They sat in a group with their parents, leaving Mom and me alone on the other side of the courtroom.

Jackson was charged with one count of second-degree mischief and one count of reckless endangerment of others, since he was the one who brought the fireworks up there in the first place. He claimed it was all innocent, that he was planning to set them off later with some friends next to their swimming pool. I will never understand why the judge thought this sounded reasonable. I can only assume his parents had some in with the judge, or someone even higher in the court system. Maybe, because they were long-standing residents and I was a transplant from the city - nobody in Elmsville liked people from the city - my punishment was far worse. Jackson, Cammie, Tan and Brent were quick to say it was me who lit the firework and threw it. This part of their statement was true, so I guess I couldn't fault them for putting the blame on me. But it wasn't like I set out that day with some twisted intent of burning down the woods.

The initial hearing was totally weird. I sat there, trying not to notice my mom's leg bouncing up and down like a jackhammer. The courtroom was dead quiet. I mean, no one made any whispered jokes or coughed, or anything. When I got up on the stand, the artist started sketching away like crazy. I tried to keep my face down to make it tougher for her to capture what I was thinking.

They charged me with six counts of reckless burning on public and private property, one count of depositing burning materials on public land, one count of second-degree mischief and one count of reckless endangerment of others. Not as bad as straight-up arson, but for throwing one firework into the sky, they pretty much threw the entire book at me. After that, I had to wait seven weeks before learning what kind of punishment the judge would hand me for these crimes.

But the sentence may as well have been handed out that day. I never got another text from Cammie or Tan. I was fired from the grocery store. No surprise. And I would have probably been let go from volleyball too, but they canceled it because of unhealthy air quality. Mom could have grounded me, and it wouldn't have mattered. I grounded myself.

I stayed in my room most of the time and when I came out, Mom and I moved around the apartment like ghosts, two troubled spirits stuck in a space somewhere between living and unliving. With

Woods Hole still closed, Mom lost her income and her only interaction with other people.

Sometimes she seemed to want to speak to me, like words were forming in her mouth. But she never shared them, instead tapping her fingers on the countertop like she was trying to communicate using some sort of code. I didn't need to hear her words. I knew they would hurt and interfere with my process of unliving.

When I came out of my room, I did a lot of cleaning. I scoured the toilet every day, removed everything from the cupboards, lining cans of soup and vegetables and kidney beans on the counter before wiping down the insides. I chipped ice from the freezer walls and threw out containers of chili I'd put in there like three months before. I spent a lot of time with my paperclip too, and as a result my cuticles stung whenever I scrubbed the sink with Lysol. Maybe that's why I became obsessive about cleaning. The burn reminded me I was still alive, even though I wasn't sure I wanted to be.

Mom said I had to put some effort into redeeming myself before the sentencing. This was probably on the advice of Tanesha, but I think she couldn't stand to be around me anymore. She signed me up to volunteer at the Morningstar Living Center. Her reasoning was no matter what happened at the sentencing, I was going to need some community service. Since the court date was a few weeks away and school would soon take up most of my time, I needed to get started now.

Morningstar Living Center was not what you'd call upper class. Old people with money went to the other facility in town, The Village. Morningstar was for seniors who couldn't afford The Village or who didn't have family with enough space, time, or desire to take their elderly parents into their home. As I drove over for my first visit, I imagined Morningstar being full of people who lived in low-rent apartments like ours and that maybe, one day, Mom and I would end up living there.

Along the circular drive leading up to the two-story building, I passed a concrete bench and a large planter full of flowers that couldn't hold their blooms under the weight of the ash covering them. Inside, the lobby smelled like a mash-up of an elementary school cafeteria and an old closet. Bad chicken nuggets and mildew. When I was in seventh grade, I played violin with a group of Christmas carolers from my music school. We visited a home that smelled just like this. The residents had mostly smiled and clapped along as we performed. Some even cried. But many remained expressionless, while caregivers shouted in their ears things like, "Isn't this fun, Marybeth?" and "Oh, don't you love this song?" I remember feeling relieved when it was over, and I could pack up my violin and go home.

A young woman, maybe a few years older than me, sat at the receptionist's desk. She was barely visible behind a large cup of brightly colored pencils, each with a silk flower attached to its end. A lady with styled gray hair and wearing a stretchy pantsuit, leaned over a cane onto the desk. The receptionist blinked up at me through incredibly long lashes. "Can I help you?"

"I'm here to volunteer."

She opened a three-ring binder. Its edges looked like it had tumbled through the washing machine a few times. "What's your name?"

I hesitated. "Tessa Hilliard." Since I was a minor, the media were forbidden from mentioning my name, which allowed me to stay anonymous throughout the hearing and, theoretically, beyond. But of course, Elmsville was too small of a community to keep secrets, and I was pretty sure everyone knew my name. I would forever be known as the girl who lit the Horseback Falls fire.

The woman glanced up at me, then back down.

"Well, I don't see you here."

"Check the file cabinet," the gray-haired lady advised.

"No, Phyllis, there's nothing in the file cabinet."

Phyllis reached her cane up and over the desk and gave the file cabinet a shove. "Right there. Volunteer files are kept right there."

"Phyllis," the young woman said in a peeved voice, batting away the cane. "I've got this."

A girl about my age, maybe a little older, sauntered down the hallway. She wore pink scrubs and her kinky hair spiraled out in a cloud above her head as she sang a song I recognized from Pandora. She broke off to shout into a doorway, "Looking good today, Mr. Roberts!"

I turned back to the woman at the desk. "Are you sure? I should be listed to volunteer five days a week, four hours a day."

"Well," the young woman closed the binder with finality. "I don't have you listed."

The singer leaned against the counter next to me. "Good morning, Ms. Phyllis!" she said in a cheery voice. She turned to the receptionist. "Are you busting her balls, Tamara?"

"She's busting her balls," Phyllis said.

"She's not listed in the book. What am I supposed to do?" Tamara was clearly irritated.

The singer reached over to grab a two-way radio and spoke into it, "Kathy, to the front desk, please. Kathy to the front." She replaced the radio and turned to me. "I'm Regina," she said, holding out her hand.

"Hi," I shook her hand and, since I couldn't avoid saying my name, "I'm Tessa."

If Regina recognized my name, she didn't show it. "Kathy will be up in a minute. See you around, Tessa." Before she walked away, she put her arm around Phyllis. "Come on, Ms. Phyllis. I need some help in the rec room." Regina and Phyllis slowly moved down the hall.

Kathy turned out to be the manager of Morningstar. She seemed nice enough, but as we began the tour, she pulled me aside. Her heavily sprayed hair wrapped around her head like a sculpted bird's nest. I guessed her age was around fifty.

"I know you've been in some trouble," she said. I flushed, waiting for what was next. "I'm willing to give you a chance because god knows we need help around here, but I don't want any funny business, understand?" I nodded. "And no smoking in the building. There's a smoking area outside."

"I don't smoke," I said.

"Any issues with alcohol, you'll be terminated immediately."

Well duh. "I don't have issues with alcohol," I said.

"Volunteers are never allowed near medications. Any volunteer who messes with medication or steals a resident's things will be terminated immediately, understand?"

Kathy obviously thought I would be trouble. At this point in the tour, which was just beginning, I was fighting my urge to turn around and leave, to terminate myself, like, immediately. I wanted to go to volleyball practice or to my job at the grocery store where I got paid to follow rules. But neither of those were options for me now. I pushed my fingernails into the scabbed cuticles of both thumbs and breathed in stale chicken nuggets. Kathy and her rules were my only option now.

"Okay," I said.

We continued our tour. Kathy showed me the recreation area where a couple of residents sat around playing a ragged game of Battleship. Several residents dozed in the TV lounge while Oprah talked on the screen. She was holding up a book that looked as though it would never, in a million years, find its way to join the shelves of paperback westerns that adorned the library section of the Morningstar recreation area.

"Hello Miss Kathy," waved a man with a fluff of white hair on an otherwise shiny, bald head. His faded plaid bathrobe hung from his shoulders. "Good morning, William," Kathy chirped. "How's Oprah today?"

"She's got a better guest than last week. That guy was a dud."

As we walked down the hall, Kathy introduced me to residents who had their doors open. Each time, I waved and smiled. Some of them waved back.

There was a sudden crash and a nursing assistant wearing scrubs ran out of a resident's room. A bowl flew after her, splattering beige goo all over her and the floor. "Oh my god," the woman huffed, wiping at the splatters on her scrubs. "She's out of control."

Kathy sighed. "Go on, get changed."

I followed Kathy as she walked through the door, careful to step over the goo on the floor. A woman sat hunched over her tray; her back was to us. She had thinning hair that hung below her ears in gray wisps.

Kathy picked up a spoon from the floor. "Effby," she said, "we talked about how to behave with the girls." Effby slammed her hand on her tray. I jumped as the remaining utensils clattered to the floor.

"I told her I don't like Cream-of-Wheat. I like Malt-o-Meal."

"Effby, you know we don't serve Malt-o-Meal." Effby looked up, registering my presence. I backed away; afraid her tray might come my way.

"Who's this? Some new lamb for the slaughter?"

"Now Effby, is that any way to greet our new volunteer? This is Tessa."

"Hello," I said. Effby grunted. Her face was a mass of lines that all pointed to a mouth frozen in perpetual scowl. Her fingers were gnarled and now that they weren't hurling things, she clasped them together as if she were going to pray. Perhaps to the breakfast gods to send her some Malt-o-Meal? Although the expression on her face looked less like she was saying a prayer and more like she was making up a curse. I took notice of the faded Avengers t-shirt that draped her tiny, bony frame.

Kathy finished wiping up the floor. "Since you've thrown out your breakfast, you'll need to wait for lunch before you get anything else to eat. Now why don't you watch a show?"

"Bunch of mind-numbing bullshit. Meant to turn us into clones," Effby grumbled.

Kathy made a start for the door, and I followed. "You'll be a clone, like all the rest of them soon enough," Effby called out. Kathy shook her head, her now lopsided bird's nest twisting with it.

I wasn't excited about going back to Morningstar after that first tour, even though Regina had been nice to me and Kathy was what you'd expect a manager to be, bossy, but not horrible. Mom was having no discussion about it. I had to go back. Anyway, I was tired of sitting on my bed day after day, night after night, doing nothing. I'd stopped checking my phone after the court date. What was the point? My so-called friends didn't want to have anything to do with me. Sometimes, I let myself worry about what they might be saying about me, what rumors they might spread, but I didn't care enough to find out. I thought about deleting my Facebook and Instagram accounts, but instead I turned off all notifications. Eventually I turned off my phone. At first, it was weird not to have it buzzing in my hand, my fingers constantly scrolling through messages day and night. But since I was still dwelling in that ghostly place between living and unliving, turning everything off became another way to shut down.

One night I stupidly opened my laptop and typed in "Horseback Falls." The facts of my fire weren't news to me - the number of houses burned, the acreage ruined, the species of animals killed. I'd seen the drawings of animals on the viewpoint sign, admired the endless canopy of trees poking up from the forest below, and seen the blinking lights from houses that scattered across the valley. The fire had caused a lot of damage, but it was the comments under the article that got to me.

The kid who started this fire should have to pay the full value of every house that was destroyed.

An entire forest devastated, thanks to one spoiled brat.

Whoever that girl is, she deserves worse than what she's going to get.

Kids these days have no respect for nature.

Lock her up! For the rest of her life.

If she had any kind of remorse, she'd quit hiding her identity and make a public appearance to apologize. Not that an apology would ever fix what she's done.

She doesn't deserve to live here. We don't want people like her.

Whenever I had a fever as a kid, I'd have a dream, the same dream every time, that I was being dragged into a fog. I didn't know what was in the fog or who or what was dragging me toward it, but it was menacing, and I somehow knew there would be no coming back. As I read the comments and felt the rage and hate coming from the people who wrote them, the words dragged me into that fog. I struggled to breathe as the sharp pain of panic gripped my chest. Just like in my dream, I felt the need to run away, to escape. I grabbed for the edge of my desk but was pulled to the floor. I heard a crash. I laid in a heap, clutching my legs, wishing I'd never opened my computer.

"Tessa? Are you okay?" Mom pushed through my bedroom door. "Tessa, what's wrong?"

I couldn't speak. My breathing came in short, labored gasps. Mom dropped to her knees next to me and grabbed my hands. "Hold on to me," she directed. "I want you to breathe in and out. Slow it down, 1–2–3-4."

I held her hand tight and did as she said. She looked me in the eye, maybe for the first time in days. Slowly, my breathing returned to normal and the pain in my chest eased. "It's going to be okay," Mom said over and over.

I just shook my head and cried.

The next morning, I called Morningstar to tell them I was sick. Mom stayed around the house, probably to monitor me, while I stayed in bed. I couldn't stop hearing those angry words in my head from people who said I didn't deserve to live. More than once, I got out my paperclip. It seemed to calm me in a way I couldn't explain. When I felt ready to leave my room, I ran my hands under cool water and bandaged them so my messed-up fingers wouldn't be the first thing Mom complained about.

I stayed home for a couple more days, but eventually went back to Morningstar. I mean, did I really have a choice? I clocked my hours and Mom checked off the boxes on the calendar as we neared the date of my sentencing.

When the day of my sentencing finally arrived, I stood in the cold, dark entrance to the courthouse, hiding under my hoodie. It took seven hours for all the victims to come forward and detail their losses.

Mr. and Mrs. Anderson owned a farmhouse with two acres in the lower mountains. They'd always raised alpacas and had ten at the time of the fire, but what happened to their alpacas after the fire? Nobody knew. They'd attempted to load them into a trailer, but the fire was too fast and furious and there just wasn't enough time to save them. Their farmhouse burned to the ground and all their belongings, including photographs of their children and grandchildren, parents, and great grandparents, were destroyed. Mrs. Anderson's voice cracked when she spoke, and the loud blowing of her red nose was followed by streams of tears.

Mr. Bracknell, the owner of a guided backpacking company, talked about the loss of revenue he'd experienced since the fire and projected losses for the foreseeable future. His daughter was a special needs child with ongoing medical expenses. He was trying to find another job, but no one was hiring because most of Elmsville was still buried under ash.

Anmarie Cross, who looked about forty, talked about the store where she sold camping supplies and offered guided hiking adventures in the forest. Her face was rough, like her skin had spent a lot of time in the sun. She wrapped her arms across her chest as she spoke of how, after her divorce, she'd saved for ten years and taken out a second mortgage to start her own business. I found her testimony especially hard to hear because she made me think of my mom. I rubbed my knuckles against the underside of the desk to distract myself so I wouldn't cry.

Kurt Callahan had been on the hot shot fire team that worked the front lines. He'd joined firefighters flown in from California to help boost local resources. He fidgeted, seeming uncomfortable in his button-down shirt and tie, as he described trudging through two feet of ash in blistering temperatures. I tried to imagine what walking through two feet of ash would feel like and wondered if ash was as heavy as fallen snow. He described snags where dead branches can fall at any moment, crushing a firefighter. And how, despite protective equipment, some firefighters had suffered ash and smoke inhalation during their long days on the job. No firefighters were killed in this blaze, thank god. That would have added involuntary manslaughter to my list of crimes.

"The thing is," he said, "all those guys fighting that fire, they're good guys. But they're doing a job. Me, I live here." He crossed and uncrossed his muscled arms. "I love these woods. It's like they're a part of me. That's why I do what I do. To protect them. This time," he looked straight at me, "I just couldn't protect them enough."

Stories like these went on and on. I listened. I kept my eyes focused on those testifying, even when Mr. Kinkaid, who lost the house he'd lived in for thirty years, pointed his finger at me and said in a quivering voice that I was rotten to the core. Tanesha jumped to her feet to object. The judge sustained, but I kept eye contact with Mr. Kinkaid for several long moments. I figured he was right. I was rotten to the core. There was no other explanation for what happened. There was something horribly wrong with me.

Repeatedly, Tanesha argued my case. She brought up my awards, my good grades, consistently noting, without directly blaming him, that it was Jackson who brought the liquor and fireworks into Horseback Falls in the first place. Arguing that the teenage brain isn't fully developed, so how could I be totally responsible.

I listened and rubbed at my bandaged thumbs as she spoke. It was bad enough being called a criminal. Now I was a half-brained criminal.

In the end, after all the testimony and Tanesha's persistent defense of my character, the judge argued I wasn't half-brained and that me and my fully functioning brain were fully responsible. Thankfully I wasn't sentenced to jail. Instead, I received 3500 hours of community service. At four hours a day, five days a week, I didn't have to use a calculator to know I'd be at Morningstar or some other place for way more than a year. They fined me nearly the total amount of calculated damages for loss of revenue, personal losses, and the cost to the city to fight the fire, including the out-of-state firefighters needed to help battle the blaze. Altogether, it was $450,000. At this announcement, there was an audible gasp from Mom.

The last part of the sentencing, the part I thought sounded the easiest, was to write an apology letter to every person who had lost property or revenue in the fire. I had 227 letters to write. Tanesha was instructed to provide me with the list of names, and I'd give her the letters as I wrote them. She was to log them into a court provided document and mail them to their recipients.

The letters were fine, but the $450,000? The 3500 hours of community service? There was no way I could ever take care of all that. People were up and leaving the courthouse, but I was paralyzed, staring at a floor tile until Mom gave me a nudge. I slowly rose to my feet and followed Tanesha outside. People surrounded us on the steps to the courthouse, news reporters at the front of the crowd. I was glad Tanesha was between me and them.

"Ms. Carlisle are you happy with the verdict?" a reporter in his mid-twenties asked, shoving his microphone toward her. Happy? I wanted to punch his ambitious, eager-beaver face to show him how happy I was.

Tanesha faced him and said calmly, "We feel $450,000 is an unrealistic fine for a first-time juvenile offender. However, my client is committed to making amends for her part in this tragedy. In fact, she's already making good headway toward her community service. No further questions, thank you."

As soon as Mom and I were back in our apartment, Mom got a phone call from Tanesha. I could tell from the sound of Mom's voice that Tanesha was trying to reassure her, explaining that the $450,000 was just to make a statement; no one would ever really expect us to pay that total amount. I didn't care about the $450,000. It was a number too large to even mean anything to me. I was already unliving. I supposed I could remain poor and unliving at the same time. I walked to my bedroom and closed the door.

I picked up my violin and placed it under my chin, letting the gentle curve of its neck rest in my left hand. I held the bow, expecting the familiar E string's vibrations to move into my arm, its sound pouring over my body like warm water washing away the day's stresses. But after a silent minute or two, I lowered the bow and packed my violin back into its case.

As I laid on my bed, the stories I'd heard from the people I'd hurt carved their way through my insides. Gone were all the things that made me me, the skills I used to gloat about. The routine that made my skin pimple-free. The tight schedule that allowed me to complete my homework, make varsity volleyball practice and work a nearly full-time job and still cook dinner every night. All gone, and on top of that, my violin was silent. It was like there was nothing left of me.

I laid like that, emptying everything inside until I fell asleep. When I woke, I kicked my violin case under the bed. There was a Nike shoebox there, empty except for the tissue paper my volleyball shoes came wrapped in. I pulled out the box and placed it on my bed, then opened my laptop. I wrote my first letter.

Dear Mr. and Mrs. Anderson,
I'm so sorry about your alpacas. And I'm sorry about your house. I didn't mean to cause you so much pain. I hope you can rebuild and purchase more alpacas.
Sincerely,

I didn't want to sign my name. Technically, my identity was hidden. Not just because I was a minor, but for my safety. There had been threats on social media and I knew first-hand how much people hated me. But it felt weird to leave it blank, so I signed it *The Girl Who Started the Fire*.

I printed two copies of the letter and sealed one in an envelope and addressed it to Tanesha. The other I folded and placed in the Nike shoebox.

Somewhere between the Nike shoes I wouldn't be using anymore and $450,000 I would never earn, between the space of my silent violin and my mother's inability to look at me, a kernel of an idea formed. It was still an invisible breath, a wisp of consciousness, like a tiny tendril of smoke that disappears before you really see it. The time it took me to write these apology letters would give me enough time to answer once and for all the question that had been nagging at me, even before the fire, even before we moved to Elmsville. Did I deserve to be in this world?

Now more than ever, I wished there was such a thing as a tesseract, a wrinkle I could step through to a time way before the firecracker, before my parents' marriage fell apart, before I needed survivor's camp. Mom had named me after endless possibilities, but

I'd gone and destroyed her dreams for me, along with untold possibilities for a bunch of other people. Yes, I would give myself the time it took to write all 227 apology letters to figure out if I deserved to be in this world, if I deserved another chance.

THE FLAME

CHAPTER FIVE

Maybe I never really knew who I was, the real me buried so deep even my mom couldn't see it. My dad never could see it. I'm not even sure I knew it was there, although, if I'm honest, there were some inklings. Before I set the fire, I could take my violin out of its case and practice for hours. I played Handel, Bach, and Brahms. I played Mozart. In my old school orchestra, I once did a twenty-minute solo. I wore a black silk dress, my posture was perfect, my notes were precise. I even got a standing ovation. But some part of me didn't want to be precise or give people what they expected to hear. Sometimes, when I was alone in my room practicing, the violin wanted to make music that was messy and lacked any sense. We fought, my violin and me, because I couldn't play the way it wanted to be played. But maybe if I could have played the music my violin wanted me to play, my world would be different now, and I wouldn't feel so helpless.

I had 226 apology letters still to write.

Glossy college brochures arrived in the mail and Mom left them on the counter where I'd see them. I dumped them straight into the recycling bin along with any thoughts of earning $450,000. There was no way to make any money right now, and I didn't even know if it would be an issue after these apology letters had been written. But I would not write the letters all at once. I was going to take my time. I knew I wouldn't find answers sitting in my bedroom, so I increased my hours at Morningstar.

The week after the trial, I stood in the kitchen of Morningstar ladling tapioca into cups the size of muffin tins. The cook, a wizened lady who looked one step away from being a resident herself, told me residents preferred tapioca to vanilla pudding. I couldn't imagine that was true as I spooned the gelatinous glop into cups. A wave of nausea came over me. I took a few deep breaths, placed my head against the cool metal of the rolling cart, and waited for it to subside. As I walked away with the cart, tapioca jiggled and styrofoam cups of apple juice threatened to spill over. Kathy stood at the front desk gesticulating animatedly, her long fuchsia nails flashing in the sun. Tamara shook her head primly.

"Seriously, she's got to stop this. I had to bribe Regina with a day shift just so she'd change the bedding in there today," Kathy said.

"Some people just don't appreciate what they have," Tamara said. "Assisted care should not be a hostile environment."

I could tell Tamara was proud of her newfound human resources terminology. I wondered if she'd been reading the employee handbook. The wheels of my cart squeaked down the hall, stopping from time to time as I delivered trays of squishy tapioca and juice.

Aileen May gave me a big smile when I came into her room. "Let me show you a picture of my great grandson," she said the moment I entered. She held up a school photo of a boy missing his two front teeth. Aileen May smelled like pee, but I pretended not to notice as I doled out comments about how smart and cute her great grandson looked.

As I rolled the cart back into the hallway, my phone pinged.

It was Dad. *How RU?*

How did he think I was? I hadn't heard from him since the day of my sentencing. He'd called to give me a lecture, as if he'd just read a book on parenting and decided to try some new tactics. But I 'd hung up on him. Not because he was annoying, though he was, but because I was too tired to listen to him. Since then, I'd left his texts unanswered.

I found Sal lying in bed watching some old TV show I'd never seen before. "I brought you a snack, Sal."

He leaned over to put his face close to the tapioca sitting on his bedside table. "Tapioca again?" He pushed it away.

"You know," I said. "Maybe I can snag you some vanilla pudding."

His eyes brightened. "Would you do that for me?"

"I'll be back in a few minutes."

He crinkled his face into a smile. "You're a keeper."

I felt suddenly lighter. None of these residents knew who I was. I was just another volunteer, not the girl who set the world on fire. A keeper who would swap out disgusting tapioca for vanilla pudding.

Effby's room was next. I found her seated in a wheelchair staring out the window at a scraggly tree next to a cement ashtray. The air outside was still gray and smoky. Many of the residents had needed to increase their oxygen. Effby didn't take oxygen, but her skin was about the same color gray as the air outside.

"Hello Effby," I said. "I have some tapioca for you."

"Take that shit away." She kept her focus out the window.

"Would you like pudding instead?"

"I don't eat sweets."

"I guess that's healthier," I said, placing the juice on the table next to her.

"I don't need healthy," she grunted. "I'm trying to die." A few flakes of ash fell like snow outside her window.

"I get that," I responded.

By the time I returned with my empty cart, Regina had joined the conversation at the front desk.

"Maybe if someone would just show up once in a while to see her, she wouldn't be so cranky all the time," Regina said. She reached over the desk to grab a binder. "Doesn't she have any family?"

Tamara swiped the binder away from Regina. "I can look that up for you, but I don't need to. She doesn't have any family. Who would want to even be around her?"

"Well," Kathy said, "if she doesn't change, she cannot stay here. I can't have her throwing things at staff. She's going to hurt someone."

"I'll do it," I said. The three of them noticed me for the first time.

"Do what?" Kathy asked.

"I'll be the person who takes care of Effby. You know, bring her food, change her bedding, whatever."

"Are you crazy?" Tamara asked, wrinkling her nose as if I smelled as bad as Aileen May. "You can't do any certified nurse assisting tasks. You're just a volunteer."

"She could do most things, though," Regina protested. I could tell she wouldn't miss visiting Effby.

"Why would you want to do that?" Kathy asked.

I shrugged. "Why not?"

"I can think of a hundred reasons why not," Tamara sniffed.

"Are you sure?" Kathy asked.

"You better get a helmet," Regina said, "you're gonna need it."

You might think it was because I never had a grandma. My mom's mom died before I was born. And my dad wasn't in contact with his parents. You might think it was because I felt sorry for her, because she didn't have any family. It was none of those things. It just seemed like she made people around her miserable. And right now, that felt a lot like me.

I'd been volunteering at Morningstar for a month when I pulled a bulging envelope from our apartment mailbox. It was white and business size, with my name and address typed on the front. Something inside was soft. I turned it over in my hand. There was no return address. I slid a finger under the flap and a pouf of gray powder exploded across my hands. It was ash and the envelope was full of it. I tipped the envelope and some of the ash fluttered out, disappearing into the air. When I walked into our apartment, Mom was at her computer. I went directly to the sink to wash my hands. Not wanting to upset her, I snuck the envelope into my room and hid it away in my desk drawer.

"It's time to get your car fixed," she started in on me the moment I came into the living room.

"What do you mean? It works fine." I knew what she meant. I'd been driving around in my ash-covered 'bitch' Subaru for almost six weeks now. She frowned at me.

"I told you I'd pay to have that taken out."

"I don't mind it," I said lightly. "I mean people drive cars all the time advertising pizza or car insurance or vaginal tightening."

"Tessa…"

"This isn't nearly as bad as vaginal tightening." Besides, it wasn't as though people wouldn't know who I was without my label. Elmsville was that small.

Mom pressed her fist to her forehead in frustration. "Would you just stop being unreasonable and take that car in? I swear I don't know who you are anymore."

"Well," I said. "You could just go look at my car."

"Tessa!" she snapped. "Knock it off."

"Fine," I sighed. "I'll get it fixed." I went back into my bedroom to try to forget about my bitch car and my mystery envelope full of ash.

The next day, I left Morningstar early to drive to an auto body shop on the outskirts of town. Kip's Auto Body was a small garage between Faye's Dry Cleaners and Fat Bob's Subs. I wondered if Kip, Faye, and Fat Bob got together for drinks after work. Or if they'd all gone to high school together and been voted "Most Likely to Never Leave Elmsville."

Several junk cars littered the parking lot. I parked my bitch car and went into the lobby, which smelled of gasoline. Kip was nowhere to be seen. There was a bell on the countertop smudged with grease. I rang it. When no one showed up, I stepped through the side door and into the shop. There were three cars inside, one missing a fender and one covered in a plastic sheet. A sound came

51

from behind the third car and sparks flew up behind it. Someone was using something that looked like the butane torch my dad used to caramelize sugar on a crème brûlée, only it was much bigger. I stepped closer.

"Hello?" The man in grimy Carhartts and heavy metal hood obviously couldn't hear me over the sound of his torch, so I waited and watched his flame melt the car paint away. When he finally noticed me standing there, he startled, and I stepped back in case his torch came flying my way. He turned it off and removed the hood from his face. He didn't look much older than me. His face was sweaty and he wore a respirator. Luckily, these days everyone was accustomed to talking to people in face masks.

"Are you Kip?" I asked.

He pulled his respirator down. "Kip?"

"Yeah, you know. Kip's Auto Body?"

"Oh," he said. "There isn't actually a Kip anymore. Kip left."

"Oh." I paused. "Well, is there someone who can fix my car?"

He stood. "Sure. Sorry there was no one at the front. Let's go check it out." I followed him out of the shop.

I'd expected someone old, or you know, at least forty. I suddenly wished I hadn't come and didn't want to show this guy my stupid bitch car. But it was too late, we were standing in front of my car. He looked it over thoroughly, taking in the slur scratched along the driver and back passenger doors. The tops of the letters reached to the bottom of the windows. It had been a thorough job.

"I take it that's what needs fixing," he said.

"Well, I think it gives me a unique sense of style, but my mom doesn't agree."

He snickered while he ran his fingers across the scratches. "I can probably do it without a full repaint," he said. "Buff it out. Bondo, then paint the two door panels."

"Okay," I said.

"It'll take me a few days. Maybe a week. Good thing they had a limited vocabulary. If they'd called you an 'uncultured blight upon existence,' it would take me two weeks."

I laughed and was caught off guard by my own laughter. I choked a little and then coughed. I hadn't laughed in months. "Good thing I didn't have a bigger car," I said.

He put out a hand. "I'm Diego."

I took his hand. It was warm, softer than I expected from someone who used a blowtorch. I hesitated. "I'm Tessa."

"Come with me and we'll get the paperwork done. Can you leave it now?" I handed over the keys and texted Mom to pick me up like I used to when I was fourteen.

That night, I wrote a couple more apology letters and then trolled the internet. I used to have volleyball, work, violin, stuff to do with friends; I suddenly found myself with long evenings and nothing to do. Mom and I weren't talking very much, but she worked at the bar most evenings anyway. I wrote my apology letter to Anmarie Cross, the woman who'd owned the equipment rental store that went out of business.

> *Dear Ms. Cross,*
> *I'm sorry for starting the fire that ended up damaging your business because no one was coming to go backpacking or anything. I didn't mean to hurt anyone. I have learned from my mistake.*
> *Sincerely,*
> *The Girl Who Started the Fire*

I printed two copies of the letter and addressed an envelope with one copy to Tanesha. Then, on impulse, I Google-searched Anmarie Cross. Of course, her store, Woodland Adventures, popped up with a message saying thank you to all her loyal customers, and announcing the store had closed indefinitely. I scrolled down past the now defunct opportunities to book a one, three or five-day backpacking adventure and propane stoves and high-end backpacks to rent or purchase. I found a photo of Anmarie Cross and a link to her blog. She wore a hat like Harrison Ford in *Raiders of the Lost Ark*, and she was tan and smiling, a mess of tangled hair down around her face. She looked much younger than she had in the courtroom. I clicked on the blog.

There were links to nearly fifty entries. Anmarie Cross had been quite a traveler and she'd detailed her trips to nearly every national park in the country, as well as to India, The Great Wall of China, some forests in Ecuador and the Scottish Highlands. It was an impressive list. I had nothing else to do, so I clicked on Yellowstone National Park and read her entry.

School was set to start in two weeks. I thought by now my phone might ring. I missed the pings that used to alert me that Geri or Tan or Cammie sent a funny gif or emoji-filled text message. I missed the volleyball practices and being part of a team, and that's why I got excited when a group email from Coach Michelle arrived in my inbox. *All right, Ladies!!* she began with her signature peppy tone. *This is our year to shine! I hope you're ready to work because I can't wait to see ALL of you and to get this championship year started!!*

The season's first practice was next Monday. I reread the message, my eyes lingering on the underlined and capitalized *ALL*. Was she trying to let me know she wanted me back? That no one would write 'bitch' or 'slut' on my locker? That burning the forest down would be an off-limit topic in her gym? *This is our year to shine!* It didn't feel like my year to shine. But then, there was that one word, *ALL*.

On the first day of volleyball practice, I didn't go to Morningstar. Instead, I bandaged my fingertips. I dusted off my Nikes and did stretches in the living room, trying to quell my nerves. I was on my tenth burpee when Mom came out of her bedroom.

"What's going on?" she asked.

"Volleyball practice," I replied, launching into another burpee. "No big deal. Just practice."

It was obviously a big deal to Mom because she busted out the first smile I'd seen in weeks. "Oh right, I forgot." I'm pretty sure she was lying. "What time does it start?"

"In an hour and a half." I pulled a knee up to my chest.

"Let me get you something to eat," she said, opening the fridge.

"Mom, I can't eat." I stopped and grasped the counter with both hands.

She closed the refrigerator door. "Drink some water then." She reached across the counter and stroked my hair. "That's my girl." There was no going back now.

Outside the locker room, I heard familiar laughter and chatter, as if it were last year and nothing had changed. Yet, everything had changed. At least for me.

"My mom made me spend all summer babysitting," Tan groaned.

"This summer totally sucked," Cammie whined. "I'm glad to get back to school. I just want to forget this whole last three months ever happened."

She was right, the summer had sucked. I was ready to put it behind me. I hefted my gym bag over my shoulder, wincing as the strap scraped over my scratched-up thumb. I rounded the corner and the group of girls, some half-dressed, froze at the same time. It was like one of those tableaus we studied in ninth grade's Introduction to Art History. *Tableau of Locker Room with Girls*. I gave a half wave to everyone while simultaneously not making eye contact with anyone. I walked steadily toward my usual locker, except Miriam was already dressing there. I switched directions and aimed for an unoccupied bench.

"Oh. My. God," Miriam said.

"Can you believe it?" someone whispered.

"No way," Cammie's voice rang out loud and clear. "This is NOT happening."

My chest clenched and I tried to control my breathing as the girls finished dressing and followed Cammie out to the gym. I'd come dressed to play, so I grabbed a hair tie from my bag and yanked my hair back into a ponytail. In the mirror, I caught sight of Randi tying her shoes. She glanced up at me.

"Hey," I said. She focused back on her shoe, then walked into the gym without saying a word.

I blinked back tears. I could play. Coach Michelle had said *ALL*. I was one of the strongest players. I would go out there and remind them how much they needed me on this team.

When I entered the gym, the familiar smell of mats and sweat made me feel at home, but that quickly faded when Coach Michelle didn't look my way, didn't even acknowledge my presence.

"Gym sprints!" she barked at the group.

I threw my all into it, bolting from one brick wall to the other. When she blew the whistle to stop, we were all breathing hard. Tan and Geri high-fived each other next to me but no one raised a hand my way. That was okay. Once we were playing, they'd remember they needed me.

"Okay!" Coach yelled. "Three on three, seven minute rotations. Tan, Geri and Cammie on one side. Deirdre, Jules, and Sasha on the other. Everyone else, line up along the wall."

Itching to get on the court, I quickly assumed the first place in line. When the seven minutes were up, I ran to my position. When the whistle blew, I bounced in anticipation. But I never got a shot because the ball never came my way. Not once. When the natural move would have been for Sandra, at the net opposite me, to spike it down, she sent the ball careening wildly toward one of my teammates, who bumped it over the net. When Christine, who was right behind me, should have bumped it up to me for a set, she bumped it over the net. The seven minutes were up before I'd gotten one hit. As we filed to the back of the line, I couldn't control my anger, I shouted, "What was that about?" Everyone just rolled their eyes at me and clustered together.

When we started the practice game with full teams on court, it was more of the same. "Here!" I called to Sami who would normally set it up for me to spike over the net. Instead, she set it to Cammie. Finally, an easy bump headed toward me. "Mine!" I shouted as I readied for the hit, but someone shoved me to one side.

"Got it!" Geri screamed. She attempted to spike the ball, but it flew out of bounds.

"What the hell was that?" I pulled myself up. "That was mine!"

"Oh," she said lightly. "Sorry."

I turned to Coach Michelle for help. "Did you see that?!"

Coach looked hardened and I realized in that moment that she'd made a mistake, neglected to take me off her email distribution list.

"Ladies," she said. "Hit the showers. Tessa, stay back please."

I felt their eyes on me as they walked to the locker room, whispering. I rubbed my bandaged thumb against my hip. "Coach," I started as the last of them disappeared. "They wouldn't pass the ball. You saw that, right?"

She folded her arms across her chest. "Tessa, you can't be on the team this year. I should have told you before practice, but I didn't want a scene."

"But" I fumbled for something to say. "You sent me an email."

"I'm sorry. I forgot to take your name off the distribution list. It didn't occur to me you'd actually show up."

"Why," I asked, "Can't I -" my voice trailed off.

"Tessa, you know you're one of my best players, but the school board has agreed that representing our school on sports teams means on and off the court. Both during school and in the summer." Her voice took on an edge. "And I think we can agree that you have

57

not represented our school well this summer. I'd say that's pretty obvious to us all."

By the time I arrived in the locker room, everyone had gone. The room smelled of sweat and hairspray, coconuts, and dirty socks. I didn't realize until that moment how much I missed that smell. I took off my sneakers and when I shoved them into my bag, I felt something wet and sticky. Whoever had done it had left the empty Gatorade bottle laying on the bench.

Thankfully, Mom was out when I got home. I didn't want to have to explain anything. I stripped off my shorts and volleyball team shirt, changing into sweats and an over-sized t-shirt. I ran my duffel bag under hot water, scrubbing out any remaining Gatorade. It was sopping wet, so I propped it open in the bathtub to dry out. Then I wrapped my dirty shorts and shirt around my Nikes and walked out to the big dumpster shared by the apartments in our complex and hurled everything inside. Back in my room, I turned off the lights and climbed under the covers.

CHAPTER SIX

The next morning, Mom came out of her room earlier than usual. I was on the couch, flipping through Netflix and idly watching movie trailers.

"Well," she said. "How was practice?"

"It was okay," I said, letting a romance movie trailer play.

"That's all I get?" she pressed. "Okay? Did it feel good? How was it with," she paused. "I mean, how was the team?"

"I'm not going out for volleyball this year." I switched to a trailer for a superhero movie.

"What? Why not?"

"It's just not going to work out this year."

She came over and sat next to me. "Honey, can you put down the remote?"

I flipped the channel once more and dropped the remote on the coffee table. A trailer for a horror movie played.

"What happened?"

"I don't want to talk about it," I said. "I'm just not going back."

"Okay," she said, "you don't have to go out for volleyball if you don't want to. But we need to get back on track now."

"Okay." I wished she'd go to work. There was no getting back on track for anything now.

"This one thing doesn't have to ruin everything."

"I kind of think it does, Mom."

"No," she said sharply. "It doesn't. Let's take one step at a time. You're doing your community service, so you'll get that out of the way."

The horror movie trailer was on repeat. A girl strapped to a chair was shrieking. "You need to get back into the college applications."

"Mom, you know I'm never getting in now."

"I don't think that's true. You can address this issue in your essays. Just write about how much you've learned and grown from this experience." Mom's voice shook a little. "Once school starts, things will get back to normal."

"I'm not going back to school."

"What do you mean, you're not going back to school? You can't just get a GED; you need a good GPA to get those scholarships."

I dug my fingernails into my palms. The girl in the movie was running hysterically through a darkened parking structure. "Mom, I can't go back to school. Everyone hates me. I can't do it."

"Is that what happened at practice yesterday?"

"Mom!" I shouted. "That's what happens every day. Everywhere! I'm not doing it anymore, okay? I'm just not doing it!" Blood ran down the girl's face. I snatched the remote, switched off the TV, and slammed it down so hard the back popped open and two AA batteries rolled under the coffee table.

There was a long silence, then Mom said, "You need to think about living with your father for a while."

I forced myself to get some perspective as I reached down and picked up the batteries. I had 208 letters still to write. Then something would change and maybe none of this would even matter anymore. But it did matter right now. I felt my eyes filling with tears and I squeezed my hands between my knees.

"You need to get yourself together," Mom said more gently. "If you can't go to school here, then transfer to a school in your dad's district."

"I can't believe you would send me to live with Dad." My voice sounding squeaky.

"It's not that I'm sending you away," she pressed. "I just think that, given the situation, maybe you need a fresh start. You know we can't move. I've already thought about that, but we have zero money right now. But you can live with your dad and start fresh."

I shook my head, willing away the tears. I knew my voice would break if I tried to talk, so I just squeezed my hands with my knees until the blood stopped flowing.

"You can transfer into school and finish there. You'll be away from all this and able to get your life back."

"I don't want to live with Dad and Tranquility. What kind of stupid name is that, anyway? Who names their kid Tranquility?"

"I don't know, Tessa, but you're not in a place to get snotty. Don't you know how hard I worked to get you here? Lessons, practices, rehearsals. Uniforms and registration fees and private lessons on top of lessons. Haven't I always been here to support you?" She was on a roll now. "Haven't I done everything I could to help you succeed?" She stood and began rattling around in the kitchen, slamming silverware into the drawer. "And what do I get in return?" Her words were sharp, they cut like pieces of glass. "What do you give me in return?"

"Mom," I protested. "I know how much you've worked. I do. I just think maybe we can try-"

She cut me off. "Listen here, Missy. You have a future. You have someone you need to be, and you don't have time for bullshit. Now, get in school, get those college applications in and quit messing around."

My tears splashed onto the coffee table. I got up and ran to my room. I pulled out my paperclip and carved into my fingertips until the pain turned to numbness and I felt like I could hold myself together again.

That night, I wrote two more letters.

Dear Mr. Halsey,
Thank you for your work in fighting the Horseback Falls fire that I started.
I'm so sorry for what I did and I'm sorry that you had to leave your family

61

and spend all that time in the woods endangering yourself. I have learned from this, and I apologize for what I did.

Sincerely,

The Girl Who Started the Fire

I put this along with the other letter in the box. Two hundred and six to go. Then I texted my dad, *Hi.*

He responded immediately. Mom must have spoken to him, which meant she'd been thinking I should leave for some time. I agreed to visit him next week after my car was out of the shop.

Later that week, Effby told me to fuck off. As a volunteer, my primary job was to play checkers with residents, paint their nails, or listen to them tell the same stories repeatedly and act like it was the first time I'd heard them. However, since I had volunteered to be Effby's caregiver, I did very little of those things. Effby informed me that checkers were for dimwits. When I suggested I paint her nails, she told me to fuck off.

The staff at Morningstar didn't tell me to fuck off, but they pretty much ignored me. Although, to be honest, I wasn't trying too hard to be friendly. I knew they all talked about me behind my back. Like everyone else in town. At least I figured Effby wasn't ignoring me because of the fire. She was just ignoring me because she ignored everyone.

As I transferred used towels into the linen basket in Effby's room, I tried to make small talk, "Effby, tell me something about yourself. What do you like to do?"

"I like to sit in the quiet of my room without people chattering at me."

"Well, we don't always get what we want, do we?" I said, hanging clean towels on the bathroom railing.

"Evidently not."

As I tidied up, I noticed a book of crossword puzzles in the trash and flipped through it. They were all completed. Since Effby wasn't much of a conversationalist, except to grumble at me or tell me to fuck off, I left to play checkers in the recreation area with Sal. He was difficult to beat.

Mom picked me up from Morningstar so she could drop me home before her shift. On my way out, Tamara flagged me down. "Oh, Tessa!" She waved me over. She was scrolling through her phone.

"What?" I asked.

"I just wanted to remind you that since you're here pretty much full time now, I'll need you to sign up for the rotation to clean out the refrigerator and tidy up the break room."

"But I never use the break room."

She blinked at me. "Well, it's kind of mandatory. We like working as a team around here."

"Okay, whatever," I said.

The next day, Effby was in bed when I arrived at ten. I sat in the chair across from her. "Why are you still in bed?" I asked. "Do you feel okay?"

Effby kept her eyes focused on the brittle bark of the old tree outside her window. "I feel like I always do. Like shit."

"Do you want some juice? Or some tea?" It was easy not to like Effby, but something about her made me curious. Plus, I didn't really have anything else going on.

"No."

"How about some TV? Should I turn on a show?"

"And kill all my brain cells so I can stare at that box drooling like a comatose vegetable all day? No thanks."

We sat in silence for a minute or two. I surveyed the room for something to prompt a conversation. She had no pictures. No books. There was a fake plant on a bookshelf I suspected was there when she arrived.

"I'm glad it stopped raining all that goddamned ash," she said suddenly. "It looked like snow. I hate snow."

As I rolled my cart of dirty linens down the hall, I heard Regina singing. Her favorites were pop songs, but sometimes she sang old hymns. Today, I heard *Amazing Grace* before I saw her. The residents ate it up, of course. If I could still play violin, they'd be all over it. My violin teacher had texted me, but I ignored her. Mom tried persuading me to go back, but I refused. I said it was because we didn't have the money. Which we didn't, but it was really because I couldn't find the music anymore. It was just gone.

Regina emerged from a resident's room. "See you later, Alligator!" she called.

Regina was a big girl. The kind of big my mom would click her tongue at and say something like 'that poor girl will be in a diabetic coma before she's thirty'. But Regina didn't seem to care about her weight. I'd seen her leaving her shift, having changed out of her scrubs. She wore tight jeans and a fitted top. Not the kind that made her spill out all over the place or anything; she just looked good. Confident. Carefree.

"Hey," she said when she saw me. "There's ice cream cake in the break room for April's birthday. Come with me."

The break room was big enough for three or four people, not the eight who were crammed around April's cake. A few seemed surprised to see me. Regina handed me a plate. "Chocolate mint, my favorite." She helped herself to a large slice. I had no appetite but didn't want anyone making a thing about it. So, I cut a piece in half then mostly mashed it around with my fork.

"How's your good buddy, Effby?" Regina asked.

"We're not exactly BFFs."

"I don't know why you volunteered for that duty, but more power to you. I owe you one."

I squished mint ice cream through the tines of my fork and lifted it to my mouth. "Does she ever even leave her room?"

"She comes out to watch *Cold Case*, April said. "I think she's into crime shows."

"So, no one ever comes to see her?" I asked.

"Nope," Regina said with her mouth full. "She doesn't have any family."

"No one? How can she have no family?"

"The hospital referred her. She's on her own. I think that's how she wanted it." Tamara and the others were throwing out their plates. There was one large piece of cake left in the box. "Hey," Regina said. "Anyone mind if I take this home? April, do you want it?"

"Go ahead," April said. "I'm stuffed." She threw her half-eaten slice into the trash.

"I'm taking it for my daughter," Regina said as she packed up the box and stuck it back in the freezer. "I'll be Mom of the year."

As I set Effby's lunch down the following day, I said, "I brought you something." I handed her a book of crossword puzzles. It had taken more courage than I cared to admit for me to run into the drugstore and buy the book. I had paid for it quickly, avoiding eye contact with the clerk.

Effby reached for it, then tossed it aside. "I already did that one."

I was glad to leave early that day. I'd stayed up late reading Anmarie Cross' blog, about how she'd hiked for two weeks through the Appalachian Mountains where mosquitoes were half an inch long. Mom picked me up from Morningstar and we drove to Kip's Auto Body. I'd gotten a text from Diego the day before letting me know my car was ready. Stupidly, and for no good reason, my heart skipped a beat when I read his text. I remembered the softness of his hands and how he made me laugh. Perspective, I told myself. I needed to keep perspective. I had 199 letters to write.

We drove in silence along the road, winding slowly out of town and toward the garage. All the roads around Elmsville eventually made their way into the forest, but fortunately, Kip's wasn't too far from town. Visiting those burned woods did not appeal to me.

Before the fire, it was routine for me to chatter on about my day. What I was working on in class. How many points I'd scored in practice. What funny thing a co-worker did at the store that day. Pretty much every day since I started pre-school, Mom had asked me to tell her at least one thing I learned, one thing that was good and one thing that was challenging. Usually, I'd babble on about more than one thing, because talking was easy, but now, my days at Morningstar didn't interest her. What interested her was anything that signaled we were getting back to where we were before. And there wasn't any of that going on.

I pushed my thumb back and forth along the rough edge of the seat cushion stitching, relishing the sting. Just as we rounded a corner, a dog darted out in front of us. "Dog!" I shouted.

Mom swerved wildly and skidded to a stop. Thankfully we missed it. I watched the medium-sized, brown and black dog dart off, its tail disappearing into the trees.

"That was close," Mom said, steering back onto the road.

The garage smelled of chemicals like paint and nail polish remover. Diego gestured toward my car, which looked perfect, as if nothing had ever happened. I could feel Mom relaxing as we surveyed it together.

"Wow, so much better," she told Diego with a smile.

"It was a little tricky mixing the paint, but I think I got it," he said. He was wearing his Carhartts again. He ran a hand over the panel on my car where the word "bitch" had been. "Much better, right?"

"I don't know," I said. "It lost a little of its personality, I think." Mom shot me a dirty look, but a smile flashed across Diego's face.

Mom paid for the repairs with her credit card and then left, while I waited for Diego to pull my car around front. He wasn't on his own today. Another worker, older than Diego by a decade or two, had been sanding the hood of a Toyota. He walked into the lobby and began tapping on the keyboard. "You like your car?" he asked.

"Yeah, it's great," I said.

"Diego does good work. He only came in today because you were picking up the car. He wanted to make sure you were happy with it."

"Oh, I'm happy with it," I said. "Why wasn't he coming in today? Is he sick?"

"He's trying to find his dog. Ran away. Goofball mutt is always on the run."

My car rolled into the parking lot. Diego stepped out. "All set," he said.

"Hey, that guy at the counter told me you lost your dog?"

"Yeah," he said. "He runs off sometimes, but he's been gone a few days now."

"What does he look like? My mom and I just saw a dog. Nearly hit him, actually."

Diego's face brightened. "He's brown with black splotches. He's got some lab, but he's a mix, smaller."

"We saw him maybe three miles from here, near Jones Road."

"Just now?" Diego seemed ready to run the three miles that very second.

"Yeah, on our way here."

"Can you show me if I drive?"

I hesitated. Not that I didn't want the poor guy to find his dog, but was it safe for me? I don't mean I was afraid of Diego, but his eyes were the same warm amber as my violin, and I could feel my heart racing. I didn't need distraction in my life right now. But then again, there was a lost dog that needed saving.

"Okay, I guess I can show you."

"Great, let's go. We can take my truck."

I climbed up into Diego's truck, a shiny Ford painted a deep blue. There was a notebook on the seat, along with half a package of Oreo Minis. The cab smelled of dog. Diego picked up the notebook as if to throw it in the back, but it slipped and dropped open on the floor at my feet. It had opened to two sketches, one of a squirrel holding a nut and the other a dog. "I don't think I've ever seen a smiling dog before. Did you draw those?" I asked.

"Oh yeah," he said, sounding slightly embarrassed. He threw the notebook in the back and placed the cookies in the consul beside an opened package of beef jerky.

"Nice truck," I said. "Did you buy it this color or paint it?"

"I painted it," he said as we pulled out of the lot. "It was safety yellow when I bought it."

"I hate that color," I said. I hated yellow like I hated daisies.

"Me too."

I pulled the seat belt across my chest and saw Diego's eyes go straight for my scabby cuticles. I buried my hands under my thighs. "The guy in the shop said your dog runs away a lot?"

"That's my uncle," Diego said. "Yeah, I've only had Rippen for a year. He's still a puppy, really. He comes with me to work, but he's a curious creature. I've noticed he has a healthy sense of adventure, just not a healthy sense of direction.

I thought of Anmarie Cross, hiking practically every state in the country and beyond. "Can't blame him, I guess," I said. "Although I thought dogs had some super sense of smell that could guide them home even when they're thousands of miles away."

"Well, it figures that the dog I'd get would be broken. I love him anyway." He held out the package of cookies to me. "Oreo?"

I hesitated for a second then took a cookie. In that moment, nothing mattered more to me than sitting in this truck with this person and eating this Oreo. "Oh, it's right over there." I pointed to the spot where Mom had almost hit the dog. "He ran into those bushes where the telephone pole is."

Diego parked on the side of the road. It was quiet outside except for a few buzzing insects. Ash had stopped falling days ago and although there was still a light haze over the forest, the sun was shining, and the sky was clear. It was late August and as we stepped out of the truck, I could feel winter sneaking into the crisp, fall air. It reminded me of school.

Diego shoved the underbrush aside and called for Rippen. I walked down the road, searching for a flash of brown and black. It would be a miracle if this dog of his, with a big sense of adventure, was still hanging around.

"There you are!" I heard Diego say. I turned to see a dog jump onto Diego as he kneeled to the ground. Yep. It was the same dog Mom and I had seen. He was clearly thrilled to be back in Diego's arms, covering Diego in dog kisses and nearly knocking him over. "Okay, okay," Diego said. "I got you, boy. Come on, let's go home."

"So, this is Rippen, the troublemaker?"

Diego stood and placed his hand on my arm. "This is your friend, bud. She saved your butt." Apparently, any friend of Diego's was a friend of Rippen's. He danced circles around me and came in close so I could scratch his fur. "Boy, do you need a bath," Diego said to his dog.

I climbed into the cab and Rippen jumped in right after. He licked my face and stepped all over my legs, trying to find a comfortable spot to lie down.

"Rippen, cut it out and sit down." Diego used a stern voice and Rippen did as he was told. "I'm sorry," he said to me. "I'd put him in the back, but I'm afraid he might see a squirrel or something and jump out."

"It's fine," I said. Rippen needed a bath for sure, and after this, I would need one as well. But when he put his head on my shoulder like he was giving me a hug, I didn't care how bad he smelled.

"He sure likes you," Diego smiled.

"I always wanted a dog," I said. "Even a hamster would have been okay, but I really wanted a dog."

"You never had one?"

"No, my mom always said we didn't have time for pets. They didn't fit into our schedule." I scratched Rippen's neck, and his back leg started kicking my thigh.

"We always had dogs. Hamsters. Cats. Lizards. Basically, I grew up in a zoo."

"Who's we?"

"I have a brother, Pablo. He'll be a junior next year. Maybe you'll be in school together?"

"I doubt it." I was reminded of a dream I sometimes had about flying. My body soars, turning backflips and twirling above the clouds, bathed in warm, glorious sunlight. I don't have any worries or cares, life is good. But then, I wake up and I'm lying on my bed, a victim of gravity, weighted down by the knowledge I will never fly like that again. Whatever lies ahead for me is an ordinary, mundane life with no wings. I sit wishing for wings, wishing to slip back into that dream where I felt special and free, but I can't. I've ruined my life, ruined a bunch of other peoples' lives, and nothing will ever be the same. I was quiet the rest of the way back.

When we arrived at the shop, I scratched Rippen behind his ears as I said goodbye. He seemed to enjoy it until he saw Diego's uncle and bounded into the garage.

"Thank you so much," Diego said. It looked like he might say something else, so I started edging toward my car.

"No problem." I wished I lived in this shop that smelled of grease and where people's worst accidents were fixed in a week or two, making them good as new.

"Hey, I'd like to thank you," Diego said. "Can I buy you lunch sometime?"

I flushed with want and desire, then came the knowledge that it was all pointless. "You know," I said, "that I'm not exactly the town favorite."

"I know that," he said. "But I don't really care what the town thinks."

I fidgeted. I knew I had to go before I flung myself at him or whatever insane thing broken people like me did. "No thank-you," I said. "I appreciate it, though. I'm glad you got your dog back."

Diego shoved his hands into his Carhartt pockets.

"Well, you've got my number if you change your mind."

"Right," I said. "I'd better go."

I drove home and tried to think about anything but Diego. But it was hard because my hands still smelled like dog. When I got home, I washed my hands and took out the apology box, to get some perspective.

CHAPTER SEVEN

The next week, I drove to see my dad. Before I left, I cleaned the bathroom and the kitchen. I put away laundry and started some soup in the crockpot. When I checked on Mom, she lay still with her back facing the door. If she was awake, she didn't let me know.

I drove along the recently opened road to Portland that wound along the edge of the mountains, a blackened hillside on my left and Cascade River on my right. It was maybe two miles across the water to woods on the other side. Thanks to heavy winds, flames from my fire had leaped the river and set the woods on the other side ablaze. For three days, two walls of fire burned along this stretch of river. I read all this online, before I'd read about how everyone in the state hated the arsonist, me. Some people said they wanted me dead. As I drove out of town, I tried to convince myself that leaving behind this town where everyone knew who I was, even though I was supposed to remain 'anonymous', would be a good thing. Leaving behind the smoky ruins of the woods, even if just for a day, would be a good thing.

Although people in my town and many of those who lived (or had lived) in these mountains hated me, the worst hate came from people in the city. Even though it hadn't been their businesses and homes that were ruined, they considered these their forests, their special vacation spots, their playground. In my newly painted car, I felt disguised, anonymous, hidden from their rage.

But waiting for me at the end of my drive would be my dad.

We hadn't spoken since before the fire, and although he occasionally sent money to Tanesha, covering a meager fraction of my legal bills, our relationship was strained. He and Mom had talked, of course, which I added to the list of humiliations I'd caused her.

When they divorced, Mom was too exhausted to fight for the house or more alimony. Too humiliated over Tranquility, who had been Dad's public relations manager before she was his sidepiece. Mom had been so overwhelmed; all she could do was trade in her Lexus for a Nissan and drive the two of us out of town to a world as different as she could find. I didn't really miss my dad. I mean, I missed who he was before his food trucks got famous and he became Food Truck Tom and I only saw him on TV. Back when I was a kid, and he'd come home smelling like deep fried onions. He'd swing me in the air, feed me delicious fried mac n' cheese bites he'd invented, and shower me with a smile that warmed my insides like a cup of good hot chocolate. But then his career took off and he smiled his hot chocolate smile at business connections, network executives and his TV audience. There was one good year, when I was eleven, but then came the next year and nothing was good after that. Seeing him would bring up those old memories. But I owed it to my mom to at least pretend I was trying to do the impossible.

I distracted myself by listening to *Crime Maven*, a true crime podcast, about the case of a woman who went missing eight years ago. They'd uncovered all kinds of weird stuff about her, like she'd been having an affair and had a bunch of money hidden away, but they never found her. How can a person disappear and never be found? If I couldn't figure out my all-important question by the time my apology box was filled, maybe I could disappear like that woman? It was something to think about.

I navigated through the tree-lined streets of my old neighborhood and found a place to park. It was the kind of neighborhood that gave the appearance nothing could go wrong. Freshly painted houses in cheery colors. Sidewalks well maintained and tidy. Wind chimes and bird houses hanging near rose bushes and in vegetable gardens that were brown and waning into fall. But I'd lived here when everything went sideways, so I knew those beautiful houses could hide all kinds of secrets.

I rolled my window down and took in the familiar smells of freshly wet leaves and pavement. A woman pushing a stroller stopped at her mailbox where she removed a few envelopes and dropped them into a basket attached to the stroller. She drank from a metal water bottle and then continued down the sidewalk away from me.

We'd moved here when I was ten, when Dad's business first took off. I saw now that he and Tranquility had replaced my mom's garden with flowering shrubs and daisies that drooped and sagged. Once upon a time, Dad had used Mom's garden produce in his restaurants, but now there wasn't an herb in sight.

A woman, two houses over, stepped out of her front door and began pulling weeds. I didn't recognize her, but I sunk down in my seat so she wouldn't see me. I noticed the light in my bedroom was on. My bedroom window opened onto a slightly pitched portion of roof. I don't think either of my parents ever knew I climbed out at night to lie on the roof, watching the moon and stars, secretly surveying the neighborhood. Hidden away from the world. Invisible.

It felt weird ringing my old doorbell. When Dad answered, he pulled me in for a hug, which I returned awkwardly. He seemed older, but good. His beard was neatly trimmed. He had more wrinkles, but they were in the right places, like someone who smiles a lot.

"You look so much older," he said. I noticed he didn't say I looked good. Just older.

"You look fed," I replied. He threw his head back and laughed like he used to, like he owned the world.

"Hi Tessa," came a perky voice. Tranquility stood in the kitchen doorway.

"Hi." I said, trying not to sound snarky. She looked older too, barely older than me.

"Come in," Dad said. "We're lunching at Alta's but first let's take a walk through the house."

"I've seen it before, you know."

"Yeah, but we've made a few changes."

"Plus, you can see where your room will be," Tranquility chimed in.

"My room wouldn't be my room?" I asked.

Dad put his arm around me. "We don't have to decide right now," he said. "Let's just have a look."

I followed him through the kitchen, which he'd remodeled with an industrial oven, two microwaves, and a much larger refrigerator. It didn't even smell like our old kitchen. It smelled like nut oil and cinnamon. Off the kitchen, and downstairs, was where we used to have the TV room. Not that we watched a lot of TV.

We headed down. The carpet had been replaced and there was a twin bed and a desk. It was an enormous space, and dark, and I was reminded why I always hated it. I didn't like being underground.

"This would be your room," Dad said. "If this works out," he added. I wondered what needed to be worked out. Was he waiting to see if I wanted to move in, or if he wanted me to move in?

"Do you like it?" Tranquility asked. "I picked out your comforter." It was yellow with a repeating daisy pattern.

I bit my lip and reminded myself I wasn't in a group home for deviants and that beggars can't be choosers.

"Yes, it's great," I lied. "What's in my old room, though? I liked my old room."

"We're using that for something else," Tranquility said. "Come, I'll show you." She led us upstairs and opened the door to my old room. It was a mess, like it was when I lived there, but this time with papers, scissors, and photos. "This is my scrapbooking room," she said proudly. There was a desk in front of the window and two large tables covered in unfinished projects. "Wanna see?" Tranquility said with excitement, grabbing a book decorated with more daisies. These flowers were her signature thing, her "brand." "I'm nearly done documenting the development of your dad's latest show." She reached for another. "And this is my favorite, our wedding and honeymoon!"

"Oh perfect," I said. "Is that the same scrapbook that documents my dad's divorce? Since it was all happening at the same time?" I couldn't help myself.

Tranquility brought one hand to her cheek as if she'd been slapped and she set down the wedding and honeymoon scrapbook.

"Okay, well, time for lunch," Dad clapped his hands together.

"I'm just going to use the bathroom. You go ahead. Be right down," I said.

In the bathroom, I opened a drawer which once held my hair bands and barrettes. It was empty except for two travel size bottles of shampoo. It made more sense to have my bedroom up here beside the bathroom, not down in a dank basement. I slammed the drawer closed. I slipped back into my old bedroom and picked-up the wedding scrapbook and began paging through it. Dad and Tranquility in Hawaii holding hands in front of an endless blue ocean. Tranquility wearing a shimmering bridal dress, cut simply but gorgeous with the sun setting behind them. They had invited me to the wedding, but I refused to go. I snapped the scrapbook shut and, without thinking, climbed onto the desk. I opened my old window and tossed the scrapbook out onto the roof.

A few minutes later, as we climbed into my dad's car, a drizzle started. I felt a pang of guilt at the idea of the scrapbook on the roof. But I shoved those feelings down as we drove away.

I was way underdressed for Alta's. The lobby was buzzing with people ready to talk business over lunch. Women in heels and slim skirts. Men in suits. Tranquility had changed into a black dress that looked like it was custom made for her petite figure. She'd draped a Pashmina around her shoulders. I stood awkwardly in my jeans and hoodie. My dad probably assumed "country hick" was my new persona. Deviant country hick. I felt an uneasiness in the pit of my stomach as I watched my dad push his way to the front of the line.

"Tom!" the hostess exclaimed. Dad leaned in and kissed her on the cheek. "Let me tell Franklin you're here." She disappeared for a few moments, returning with a man in his late twenties.

He grinned eagerly at my dad. "Tom! Good to see you!"

"You're doing a brisk business, Franklin. I always knew you would." They clasped hands and gave each other a quick hug.

"Not without your help," Franklin replied. "Hello Tranquility." He gave her a kiss on the cheek. "I have the perfect table for two." He didn't realize I was part of their group.

Dad gestured me forward. "This is my daughter, Tessa."

Franklin glanced at me with renewed interest. "Welcome Tessa! Just follow me."

It had been a long time since I was in a restaurant that offered more than cheeseburgers or tuna melts and it had been weeks since I was even in public. Clattering glassware, a cascade of voices all around me and bright spotlights bearing down from above all combined to make me feel a little shaky. It was a lot to take in all at once. I sat down and focused on the menu handed to me, where I first noticed prices before items. Since the divorce, I always skimmed for the cheapest plate because whenever I went to a restaurant, it was with my poor mother.

Two ladies on my right were enjoying wine, their long, false nails tapping their glasses to the music. Shopping bags from Nordstrom laid at their feet. A woman on my left picked at her salad while discussing revenue gains in the third division with the man across from her. I wanted to yawn.

"So," Dad said as we waited for the server. "How are you doing?"

It was the sort of question people asked when they wanted to hear everything or nothing. I went with nothing.

"Okay." I said, my eyes on a server placing a cup of black coffee in front of the woman with the salad.

"Are you working?"

"I'm volunteering at an old folks' home."

"Eww," Tranquility said. "Those places depress me."

Dad lowered his voice. "I know you'd have to do community service here too, but I think we could get you into a better place. I have some restaurant connections that do outreach. Deliver organic vegetables and stuff like that to people in need."

Our server arrived. I ordered a white cheddar grilled cheese with pickles and a cup of Italian wedding soup with ice water to drink.

"It would be better than working in a smelly old people's home," Tranquility said.

"And for you?" Tranquility ordered grilled salmon with truffle mashed potatoes, a small Greek salad, and a glass of white wine. I tallied it up in my head. Her order was three times the cost of mine. Dad ordered a steak.

"Hold on," I said before the server stepping away. "I'll have what she's having," I gestured to Tranquility. "But with a huckleberry lemonade."

"Tessa," Dad said as he leaned over the table toward me. "I know we haven't had the greatest of relationships."

"You think?"

"But if I can be here for you, then I will try. I don't know what happened, where things went wrong, and I'll take some blame-"

"It's no one's fault but my own," I interrupted.

"Well, what do you say we start over. You can enroll in school, take care of your obligations, and get on with things. I mean, what do you want to do after high school?"

"You know, Dad, I really can't think that far ahead right now."

"When I was in high school, I wanted to be an actress," Tranquility said. "But I knew I needed more realistic goals. Having goals is important. I've been reading about setting SMART goals. You know, "S" for specific," "M" for measurable, "A for--"

I cut her off with a withering glare. "I know about goals, Tranquility."

"You were doing so well," Dad said. "Whatever happened, whatever crowd you've been running with, let's get you back to where you need to be."

I wished the food would hurry and arrive so we could do something besides have this painful conversation. "I need the bathroom."

"I'll go with you," Tranquility piped up.

I sat in the stall, trying to pee. Of course, I couldn't because I didn't have to. I just wanted to escape the conversation. I eventually gave up and joined Tranquility at the mirror where she was applying lipstick and smoothing her hair. I washed and dried my hands.

"You know," she said. "I think it would be fun if you lived with us."

"Really," I said.

"Definitely!" She checked her eyebrows where I assumed there must have been one hair out of place. "We could be friends. I could, you know, mentor you."

"You're going to mentor me?"

"Sure," she said. "I know you've made some bad choices, but maybe I can help. We can set some SMART goals."

I had hoped if I lived with them, I could just pretend Tranquility didn't exist. If she was going to mentor me, that was a whole different story.

"I don't need any mentoring."

She put her makeup back in her purse. "Some people may disagree," she said. "If you want to live with us, you'll need to pull your image together. I'm still your dad's public relations manager, you know. I'm responsible for how the world sees him. Sees us."

"Are you worried I'm going to hurt his brand or something?"

"Well," Tranquility said, meeting my eyes in the mirror. "Look at you."

When we returned, our food was on the table. I had hardly any appetite, but I forced myself to eat some salmon.

"I just want you to think about it," Dad said. "Both Tranquility and I are on the road a lot, so you'd be on your own sometimes." That was a relief. This arrangement sounded better and better with every bite. He continued, "so we'd be trusting you to make good decisions on your own."

"Dad, I'm not a total delinquent."

We ate without talking for a long while and I tuned into the conversation between the ladies on my right who were now well into their second glass of wine.

"Just horrible," one of them said. She wore her reading glasses on top of her head.

"I know. Think of the cost," the other replied.

"Those poor firefighters. Such a tragedy."

I flushed when I noticed the tension at our table and realized I hadn't been the only one eavesdropping. My hand, the one holding my fork, froze over a stalk of broccolini.

"And all because of a teenage girl, can you believe it?"

"What is wrong with kids these days?"

If I could have fallen through a crack in the floor and never come up for air again, I would have. I felt Tranquility's eyes on me as if to say, "I told you so." Dad appeared suddenly very interested in cutting up his steak. I had to pee for real now, but I couldn't move. It was like I was paralyzed in some crazy nightmare I couldn't escape.

"I heard she's only sixteen. At that age, it's really about the parents. I heard she's been raised by a single mom."

The other lady sniffed. "That's who should be held responsible."

I slammed my fork down on the table. Everyone around me, the ladies, Tranquility and even Dad, jumped in their seats.

"What do you know?" I snapped over my shoulder. "You don't know anything, so shut your rich lady traps."

"Oh my gosh, I'm so sorry," Dad said to the women at the table. I glared at him. "Come on," he directed sharply. "Time to go." He pushed his chair back and grabbed his jacket.

"My goodness," one of them exclaimed. "How rude."

"You're just going to let them talk like that?" I demanded. Dad started to put one arm into the sleeve of his jacket, then gave up. He took hold of my elbow and guided me toward the door.

"I'm so sorry," Tranquility said to the women, "your lunch is on us."

"Stop this," Dad whispered to me. "People know me here."

Customers were moving out of our way as I let Dad drag me through the restaurant, my eyes filling with tears. I didn't go back into their house. Not even to pee. I drove away and used a restroom at a gas station just outside the city. I sat on their grimy toilet, pressing my hands into my eyes, taking deep breaths to keep from crying. I scratched the tops of my fingers until I could breathe again. Then I got into my car and drove home. No matter what Mom wanted, I wouldn't be living with my dad. Not now. Not ever!

CHAPTER EIGHT

Dear Ms. Fitzimmons,

I'm sorry that your coffee and ice cream shop has lost so much money this summer because of the fire I set. I didn't mean to cause you harm. I like The Plaid Cow and always enjoyed the pecan ice cream there. I'm truly sorry you had to shut down for the season, I know this is your busy time. I apologize for what I did. I hope you can open the shop again next summer.
Sincerely,
The Girl Who Started the Fire

It was a relief to be back at Morningstar after my disastrous visit with Dad. The residents didn't seem to know who I was and none of them acted like they knew a SMART way to fix me.

"Good morning, Dolores," I called as I wheeled a breakfast tray down the hall to Effby's room. Dolores drooled. She always drooled.

Effby had an oxygen tank beside her bed. Tubes went from the tank into her nose.

"Good morning," I said. Effby grunted. "That's new." I gestured to the oxygen tank.

"I'm accessorizing," Effby said in a voice that didn't welcome any follow-up questions.

I set the tray down beside her. "Time for breakfast."

"What is it?"

"The chef has prepared a culinary masterpiece of al dente scrambled eggs, smoked bacon cooked to medium perfection, and blackened toast topped with a dollop of fruity preserves. Bon appetite." I thought if I made her bland breakfast sound like something off the menu at Alta's, she'd be all over it.

"What kind of fruity preserves?"

"Strawberry."

She reached for the toast. "I like strawberry."

I sat down in the chair opposite her, savoring my first positive statement from Effby. "I got sick on strawberry jam once," I said. "When I was three. I haven't been able to eat it since."

Effby smeared the jam across her toast. "More for me."

I noticed the crossword puzzle book I'd given her was wedged in between the cushions of the armchair I was sitting in. I pulled it out and flipped through the pages. She'd completed all the puzzles. "Effby, how did you get your name?"

"It's short for Frances Belinda."

"What?"

"Frances Belinda Hartson. F.B."

I started laughing. "Oh, I get it, your initials without the H!"

She shook her head. "Call me whatever you want. But not Frances Belinda."

Effby swallowed the last bite of toast and sat back, licking jam from her lips. A hummingbird hovered outside the window for a few seconds. Effby raised a finger to it. "Fast little buggers," she said.

"Hey," I said. "Did you hear about that woman who went missing in Pennsylvania eight years ago and they only found her shawl and tennis shoes?"

"Murdered?" Effby asked.

"Who knows," I said. "They didn't find out until later that she'd been having an affair."

"It was the husband. It's always the husband. Or the lover."

"Well, they never found out for sure. It's a mystery."

"Hmmph," Effby huffed. "Amateurs."

"Do you ever listen to *Crime Maven*? It's a podcast."

"Do you see me with a goddammed iPhone? How am I supposed to do that?"

She had a point.

Kathy pulled me aside later that day. "Hey, I just want you to know you're doing a good job with Effby." She lifted a chart from Tamara's desk. "She needed the oxygen. COPD's gotten worse."

"What's COPD?"

"Chronic Obstructive Pulmonary Disease. It's what everyone gets after smoking one or two packs of cigarettes every day of their lives. It's a lung disease. Over time, it gets worse. When she came here, it was after she'd been in the hospital with pneumonia and needed to recover, but you never really recover from COPD. Anyway, you're doing a good job with her."

Tamara swiveled in her seat to grab a file. "She's still a brat."

"See if you can coax her out of her room," Kathy said, "be a little social."

I didn't think it worth mentioning I was probably not the best person for teaching anyone social skills.

Kathy continued, "We got a donation of books for the library. The boxes are in the storage closet. Can you get those put away in the rec room?"

"Sure."

I was glad to have Effby. As cranky as she was, she was the only person who talked to me these days besides Kathy telling me what to do. Dad had stopped texting, and Mom hardly said two words. Not that she refused to talk with me, but more like she left the best parts of herself at Woods Hole every night. I told myself I deserved it, but it still hurt.

One night, after I'd waited up especially late just to chat with her, after asking loads of questions and her not responding, I switched tactics. I went back to something that had worked for us in the past, something that had been part of our regular schedule since I could remember. I told her about my day. I talked about Effby. How I wanted to buy a hummingbird feeder to hang on the tree outside Effby's window.

Mom nodded and said, 'That's nice', but I could tell she wasn't really listening. She did a lot of staring into her mostly empty glass of wine. I continued talking about the happenings at Morningstar, until out of the blue Mom said, 'It's not too late,' relevant to absolutely nothing I'd been talking about, but I knew the rest of her sentence would go something like 'to go back to school this fall'. The first day of school was one week away, but I'd already decided. I wasn't going.

Back in my room, I opened the thick manila envelope that had come through the mail earlier in the day. For the tenth time, I pulled out a charred piece of wood. It had broken apart and blackened the inside of the envelope, which came with no note or explanation, just my name and address scrawled with a thick, black Sharpie. There was no return address, just like the first envelope I'd received some weeks ago. My thumbs and fingers became covered in charcoal, and I was grateful my mom was too out of it to notice.

The moment I hung the hummingbird feeder, Effby asked me to move her chair closer to the window, which made me happy because it meant she liked it. After that, I'd come on shift most days to find her sitting by the window more often than lying in bed, sometimes with her forehead pressed to the glass.

"How many have you seen this morning?" I asked.

"Four," she said. "One of them came right up to me. I didn't have my teeth in. Probably scared the crap out of him."

I pulled out the iPad and flash drive I'd brought. "I've got something for you, in case you want to listen to something while you're terrorizing birds." I put the flash drive in. "I downloaded three episodes of *Crime Maven* for you. You remember, the true crime podcast. My favorite is about this guy who makes jewelry." I handed her the iPad and a set of earbuds. "Here. I won't tell you what he does with it." She took the iPad, dropping it in her lap.

My phone pinged. I didn't recognize the number until I saw Rippen's face with his big doggy grin. The text under the photo said *Rippen says hi.*

It had been two weeks since we'd found Rippen, and I'd thought about him nearly every day, wondered if he'd run away again. Well, to be honest, I'd been thinking about Diego more than his dog. He may have asked me out, but I knew once he got to know me, he wouldn't want anything to do with me. I mean, who wants to hang out with a convicted arsonist? I slipped my phone into my pocket.

"Come on Effby, let's take a walk."

"And do what? Swap war stories with the other inmates?"

"Let's go to the rec area. We can play a game or something. True crime can wait."

"Delightful. A stimulating game of Candy Land, perhaps? It fits, since all the clones who work here talk to me like I'm three years old. They use that stupid voice when pretending they're happy to see me. I hate that stupid voice." She shifted in her seat. "Who texted you just now?"

"What?" She'd never asked me anything about myself.

"Are you deaf? I asked, who texted you."

I pulled out my phone and showed her Rippen's picture. "A dog texted me. See?"

"You gonna text your dog friend back?"

"I doubt it."

Effby fidgeted with the thumb drive and iPad, while I straightened her bed and fixed her pillows. She placed the iPad on the bed tray. "Okay, let's go on this big recreation area adventure you promised," she said. "I'm sure it will be the thrill of a lifetime."

I loaded Effby's oxygen tank onto the back of her wheelchair and put a blanket over her frail legs before pushing the chair out of the room. We rolled past William, who was sitting in his wheelchair in the hallway.

"Hello there!" he said cheerfully.

"Hello William," I said. Effby gave a small wave.

"Dullard," she muttered when we were out of earshot.

Tamara's eyebrows raised as we wheeled past the receptionist area. "Hello!" Tamara said in a sing-songy, high-pitched voice. "Effby, it's so good to see you out of your room!"

"Told you," Effby said to me.

In the rec area, several residents were watching *Judge Judy*. We wheeled up to a table with a smattering of art supplies. "There's some high-quality entertainment," Effby said, gesturing at the TV.

"Here," I said. "Let's paint a picture." I gathered some blank papers and brushes.

"I can't paint anything. Or draw."

"Me neither," I said.

Effby picked up the local newspaper, *The Elmsville Connection*. "Can you believe this is the only paper they get here? These articles are crap." I dipped my brush into a watered-down blue color and painted a streak across the paper. "I wrote better material when I was writing obits in my twenties," she said.

"You wrote for the newspaper?"

"Yes, I did. For most of my life. Wrote for *The California Chronicle*. I was a reporter. And a good one. Not that it matters anymore." Effby was making small splotches on her paper with black paint. I tried imagining a young Effby, the intrepid reporter, bullying her way into a room with her notebook and pen, asking tough questions. I could kind of see it.

Kathy noticed us and hurried over. "Effby!" she said in the same high-pitched tone Tamara had used. "That's a wonderful picture! What is it?"

"Self-portrait," she said, putting down her brush.

"Oh," Kathy said, confused. "Well, keep up the good work, you two Picassos!" She flittered off.

"How long did you work for *The Chronicle*?" I asked, eager to move on from Kathy's interruption.

"Most of my career," she said. "Started there after I moved from Iowa."

I had thought little about where Effby might have lived or what she'd done in her life before Morningstar. I'd sort of assumed she'd always lived in Elmsville, or at least in Oregon.

"Wait," I said, trying not to sound like an investigative reporter. "When did you move from Iowa?"

Effby put her paintbrush back in the water with a shaky hand. "I'd like to go back," she said gruffly.

Effby remained quiet all the way to her room. She climbed into bed and rolled onto her side. "Effby?" I said, "you need anything?" She shook her head. I placed our paintings on her bookshelf. One, a bunch of black splotches, and the other, three big blue lines. If you squinted and looked sideways, they sort of resembled people, at least people who'd been painted by a three-year-old.

"Tessa," Effby said.

"What?"

"You should text that dog friend."

As I left Morningstar that evening, I sent a text. *Hi Rippen.*

Maybe it was because Effby had shared something about herself. Or maybe it was because when I went to the library to borrow past issues of *The Washington Post* and *The California Chronicle*, no one glared at me, or even seemed to notice who I was. Maybe it was because the sun was shining, and the sky was clear of ash for the first time in weeks. It looked normal, and I felt like my old self again, or at least normal.

CHAPTER NINE

We met at a park on the outskirts of town. I saw Rippen before I saw Diego. Rippen ran up to me, his tail wagging and the whole back half of his body wagging along with it.

"Hey, Buddy," I said, "I can't believe you remembered me."

"He remembers everyone," Diego said. "He's not the best-behaved dog in the world, but he might be the smartest." Diego stood with a backpack slung over one shoulder, holding a ball launcher in the other hand. My stomach flipped when Diego smiled at me.

"I hardly recognized you without your Carhartts," I said.

"I can streak some grease on myself, if that will make you feel more comfortable." He was wearing jeans and a long-sleeved shirt that was just tight enough around his arms to show the muscles underneath. I bent down to scratch Rippen behind his ears.

The day was chilly, but the sun was out. "Want some hot chocolate?" Diego asked, opening his backpack. We sat on top of a picnic table. Steam from our cups took the chill out of the air.

"So, I don't know much about you," Diego said.

"Everyone knows about me."

"I don't mean that," he said. "I mean, everything else. Like what do you like to do? Do you work? What year are you in school?"

Rippen was running in the field past a play structure. I envied him. It felt like every question was more complicated to answer than it should be. I skipped most of Diego's questions and instead told him about Morningstar. I told him about Effby and the hummingbird feeder and *Crime Maven*. I described our horrible paintings and how, sadly, they were the only things on her bookshelf. I told him how she would eat strawberry jam, but no ice cream or pudding. I told him she liked to swear and how she needed oxygen because she had COPD. At a certain point, long after I'd finished my cup of chocolate, I realized how happy I felt talking to someone who was truly listening to me.

"Sorry, I think I just talked for like, an hour straight."

"Hardly," he laughed. "I loved it. It sounds like a pretty amazing job."

"Well, it's not exactly a job. I volunteer there." I paused. "I have to do community service as part of my sentence."

"Yeah, Pablo had to do a bunch of community service last year when he got his MIP." Diego stretched his legs out. "But all he could find was trash pickup along the highway. Yours sounds way better."

"Did he get it all done?"

"Yeah. He's done. It's just him and me, and our dad, but he's hardly ever around. Pablo's got a wild side."

"What about your mom?"

Diego's voice shifted tone a little. "She passed away a couple of years ago. Cancer."

I wished I hadn't asked. I knew right away how tired Diego was of answering this question. "I'm so sorry."

"Yeah, it sucked." He grabbed the ball launcher. "Time for Rippen to get some exercise."

We took turns throwing the ball, watching Rippen hurtle across the field, sometimes losing control and somersaulting to a stop. After a while, I climbed up a rock wall in the play area, scaling quickly to the top. I jumped down, then grasped the bars and pulled myself across, swinging hand-over-hand, lifting my legs out straight in front of me several times. It surprised me how strong I felt despite not using my muscles like I did when I was playing volleyball.

Diego grinned. "You should do one of those obstacle course TV shows." He climbed up beside me. "That was impressive."

"The kind where giant foam mallets hit you in the face? No thanks. How did you end up at Kip's?" I asked him, afraid he'd ask me more questions about me, and I'd blather on for another hour.

"My uncle taught me. When I graduated from high school last year, I needed a job. I'm pretty good with details and doing stuff that most people think is tedious. You know, sanding metal to the exact right smoothness. Or mixing paint to the perfect color and consistency. It's not exactly the type of work that thrills most people, but I like it."

"You didn't want to go to college?"

"I couldn't afford it. But even if I could, it's not what I want. At least not right now. I'm happy where I am. And besides, I wanted to stick around to help Pablo through his shit. Make sure he stays in school and out of trouble."

"What about those sketches I saw? Do you draw a lot?"

"Yeah, it's a kind of stress reliever for me, I guess."

I took a breath. "I'm supposed to start my junior year next week, but I'm not going back to school." It was the first time I'd said it out loud.

Diego was quiet. "What are you going to do instead?"

"I don't know," I said. "But I can't go back there."

He swung his legs gently until they dangled down from the play structure. "Do you ever think how every decision we make takes us in a different direction, but maybe we have other lives happening at the same time? Like you could go back to school and live that life, but also live a different life where you don't go back to school. And those different lives could be happening at the same time."

"Yah, I do sometimes wish I could switch. Jump into one of those other lives."

"Yeah, me too. But the thing is, there are so many directions. So many pathways you could take."

I looked out at the low-lying sun. I tried thinking of directions and pathways. It didn't feel like I had all that many to choose from.

We said goodbye sort of awkwardly in the parking lot, with Rippen leaping around, then finally sitting on my feet as we talked in vague terms about getting together again. By the time I pulled into our apartment parking space, Diego had texted. *That was fun. Next time I'll bring more hot chocolate.*

I texted back. *Sounds good.* Then I noticed Mom's car. She hadn't gone to work again.

I found her sitting at the kitchen table when I entered the apartment. The sun had nearly set, and our apartment was dark. I flipped on the lights. "Mom, why aren't you at work? Are you okay?" She was wearing sweatpants and an oversized t-shirt. I dropped my bag and came to sit across the table from her. "Are you sick?" I asked. There were dark circles under her eyes and her hair was a tangled mess.

"I just couldn't go in," she answered, "I'm too tired."

"Maybe you're coming down with something," I said. "Have you eaten anything today?"

"I think so."

I went to the fridge and pulled out makings for sandwiches. "Mom, maybe we could color our hair tonight. You know, kind of like a spa night."

"I'm going to let mine grow out," she replied. "Save money."

The bread was a bit stale, but I would make it work. I opened a package of ham and lathered on some mustard.

"Let me tell you about my day," I said, as I put two plates of sandwiches on the table. "I brought Effby some more newspapers and she listened to all the podcasts I gave her. I'm going to download three more tonight. She figures out who the killer is before I do almost every time."

Even though I'd been talking, I'd finished my sandwich. She had made no move to eat hers. "And," I said. "I went to the park. With a friend." I felt a wave of happiness. "I have a new friend. I think he's a friend, yah, I'm pretty sure. You've met him. The guy from the garage." When Mom didn't respond, I said, "Mom, please eat your sandwich."

She picked it up. "I'm sorry if I can't be excited for you," she said, tossing it back on the plate. "I just can't find my way out of this right now."

Anger bubbled up inside. Couldn't I just feel good about this one thing? Didn't I deserve to feel some happiness after everything that had happened? Just when it felt like things were returning to normal, she had to tell me she couldn't be excited for something good finally coming my way.

"Mom," I reached across the table to touch her hand. She was clearly hurting. "It's going to be all right."

"Tanesha called today."

I pulled my hand away. "What is it?"

"We have an appointment with her to talk about the fines. The $450,000."

"I thought she said that amount was just for show. To make a statement. That it wouldn't stick."

"Tanesha said we have to start paying on it, to show good faith. But even if the amount changes, we still can't afford it." She slumped back in her chair, dropping her arms into her lap.

"Mom, we'll figure it out. I'll figure something out. Mom, I'm worried about you." I pulled a piece of crust from her sandwich and rolled it between my fingers. "I'm worried you're going to, you know, become like you were before."

She sighed. "It's just a hard time."

"I know, believe me, I know how hard this time has been, but maybe you could use some help before things get worse."

"Did you know when I was young, I was a dancer?" My mom seemed to be speaking to someone else, the way her eyes looked straight through me. Once, I'd found an old picture of my mom, dressed in a white snowflake costume from *The Nutcracker*. She was about sixteen in the photo, maybe younger. She stood *en pointe,* balanced on the toes of one foot with her other leg extended gracefully behind her.

"I was *en pointe* for three years," she said. "Before most girls. I practiced every day. Strengthened my ankles so they could support me. It was what I loved most of all."

"What happened?"

"My mom became sick with kidney disease. We had so many medical bills, we couldn't afford ballet anymore. Besides that, I was needed at home to take care of her. I dropped lessons, dropped out of school and stayed home." She took a drink from the water glass. "I don't regret being with her, of course, but-" She shifted her weight and turned to face me. "I was going to be great. If things had been different, I'd have-" Her voice broke, "I was going to be great, and it was taken away from me."

"Mom," I said, but she pulled away.

"You," she pointed her finger at me. "I did everything for you, and you took it away from yourself." She sat back, like a balloon totally deflated. "I just don't understand."

"Mom, I didn't mean to…" I trailed off. I didn't know what I wanted to say. Didn't mean to start the fire? Didn't mean to totally screw up my whole life? Mom always believed I was destined for greatness, Miss Possibilities. Maybe I didn't mean to mess that up. Or maybe I did? Maybe I was just waiting for the right moment to sabotage everything. Which sort of made everything a hundred times worse. I took my plate to the sink.

"I'm going to bed," she said.

She'd been like this before, back when I was twelve. I'd seen her close in on herself, lying in the darkness of her bedroom all day and night, pushing aside food until she was pale and gaunt. I thought we'd left all that behind, after the divorce, before we moved to Elmsville, but looking at her now, I guess we didn't.

In my room, I opened my bottom dresser drawer and pulled out a soft piece of fabric I'd buried toward the back. It was a small square with three ducks, cross stitched clumsily with the words "For my brother." I'd spent a lot of time working on those letters, which, for an eleven year old, wasn't easy. I'd been excited to make my brother something nice, and I remembered those days we spent getting ready for his arrival as probably the best time for my family. Dad stopped traveling so much. My parents hardly fought. I'd catch them kissing in the kitchen, Dad's hand resting on Mom's belly. What I didn't really understand at the time was how my unborn brother was the glue that kept my family together. But then Mom came home from the hospital without a baby.

Dad threw himself into work and was away most all the time. Mom wouldn't come out of her bedroom. For many nights, weeks on end, I sat outside her bedroom door and talked about my day. She didn't reply, not even a 'that's nice', but I kept going. I sat in the hallway and told her what I'd done at school that day, about the good grades I'd received, the science competition I was preparing for, after school soccer games my team had won. I talked and talked and talked and finally, after several weeks, she came out of the bedroom. I made her tea and from that night onward, sitting at the kitchen table was part of our routine.

In those first few days, she said nothing. I'd never felt so alone. I'd curl up at night with my duckling cross stitch and cry for my brother who never came home. But during the day, I did my homework, I even did extra homework, helped my teachers tidy up after school. I joined as many school clubs as I could, just to be sure I had enough to talk about with Mom each night. This time, however, it was me who put her in this dark place and no matter what I said, there was no talking my mom back from the ledge she was standing on.

I carefully folded the delicate fabric and placed it in the back of my drawer. Then I laid in bed, imagining my life as branching lines through space. If I could jump from one to the other, switch to a life where there wasn't so much pain, I would do it. But I was stuck on this line, and I couldn't see where it was going or where it would end.

CHAPTER TEN

There were a hundred reasons not to see Diego again. In fact, there were 145 and 82 more in the box under my bed. But being with him made me forget about that damn box. Made me forget the reason my mom was withdrawing from me and why she sometimes didn't eat, or shower, for days. Diego made me forget how much I missed volleyball and playing my violin. Made me forget about another envelope that came in the mail. This time it was an article detailing the extensive damage my fire had caused and how long it would take the forest trees to heal.

So, when Diego texted me, I texted back.

At Morningstar, Effby and I painted pictures. My picture of summer flowers, 'Monet style', looked like someone threw up a sunflower field. I texted it to Diego with the caption, *almost as good as u.*

A minute later, I got a text back. *U've been hiding ur talent.*

Another day, while I was bleaching the kitchen counters at home for the second time that week, my phone pinged. It was a link to a video of two dueling violin players, both playing versions of Metallica's "Enter the Sandman". A couple days later, he texted, *What time RU off tonight? Hang out w me?*

I hesitated. Texting was a harmless distraction, but seeing him in person seemed wrong, like it was off-limits. Happiness I didn't deserve. I wrote, *Working til 10. Sorry!*

I was really off at seven. Mom was working an early shift today and I wanted to be home when she got there, to convince her to watch a show with me. Anything besides sitting at the table staring at nothing until it was time to go to bed.

Later, as I replaced board games in the rec area, I got a text from Mom. *It's busy here, working late. Roast chicken in the fridge.*

In the world of Mom's texts, this wasn't spectacular, but given everything that was going on with her right now, it felt monumental. Things almost felt normal, like she hadn't spent the last two days in her bathrobe.

I texted her back. *Kk, love U.*

Then I texted Diego, *What about tmrw?*

I met him at Kip's the next day just after five. Effby had watched me run a brush through my hair, as I examined myself in her bathroom mirror. "Hot date?"

"No," I said, prickly heat spreading across my cheeks.

"Right," she said.

"It's not a date."

"Of course, it's not. Have fun on your not-date. Remember Amanda Lee was on a date, except they found her in a fridge at the bottom of the lake."

"Thanks a lot, Effby. No more podcasts for you." I left her chortling to herself.

When I walked into the lobby of Kip's, it was empty, so I peeked through the door into the shop. Diego was on the far side polishing a teal-colored Honda Civic. I was about to call out, when someone yelled "Yo, D!"

A guy, about my age and wearing jeans and a black t-shirt, walked through the door. His long, shaggy hair fell around his shoulders. I could tell right away he was Diego's brother. I hung back, not wanting to interrupt.

"What's up?" Diego stood.

"You got some cash, man? I'm out. Jay and Carlos want to hit the cheap night movies." Pablo stood against the Honda with a lazy confidence. It occurred to me that Diego's brother could be trouble. But then, I was in trouble, too.

"What happened to the forty I gave you last weekend?"

"You know I had to pay fees for that chem class at school. Come on, man. I should've asked Dad before he left, but I got busy."

"Got busy doing nothing," Diego said. There was an edge to his voice I hadn't heard before.

"Dude, I need cash sometimes."

"Dude," Diego said pointedly, "you need a job."

"I know, bro, but come on, just for tonight."

Diego twisted a rag in his hands and finally nodded. "Go on, grab forty from the register. I'll take care of it when I'm done here."

Pablo brightened, giving Diego a light punch. "Thanks, man. Hey," he gestured to the Civic. "You do this job? It's sweet."

"Thanks," Diego said. "Hey, check this out." They headed in my direction but became engrossed in a lime green Mustang Gran Torino.

"Whoa," Pablo said, admiringly.

"Yeah, pretty awesome, huh?" Diego said, then noticed me. "Hey," he grinned and waved.

"Hi." I wondered what Pablo had heard about me. Apparently not much by the way he gave me a once-over.

"Got to go," he said. "Thanks, dude." He sauntered over to the register.

"Sorry, I'm a little behind," Diego said. "I have to run a car through the car wash down the street. It'll be faster than me washing it myself. Come with me?"

I climbed into the passenger side of a Mazda that smelled like coconut oil. A book from the *Twilight* series was on the seat. I picked it up to sit down.

"Yeah, I got caught up with that Civic. Sorry." He started the engine and backed out of the driveway.

"Well, this explains the coconut smell in here," I said, holding up the book. "Glitter vampires."

"Have you read it?" Diego asked.

"Isn't it a little early in the night for true confessions?"

"I take that as a yes."

"I didn't see the movie, though. Did you?"

"No." He pulled out into traffic. "Not my style. I'm more of a *Napoleon Dynamite* kind of guy."

I turned to him. "I love that movie," I said. "None of my friends would watch it with me, but I streamed it on Netflix at least once a month back in Portland."

"Sweet," he replied. "You know, you remind me a little of Deb. If your hair was in a side pony."

"Whatever," I laughed. "So, that's your brother?"

"Yeah," he said, and I felt a slight tension in his voice. We drove down the block, turning the car into the Quick Quack Car Wash. A worker waved Diego through. "I come here a lot," he said.

"You should get a punch card."

"I wish they sold milkshakes. It's a nice break just sitting here."

The car moved into the tunnel. A purple light glowed as water fell all around. It was loud, like heavy rain outside your window that your brain shuts out when there's something more interesting to focus on.

"I like going through the car wash," I said. "When I was little, I used to pretend I was going through some kind of portal."

Diego turned toward me, leaning back against the driver's door. "A portal to where?" Suds cascaded down the window behind him, dimming the light. Nothing outside mattered. It was just me and Diego sitting in some anonymous person's car that smelled like a tropical island.

"Any place, I guess," I said. "Just someplace more interesting than where I was."

Diego held my eyes, and I felt my stomach twist in on itself, but I didn't look away. The suds slowly disappeared, and the light changed to blue. "I've always liked the car wash," Diego said. "I could ride this slow track forever, you know?"

I felt my breath quicken. "Yeah," I said. "I know."

The polish cycle flipped on as another round of spray came at us from all sides. In that moment, I wished with all my heart this was a portal. For us to come out of this car wash into a different reality where everything was clean and shiny and bright. And then to go through it all again, an eternal loop of wash, rinse, and polish. Just being under cover of suds with the changing lights with this boy who was moving closer to me until our lips touched, brushing against each other as the light changed from yellow to green and the car lurching forward until it rolled off the track felt, for a second, like my dream wings had come out and I was flying toward another world.

CHAPTER ELEVEN

Dear Mr. Collins,

Thank you for your efforts in fighting the Horseback Falls Fire. I'm sorry that you had to put yourself in danger and be away from your family and breathe all that smoke. I apologize for what I did, and I've learned from this experience.

I didn't mean for this to happen.

I'm sorry.

Sincerely,

The Girl Who Started the Fire

Someone had decorated Morningstar with ghosts, jack-o'-lanterns, and large furry spiders for Halloween. Kathy's face was green under the sagging brim of her witch's hat. Tamara wore cat ears and had drawn whiskers on her nose with eyebrow pencil. I suspected her real costume was at home. A 'sexy nurse' or a 'sexy plumber' or a 'sexy potato' perhaps? My costume was a small spider drawn on my face with Mom's liquid liner, because that's about as much spirit as I had this year. I was meeting Diego at his place to hand out candy later. He'd invited me to a Halloween party, but I was too nervous about encountering local people.

Aileen May waved at me. She was wearing a headband with orange streamers. "Happy Halloween," I said.

She held my hand as I leaned toward her. "I hope the children come this year. Do you know if the children are coming? I have a whole bag of Tootsie Rolls."

Phyllis came toward us, wearing a bumblebee headband and a black and yellow striped shirt. "Aileen May, you know the church group is coming just like they do every year. Now, be at your station by five and the kids will come through." She pursed her lips. "And do not allow them to grab candy by the handfuls. Give them two and no more." Phyllis bustled away, her bumblebee antennae waving.

Aileen May motioned for me to lean in. "I'm giving five each," she whispered. I didn't tell her that Tootsie Rolls were hardly going to be a big draw.

I knew Effby wouldn't be caught dead in a Halloween headband. And I was right. She wore her usual sagging t-shirt and a pair of stretchy brown pants.

"I see you're dressed as a grumpy old lady," I said.

"I don't have any candy," she grumbled. "No one better ask me for any."

"Come on, let's go out to the rec area." I reached for her wheelchair.

"No, I'm not going out there today. Too much ruckus. I'll just sit here and read The Post so I can keep track of the criminals in Washington."

"Here, I brought you a couple more issues."

She'd read every issue of *The Washington Post*, *New York Times*, and *The California Chronicle*, back-to-back. She'd brought up the latest insider trading scandals and a story about compromised water supply in California, among others, so I knew she was reading them. It was nearly worth sitting in my car for twenty minutes, working up the courage to enter the library. It was almost laughable how I'd skulked in, beelined for the newspaper shelves, and avoided all eye contact. For all I knew, the librarian could have been on my list of apology letters.

I yawned, sinking into the seat across from Effby. I'd been up late revising an essay for one of several online tutoring jobs I'd picked-up, helping people with homework assignments or assisting terrible writers with their college admittance essays. It stung a little that I wasn't snagging scholarships out from under these kids from privileged backgrounds who, rather than work a little harder, paid me to do the work for them. I couldn't complain. I was making money, which I dutifully transferred into my mom's account.

Effby rattled the paper decisively. "I hate writing that drags on. Get to the point. Damn English majors think they're journalists."

"Tell me about when you were a reporter," I said. "How did you learn to write like that?"

Effby peered at me over the paper. "I was never one of those flowery writers that meanders around forever getting to the point. I didn't have time. I needed money and I was paid by the story, not by the word. So, when I finished enough stories, I could pay my rent."

"What was the hardest thing about your job?" I asked.

"Well, I didn't much care for how my first boss slapped me on the ass and made me get his coffee."

"What?" I asked. "He actually slapped your ass?"

"It was the way things were back then. A lot of bosses did worse than that. I was lucky. I left that paper to work for *The Chronicle* where I made twice as much as my old boss by the time I left."

"You mean when you retired?"

"I never retired. Unless you call having a stroke retiring."

Effby still hadn't told me anything about her family. Or friends. Or husband. I understood not wanting to talk about some things, but I also understood wanting to talk about stuff and not being asked. So, I asked.

"Why did your family move you here?"

"They didn't. I moved here on my own."

"But why didn't you stay in California?"

Her hands clasped around the newspaper. "Assisted suicide. Oregon has assisted suicide."

I didn't know what to say. I tried catching her eyes, but she focused them outside. There were no hummingbirds, not until next year. The feeder was empty, but it was the only bright spot against the dying tree.

"What about your family? Did you have a husband? Where are your children?"

"Nope and nope," she said swiftly. "No friends either, in case that's your next question. Didn't need any. Didn't want any."

We sat in silence for a while. Effby fidgeted with the paper. "I could use some tea," she said, "black tea."

"I don't believe you, Effby," I said.

"You don't believe I want black tea?"

"I don't believe you had no one you cared about." I stood up. "But I'll get you some tea."

As I waited for the water to heat, Regina came into the kitchen. She was dressed as a princess with ribbons braided through her hair and her cheeks sparkling with glitter.

"Nice costume," I remarked.

From the refrigerator she pulled a tray of individual cups of tapioca, colored orange for the occasion. "That's disgusting," Regina said, making a face not usually associated with a princess.

"What's your daughter dressing up as?"

"We're matching princesses. If I can ever get out of here. I'm supposed to take her out trick-or-treating, but I'm not sure I'm going to make it."

"What do you still have to do?"

"I need to check meds and some vitals for Wing Four, but this Halloween thing is throwing me off." She pulled plastic wrap from the sheet of tapiocas, wadded it up and tossed it into the bin. "Tapioca and zombie cookie delivery, then I've got to dole out all the candy for them to give to the kids, plus all the linens."

I stirred Effby's teabag. "Let me deliver this, then I can help with the food and linens. You do meds and whatever else I can't do."

"Are you sure? That would be amazing."

"No problem."

After she left, I texted Diego. *Might be later than I thought. I'll text b4 I leave.*

Diego and I saw each other around once a week. It was getting too cold to hang out at the park, so instead we walked Rippen, or I'd wait for him at the shop and then we'd hang out at his place. His dad traveled for work and wasn't home much. Pablo, the few times he was around, seemed suspicious of me. I was sure he knew who I was, but he said nothing.

I was looking forward to seeing Diego, although I should have been home reviewing essays and writing letters. But Mom mostly worked or stayed in her room with the door closed, and our little apartment was just too quiet and dark for me. Diego's house was easier. Diego was easier.

I let myself feel a little Halloween spirit as I made my way through each wing, distributing bowls of candy. Many residents wore funny hats or glasses. Several were being visited by great grandchildren dressed as Marvel characters or Disney princesses and, as they smiled for photographs, I could see they were excited to get to the next thing, the real trick-or-treating. As I headed back to the kitchen, the church bus pulled up. Regina was just leaving and waved at me as a gaggle of costumed kids unloaded.

"I owe you one!" she called.

I knew no one in school who had a kid. All my friends were busy with sports or groups. Someone like Regina would never have been in my circles. Which was too bad, because maybe I needed someone like Regina. Someone who did her own thing. Someone with important stuff to think about.

April and I held the doors as kids paraded in. A fairy got her glittering green wings stuck in the doorway for a moment until she thought to move sideways. Kids skipped and stumbled over one another on their way to the lobby. "Happy Halloween," they said.

After I'd finished loading the hamper with linens, I stopped by Effby's room. Trick or treaters were just starting down her hall. I opened her door to find her reading *The Chronicle*. "Come on Effby, keep your door open and hand out some candy." I put a bowl of Jolly Ranchers into her lap.

"Fine," she groused. I wheeled her over to her doorway.

"How come you're not dressed up?" Asked a girl wearing a pirate's costume, complete with a dagger in her belt and an eye patch on her forehead, as if covering a third eye.

"I am dressed up," Effby grumped. She dropped some candy into the girl's bag. "I'm dressed as your future. Scary, isn't it?" The girl scratched her eye patch, looking confused. Effby gave a loud cackle and the girl scuttled off.

"That wasn't very nice," I said.

"You were right," she chuckled. "This is fun."

As kids came in groups of twos and threes, Effby dropped pieces of candy in each bucket. The little fairy with green wings who'd been stuck in the door came skipping up. "Trick or treat," she said. Effby didn't move. She stared at the girl, moving her fingers through the bowl as if they couldn't find anything to grab on to.

"Trick or treat," the girl tried again.

"I'm done," Effby snapped. She gripped the wheels of her chair and began to roll, the bowl of Jolly Ranchers emptying out onto the floor.

"What's wrong?" I asked.

"I'm done. Shut the door."

I grabbed a few pieces of candy and dropped them into the girl's bucket. "Happy Halloween," I said. "Go on to the next room, there'll be more candy there."

I wheeled Effby inside and closed the door.

"What just happened?" I asked. "Are you okay?"

Effby was slumped in the chair. "I'm fine. I just want to go to bed. Can you get me into bed?"

"Let me call a CNA," I said. "I can't do that myself. Are you sick?"

"No," she said. She hung her head. "I'm just done with today."

After April had helped Effby into bed and left the room, I tucked the covers around Effby's shoulders and set a glass of water beside her bed.

"Go on," she said, "leave me alone."

This moment with Effby reminded me of my mom, all those years ago, sitting in her bedroom after coming home from the hospital without my baby brother, telling me through the door that she wanted to be left alone.

"Goodnight Effby," I said, pulling the door shut.

CHAPTER TWELVE

Diego's driveway was slick from the day's rain. As I dribbled the basketball, jogging in for a lay-up, I skidded into a puddle. Miraculously, the ball swooshed through the hoop.

"That makes four to two," I grinned. "So, when am I going to feel that agony of defeat you were talking about?"

Diego bounced the ball between his legs. "I'm obviously letting you build a false sense of security before blasting you with my athletic prowess."

"Obviously."

It felt good to be running, dodging, and weaving. Basketball wasn't my thing, but my body was craving a good workout.

Rippen trotted back and forth across the court, watching as the ball moved between us. Diego's driveway was hemmed in on one side by garbage bins and on the other side by two rhododendron bushes in desperate need of trimming. His house, a small three bedroom, needed a coat of fresh paint. The deck overlooking the backyard sported two soggy lawn chairs that hadn't made it to storage at the end of summer. Ash had turned to gray puddles and settled in the cracks of the cushions.

His neighborhood wasn't as nice as my old Portland neighborhood, but it was definitely a few steps up from the apartment complex where I lived.

Diego dove in for a run at the hoop. I swerved to block him, getting a face full of wet rhododendron leaves. A car came up the drive and Pablo stepped out from the passenger side. Diego paused, watching Pablo give a short wave as his friend pulled away.

"S'up?" Pablo said with a general nod in our direction as he walked past, his backpack slung over one shoulder. He kept walking to the house.

I felt a few raindrops. Diego looped his arm up and swished the ball through the hoop.

"Unfair height advantage," I said.

The door opened. "Did you eat all the turkey?" Pablo shouted.

"I don't know," Diego replied.

"Well, the turkey's gone."

Diego dribbled the ball between his legs. "There's roast beef. I just got it yesterday."

"I don't like roast beef." Pablo let the door slam as he went back inside.

Diego shot and missed. "Get your own food then," he muttered.

It was raining now, and the ball was slick in my hands.

"Come on," he said, "let's go in. You want a sandwich? Evidently there's only roast beef."

Diego's house smelled of unwashed socks and dirty dishes. Laundry was piled on the floor, unfolded, and Pablo's belongings littered the place. I plopped myself on a kitchen barstool and grabbed a napkin to wipe the rain from my face.

Pablo was peeling pre-cut slices of cheese from a package. Rippen shook off a crazy amount of rain and then sat gazing imploringly at Pablo. Diego grabbed two plates from the cupboard and a package from the refrigerator.

"Who was that who dropped you off?" Diego asked.

"Kyle," Pablo said. His toast popped up, and he began layering cheese on top of it.

"Do I know him?"

Pablo shrugged, adding a fourth slice of cheese.

"Hold up on the cheese, bro," Diego said. "I just bought that yesterday."

Pablo sighed. He pulled off another slice and dropped it on the floor in front of Rippen, then pushed the package toward Diego.

"Mayonnaise?" Diego asked me.

"Just a little."

Pablo had Diego's same dark eyes and lashes, but his hair was more unruly and long enough to put in a ponytail. He pushed it back from his face as he reached up for a glass.

"We need some more food," he said. "When are you going grocery shopping?"

"I told you I bought food yesterday." Diego spread a thin layer of mayonnaise on the bread and removed a couple of strips of roast beef from the package. "There's stuff to eat. Make some beans and rice or something."

"I don't have time to cook beans, dude. Kyle will be back in an hour."

Diego paused. "You're going out?"

"Yeah."

Diego pushed a sandwich toward me. "Don't you have midterms coming up?"

I didn't have any interest in being part of this evolving family drama, so I took my sandwich into the living room. I pushed aside Pablo's backpack and sat down. Since there was only a partial wall between the living room and kitchen, I could easily hear the argument heating up on the other side.

"Why you always ridin' me, bro? I got it handled," Pablo said.

I took a bite, flipping through Diego's sketchpad which lay on the coffee table.

"Sure, just like you had it handled last term? When you almost flunked out?"

"Why do you even give a shit?" Pablo snapped.

I turned a page and saw a portrait of me. It was not a pretty likeness. Not ugly, but sad, especially around the eyes.

Diego's voice was cutting. "Pablo, you drop out and you got nothing. Got that? Nothing. And you can't afford to have nothing."

I didn't want Diego to draw me this way. I carefully tore the paper, folded it, and shoved it into my back pocket. I wished I'd driven myself. Then I could sneak out, get in my car, and drive away.

"Quite acting like my dad," Pablo shouted. "Go get yourself a life for a change!" He stormed into the room, with Diego following.

"Where are you going?"

"Out. I'm walking. Fuck this shit. Have fun with your *gringa*." He said, "*Tu novia la pirómana.*"

"*Cállate la boca!*" Diego said sharply.

Pablo snatched his backpack and a vape pen rolled out onto the floor. Since Diego was behind Pablo, he couldn't have seen it. Pablo's eyes met mine. He reached for the vape and stuffed it into his backpack. Then he left, slamming the door on his way out.

Diego turned to me. "Shit. I'm sorry."

"I think I'd better go," I said. "Can you take me home?"

"No, don't leave," he came toward me. "I'm sorry. I shouldn't have let that get out of hand." He sat next to me. "He's just so aggravating. I mean, he needs to grow up. I wish he'd see I'm just trying to help him graduate, for Christ's sake."

My mouth struggled to form words, "Because if he doesn't graduate, he's a total failure, right?"

"No, of course not. It will just be harder for him, and it's been hard enough already."

"You remember," I said, standing, "that I'm not a graduate. I'm currently doing nothing. So, I guess in your world that makes me a failure too, right?"

"No," he blurted. "No, you're not at all and it's a totally different situation."

"How's it different?" I moved to stand beside the fireplace.

"It's, well, you're in a tough situation. Pablo's different. He's not in a tough social situation, he's got too many friends. But he's lazy. You work hard, you're doing something."

"Not really," I mumbled.

"He's just hanging out. The kid is too flipping smart for that. He's wasting this opportunity. But you're not wasting anything. You're just, you know, taking a different direction."

I was pretty sure I wasn't taking a different direction. I'd stalled, biding my time until I figured out my next move or hit rock bottom.

I ran my fingers across the mantle, allowing them to come to rest on a picture of Diego and Pablo. Diego looked about eight. He wore slacks and a button-up shirt like a grown man. His arm was around his brother, who was maybe three. Pablo's hair was combed neatly across his head.

"What did he say about me?" I asked.

"What?"

"In Spanish. I know what *gringa* is. Obviously. But what was the other thing? *Pirómana*?"

Diego came to stand beside me. "It doesn't matter. He was just spouting crap."

"What does it mean?"

Diego sighed. "Arsonist," he said. "He said 'your girlfriend the arsonist."

"I need to go."

"No, please," he held my arm lightly. "I'm sorry about him, and I'm sorry I let him get that way. I shouldn't have pushed him." He reached to touch my face and I let him. "It was me. I think I didn't want him getting the better of me in front of you. So, I kept pushing when I should have just dropped it."

"He's right about me."

"No, he's not. He doesn't know what he's talking about."

I pushed the nails of my right hand into the cuticles of my left. They felt raw and pulsed with pain.

"I don't know why you hang out with me."

He stepped closer. "Maybe because you're funny and you surprise me."

"How? With my criminal tendencies?"

"No, with how you see the world. I mean, not all the time. But sometimes you show me the good stuff in the world."

"Whatever," I grumbled. I wasn't sure I even saw the good stuff myself.

"Plus," he reached his hand behind my neck. "You're smoking hot. Come on," he pleaded. "I'll take you home if you want, but please stay. We can watch some Netflix. I'll make popcorn?"

I should have left. Pablo was right. I set the fire. I was an arsonist. *La pirómana.* Deep down, Diego probably thought the same. But his face was close to mine and his hands were on my cheek, and I wanted to pretend what Pablo said about me wasn't true. So, I stayed.

CHAPTER THIRTEEN

Dear Mr. and Mrs. Clark,

I'm so sorry I started the fire that took your house. I know you had lived there for almost twenty years. I hope you can rebuild. I'm sorry for all the things you lost in the fire that were important and special to you and that can't be replaced. I didn't mean for this to happen, but it did and I'm sorry.
Sincerely,
The Girl Who Set the Fire

Effby rattled her copy of *The Washington Post.* "Lunar eclipse tomorrow night," she announced. "Probably my last one and I'll be locked-up in here like the inmate I am."

I gathered Effby's empty bowl. I'd ordered Malt-O-Meal from Amazon and brought it in last week. It was the happiest I'd seen her since Halloween. She'd barely spoken to me for almost two weeks, and I still couldn't figure out why, but thanks to that little box of cereal, she was coming out of her funk.

"Do you need special glasses for that?" I asked.

"No, that's only for a solar eclipse. However, watching a lunar eclipse requires one to be outside."

"Can't you ask to go outside?"

"At 12:30 in the morning? Way past our curfew."

I knew she was right. Residents were required to be snug in their beds by ten. "Maybe I can film it for you?"

"If I wanted to watch a natural phenomenon on a screen, I'd use the internet. Besides, I assume you have other things going on at 12:30 at night. Like hanging out with your boyfriend."

"He's not my boyfriend," was my automatic response.

We hung out at Diego's house once or twice a week, although since the Pablo episode, I drove myself. I knew I shouldn't be hanging out with him at all, but home writing apology letters, keeping to myself, maintaining my perspective. But on Mom's days off, she rarely came out of her bedroom. When she did, she'd asked what I was doing and before I'd finished my first complete sentence she'd already walked back into her room. Most nights, I laid under my covers with my phone, waiting for it to light up with a text from Diego.

As if on cue, my phone vibrated. I pulled it from my pocket expecting to see a message from my not-boyfriend, but it was my dad. *How RU? Going to LA tomorrow for 2 wks. Filming for nxt season. Call me?*

Dad and I still hadn't talked, but we texted every now and then. He was my dad, after all, even if he was a self-centered narcissist. But I still wasn't sure about calling him.

April walked into Effby's room, dragging a bag full of clean linens. "Here, Essie," she said, using her pet name for me. She handed me a few towels to put in the bathroom. I followed her out of the room when she left.

"Hey," I said. "Are you working swing tomorrow?"

April flipped her hair. "No," she said. "I'm going out tomorrow. I think Regina's on swing."

"Did you know there's a lunar eclipse?"

She paused, readjusting her grip on the linen bag. "Do you need special glasses for that?"

"No," I replied. "No glasses."

"After I get these linens done, I'm going to go smoke. You want to come?"

"No thanks," I said.

She shrugged. "Suit yourself."

I found Regina in the rec room, playing chess with Sal. "Who's winning?" I asked.

"Like you need to ask," Regina frowned.

"You're improving," Sal observed. "But alas, checkmate." He added Regina's king to the pile of white pieces on his side of the board.

After we'd cleaned up the game and Sal had left, I broached the topic with Regina. "You're working swing tomorrow?"

"Yeah," she responded as we headed toward the kitchen to prepare snacks.

"You know it's a lunar eclipse?"

"Yeah, a full one," she replied. "They only come around once every couple of years."

"Remember how you said you owed me one for Halloween?"

Mom was still at work when I left our apartment shortly after eleven. The lights in Morningstar's lobby were just as bright as during the day, but I found the quiet unnerving. A bored-looking security guard sat where Tamara normally sat.

"Hi," I said, a little uneasy.

Just then, Regina swung around the corner. "Ken, this is Tessa. The one I told you about."

Ken nodded. "Oh right. Helping with the re-org in the supply room."

"Come on," Regina said to me. "Let's get started." I followed her down to the supply room. Once inside, she said, "I had to tell him that. We'll have to make sure he's busy when you take her out." This suddenly didn't seem like such a great idea. I wondered if Ken was going to catch us and then if I'd get fired, or, as Kathy put it, terminated immediately. "Are you ready? I'll have to help her into the wheelchair, then I can keep Ken distracted while you get her outside."

I checked my phone. It was midnight. "Aren't you supposed to be off now?"

"I can stay for this," she grinned. "I don't usually get to facilitate midnight breakouts on my shift."

I felt like a trespasser, sneaking into the dark of Effby's room. I hoped she wouldn't scream when she saw someone standing beside her bed. She was a small lump in the darkness against the bright moonlight that fell across the room. The night was clear, which I felt was a good sign. "Effby," I whispered.

She jolted, raising herself part way, and peered toward me. "What is it? Who's there?" Her face was unfamiliar, sort of like it had fallen in on itself.

"It's Tessa and Regina. Remember how you wanted to see the eclipse? It's almost time."

She pushed herself up, then reached over for her false teeth and stuck them into her mouth. It relieved me when her face was back to its normal proportions. "You're taking me on a midnight escape for an eclipse?"

"Yes," I said, "You still want to go, right?"

"Hell, yes," she said. Regina transferred Effby to the wheelchair, and I tucked a blanket around her and handed her a sweater, which she shoved her thin arms into. Regina strapped the oxygen tank to the chair while Effby hooked the tubes into her nostrils.

"Okay," said Regina. "I've disabled the emergency exit alarms, so just take her straight down the hall and out. I'll distract Ken. Text me when you're coming back, so I can make sure he's not at the desk. Are you ready for this? It's go time."

"Let's do it."

Regina headed into the hallway and after a while, I heard her chatting with Ken. I kept my ear to Effby's door. I heard Regina say something about the kitchen and then her voice died away. I peeked out. The receptionist's station was empty. My heart was racing, as if I was an operative in an *Ocean's Eleven* heist.

"Here we go." I wheeled the chair out, resisting any urge to sprint down the hall. What if William or Aileen May stepped out at the exact moment I ran past? What if they reported us? I hesitated at the emergency exit doors. What if Regina had set me up so I would get terminated immediately? I took a breath and pushed the doors open. The night was blessedly quiet and cold.

I propped the emergency door open with a rock. It wouldn't do to get locked out. "Where should we go?" I whispered.

"Can you push me to California?"

"Not quite." I wheeled the chair over to a grassy patch with a concrete bench and some flowerpots with scraggly stems poking out of the dirt. I pulled my sweatshirt tighter around me. I was grateful for the unusually clear November night, but it wasn't exactly balmy. The moonlight I'd seen on my drive to Morningstar was getting dimmer by the minute. A slight wind blew through the trees, rustling branches and sending the last of the fall leaves twirling to the ground.

It was fifteen minutes past midnight. The moon, partly in shadow, showed less than half of its silvery surface. Effby craned her neck to see it.

"Does that hurt your neck?" I asked.

"I feel like I'm in the first row of the movie theater," she said.

I texted Regina and within a few minutes she appeared, walking softly toward us.

"Wow," she said, taking in the moon.

"How's it going in there?" I whispered.

"Just fine. I've got Ken lifting some boxes of supplies for me. It'll keep him busy." She leaned over to Effby. "Want to lie down so you don't have to twist your neck?"

I laid Effby's blanket on the grass and Regina hoisted her onto the blanket. She shifted the oxygen tank and handed Effby the nostril tubes, but she waved them away. "I don't need those out here."

"Is that better?" I asked as Effby laid looking up. The sky was almost completely black. I could barely make out Effby's face, even though she was only a few feet from me.

"Better," she said.

I plopped down beside her. "Come on," I said to Regina. "I think it's almost at a hundred percent."

"Might as well," Regina said. She reclined on the opposite side of Effby.

As the night went black, I shivered. "So, is this all it is? The moon just goes away?"

"Just wait," Effby said.

Suddenly, the moon reappeared, but now it was a warm orange. It moved into view a bit at a time, the soft orange glow changing to a fiery red.

"Whoa," Regina said.

I forgot about the chilly air around me and stopped worrying that Ken would finish moving boxes early and come searching for Regina. Forgot that home was a dark and lonely apartment full of dead memories. I even forgot I was a *pirómana*. Lying beside Effby and Regina, the only thing that mattered was the magical red moon dominating the sky above our heads.

"Nothing like it," Effby said softly.

"It's like the moon just discovered its superpower," Regina said.

"Like it turned into something completely new," I said.

We watched until the moon re-emerged as its normal self, as if it hadn't just transformed before our eyes.

"Welp," Effby said, "that's a wrap."

I wasn't ready to go inside, but we needed to, and fast. We managed to sneak back without being discovered, and once Regina had transferred Effby to her bed, I made sure she had double blankets to curb any lingering chill from the outside air.

"All good here?" I yawned. She reached for my hand and squeezed it.

"All good," she said.

It was dark in her room, but I'm pretty sure she was smiling when I left. On the way home, I whispered to the moon, "I know what you really are.

THE FIRE

CHAPTER FOURTEEN

The next week, Mom set a face-to-face meeting with Tanesha. Somehow, between caring for Effby, spending time with Diego and being enchanted by the moon, I'd forgotten the responsibilities that came along with being an arsonist. I hadn't written a single letter. I hadn't even taken out my paperclip. A visit with my lawyer was just I what I needed to remind me that everything still sucked.

As we drove to the meeting, I leaned my head against the window, feeling the silence between Mom and me as if it were a tangible thing, like there was a stranger sitting in the car with us. I tried not to dwell on it and instead focused on the trees whipping past my window.

"You have the entire day off from Morningstar?" she asked. I nodded. "Because we can be back by two, if you want to go in for a couple hours."

"No, that's okay," I mumbled. She turned on the radio.

It was so seldom my mom was out of her room I felt like I should talk with her. Part of me wanted to talk to her. But without school or violin or volleyball, there was nothing to talk about. All the words that should be spoken, she was too scared to bring up. Or maybe it was me who was scared. For the two hours car ride to my lawyer's office, the radio did all the talking.

Tanesha's office was in an old nineteenth-century house converted into office space. I brushed my hand over the ornately carved, dark wood banister as we climbed the stairs. I thought briefly of all the people who had walked these stairs before. Their ghosts still lurked in the shadows, their vacant eyes watching Tanesha as she read law books and sifted through files. Maybe one day Tanesha would be a ghost here too. Maybe one day I would be.

Upstairs was a narrow hallway ending at a window overlooking the neighborhood. The space was smaller than our Elmsville apartment. Two chairs were wedged next to the window. As Mom and I walked toward them, Tanesha stuck her head out. She held her cell phone to her ear while motioning for us to wait. Mom and I squeezed into the chairs, our knees nearly touching.

I used to think all lawyers worked in high-rise buildings downtown where they rode the train into work and ate lunch in chic restaurants. Like my dad's lawyer. But Tanesha's office was in a funky part of town that had built up around old houses, leaving most of them intact. Out the window, I could see a super cool vintage clothing store in an old Victorian house, and a vinyl record store next to a tiny crepe café. Next to that was a southern food restaurant where a line of people, some with beards and checkered shirts and Northface jackets, stretched down the sidewalk. I wondered if any of them had made death threats against me in the newspaper comments section.

Tanesha opened the door and smiled. She shook both of our hands as we approached. "Can I get you some coffee?" she asked. "Water?"

We followed her into her office where a modest desk was surrounded by tall stacks of law books, a few live plants, and a fish tank about the size of our flat screen. A bright blue fish swam idly in the tank, its unblinking eyes following me to my chair.

"How are you?" she asked. "Both of you."

"It's been tough," Mom said. "But we're okay."

"Tessa?" Tanesha prodded.

"Okay," I said. The fish reached the end of the long tank and made a slow, wide turn.

"I see your community service is going well. You're getting regular hours in."

"I'll be doing regular hours at Morningstar until I'm ninety," I replied, "and then if I'm lucky, I'll be a resident." I was trying to be funny, but no one laughed.

"The judge will reduce those hours. That's how it works," she said. "The hours, the fines, all of it. But we must show a good faith effort by making progress in each of these areas first."

"The fines too?" Mom said.

"Yes," Tanesha said. "We've got to pay on them."

The blue fish had reached the tank's far end without so much as lifting a fin. I wondered if, as he swam the rounds in his tank each day, he thought of himself as living or unliving. Maybe he wasn't even real?

"We're barely making ends meet as is," Mom said. "I mean, with bills." I knew she meant Tanesha's lawyer's fees, but Mom would never say so.

"I can do more essays. I review them online. Plus, I tutor."

"That's good." Tanesha nodded.

"It doesn't pay much, but it's something," I said.

Mom leaned back in her chair, her hands lying open in her lap as if she was waiting for bags of cash to drop out of the sky.

"Whatever we can pay, it will never be enough," she said.

"It will," Tanesha said. "We'll chip away at it for six months and then we'll go back to the judge. Ask for a review and I'm sure she'll reduce it. Ellen," She paused, "you shouldn't have to do this alone."

I knew what Tanesha meant. We should hit up celebrity chef Food Truck Tom, that he should contribute more toward his dysfunctional daughter's legal fees. We, Mom and me, knew that would never happen. Because Mom would never ask.

"I need the restroom." Mom got up and left the room.

"Tessa," Tanesha said. I pulled my focus away from the fish. "Are you alright?"

I wanted to say, 'Sure. I mean, apart from carrying the weight of ruining my life, my mom's life, and everyone else's in the town of Elmsville. I'm just peachy'. But instead, I answered, "I'm fine."

"I think your mom is having a hard time seeing through this right now."

"Can I feed your fish?" I asked suddenly.

"Oh, okay, sure," she reached into her desk and handed me a jar of fish food. "Just a pinch."

A strong odor filled the room as I lifted the lid. I dropped in a few pellets and watched the fish poke at each piece as it floated, weightless, in the water. The way he swam around the food made me think he wasn't hungry so much as looking for a distraction from the endless loop of his ghostly existence.

After the meeting, we headed in the freeway's direction, but instead of taking the on-ramp, Mom turned the car toward the south-eastern part of town, where Dad and Tranquility lived. The Whole Foods parking lot was packed and, even in the drizzling rain, sidewalks were busy with people. Greenery and soggy red Christmas bows decorated streetlamps, even though Thanksgiving wasn't for another week.

"What are we doing?" I asked. "I don't want to go to Dad's."

"Ugh. No, me neither."

She pulled into the tiny parking lot of A Lotta Gelato. We hadn't been there in years, even though, before the divorce, it was one of our favorite places to go after practice or orchestra rehearsal.

"Come on," she said. "We need gelato."

Seeing the soft mounds of pastel colored deliciousness made me feel thirteen again. That childhood excitement I used to feel when trying to settle on a flavor came rushing back. I could never decide between so many choices and always asked for samples. But this time there was no need for the cute little spoon testers, I went straight for coconut. Mom ordered pistachio, as she always did.

We sat in a corner booth, our cups of gelato on the table in front of us. "I miss this place," Mom said. "There's no gelato in Elmsville."

"There's Baskin and Robbins," I volunteered.

"Not the same." Mom took a bite. "When I was a kid, I was all about Bressler's 31 Flavors. We had one right down the street. My mom would take me there after ballet lessons."

"Was pistachio one of the 31 flavors?"

"Maybe, but I didn't like it back then. Bubblegum was my flavor, I remember it was bright pink with real bubblegum balls."

"What? You would never let me eat bubblegum ice cream with real bubblegum balls."

"Nope," she said. "Because I choked on a bubblegum ball once. Someone saved me with the Heimlich, you know, where they squeeze you from behind until the thing you're choking on comes flying out. It was so embarrassing."

"You're lucky you survived childhood. No seatbelts. Ice cream cones of doom." Mom chuckled and the air between us suddenly felt lighter.

The door opened and three girls burst in laughing and chatting to one another. They looked close to my age, wearing short skirts in muted colors with tights and leather boots, as if they'd all found the same sale at American Eagle.

"Now don't take forever," one of them said. "We have class in twenty minutes."

"Yeah," another girl added. "If I'm late to fifth period again, I'll get a referral."

The third girl held her long, wavy hair to one side as she peered into the gelato case. "I can never decide between orange and strawberry."

"Hey, you want to go to Claire's after school. I need some earrings for the Christmas Formal."

I watched my mom watching the girls. There was longing all over her face, like what she really wanted was a bubblegum gelato, but it was out of reach and slowly and painfully receding from view. She caught me looking at her and immediately dipped her spoon into her cup.

"Anyway," she said. "I prefer pistachio to bubblegum now."

"Christmas Formal," I muttered. "Otherwise known as 'date-rape night'."

Mom slapped her plastic spoon on the table. "Knock it off. Why do you have to be so ugly?"

"Why do you have to be so dim?" I shot back. "As if those girls aren't totally vapid. You look at them like they're something special. Well, they're not."

"Keep your voice down," she whispered. "You're just jealous."

"Hardly," I scoffed. "And I'm tired of being told to keep my voice down."

"Come on, let's go." She stood and threw her half-eaten gelato in the trash.

I was grateful when the door swung closed behind us and shut out the girls' conversation. I pulled my hood over my head and slouched into the passenger seat. I knew there was a long ride ahead. By the end, my anger would have morphed into another crushing wave of guilt, and I'd be searching for a way to redeem myself in my mother's eyes. Until then, I closed my eyes and swam alongside Tanesha's ghost fish.

CHAPTER FIFTEEN

I hadn't planned to break up with Diego. It was a Sunday afternoon, and we both had the day off. Mom didn't work that day either and I'd left her sitting at the computer poring over her electronic bill pay. I lingered near the door. "I think I'll have fifty more dollars by the end of the week," I offered.

"That will help," she replied.

I couldn't think of anything else to say. A few drops of rain fell from very dark clouds. I reached for my sweatshirt, then hesitated. "Okay, bye," I said, thinking of the hundred and fifty times a month Mom would warn me about going outside without a coat or sweater, 'You'll catch a death of a cold', 'You'll regret it later', 'Where do you think you are, Hawaii?'. But today, her focus was on the computer screen. I left without my sweatshirt.

I cranked up the heat in my car and turned on the windshield wipers. The dreary weather made it feel later. As I drove toward Diego's house, I thought of my mom the entire way. No, that's not true. I thought of the worst year of my life when, as a twelve-year-old, I'd endured a long, lonely year of my mother's silence. It was the sound of my voice that eventually dragged my mother out of her depression. Why was I thinking of this now? Oh, I know, because this year was turning out to be far worse.

When I was twelve, afraid and confused, thrown into a situation I didn't create nor understand, I scavenged for happiness. I grasped at any bits of hope offered to me and consumed them like they were my only food. This time around, the worst year ever was my fault. I only needed to read the judge's sentence or pull up Facebook or old news coverage of the fire. I only needed to look in my Nike shoebox. I had 98 letters to write, and yet, the more letters I added to the box, the more confused, lost, and lonely I became.

Thank god for Diego. He was an oasis. I gobbled him up like those morsels of hope. When I was at his house, shooting hoops, or flipping through his sketchbook, I felt warm inside, even hopeful, like a good person with a normal past and limitless possibilities for a future.

A few days ago, when we'd taken Rippen to the park, I sat on the swings. I twisted the chains to almost breaking point, letting them unwind as the ground spun under my feet. Diego sat in the swing beside me hurling the tennis ball for Rippen. Geese flew above our heads. There were hundreds of them. I tipped my head back to watch them pass. Diego reached for my hand and in that moment, everything was close to perfect, like the geese flying in V formation.

But then he talked about his future, and some of that talk involved me. Without using his words exactly, he asked me to think about a future, as if I had one. As if I didn't owe $450,000 to the people of Elmsville. Or I didn't have apology letters to write. As if I had direction, like the geese flying overhead.

By the time I parked my car in front of Diego's house, rain was coming down in sheets. I didn't even make it to the door before Diego met me.

"Come on," he said. "Let's go. We'll take my truck."

He seemed to want out of there, so I didn't argue. I climbed into the truck, picking strands of wet hair from my face. "What's going on?"

"My dad's just being a jerk right now," he said. He shifted into reverse and the truck lurched back. "When he gets that way, I try to avoid him."

"Where's Rippen?" I asked.

"Lying by the heater and not at all excited about going out in the rain."

"Smart dog."

He cranked up the heat and soon I felt warm air blowing onto my soggy tennis shoes. "Where's Pablo?"

"At his friend's. He knows to avoid Dad, too." He glanced at me quickly. "It's not that my dad is really mean or anything, he just gets in a mood, since my mom passed."

According to Diego, their mom's passing sent Pablo off the rails, and from what I could tell, Diego was the only thing keeping his brother grounded. Rain splashed against the window. Thanksgiving was a few days away. I didn't figure that was a super awesome time for Diego's family. It wouldn't be for my family either. Mom and I were trying not to spend any money and although I should have a long list of things to be thankful for, like not being in prison, I was having a hard time coming up with anything. I wasn't starving or homeless or living in some war-torn country and I had people in my life, like Effby and the Morningstar crew, and of course Diego and Rippen and Mom, but I wasn't feeling overwhelmed with gratitude. In fact, most of the time I wanted to punch something, but I wasn't sure what. Mostly I think I wanted to punch myself.

"Let's get some pie," Diego said with a big smile. "They have the best pie at Sill's Café and around this time of year they always have pumpkin."

Diego and I had been hanging out for almost two months, but we'd never been on an actual date. Never been to the movies, or out to dinner, or even to a coffee shop. Going into a café where there'd be other customers scared the hell out of me, for obvious reasons, but I didn't say anything.

My nerves calmed when I saw the café was deserted. Who else in their right mind would come out in this weather for a slice of pie? Plus, it was mid-afternoon, the lull between meals.

We sat in a booth with red vinyl seats and two ceramic coffee mugs beside utensils wrapped in thin paper napkins. They were heavy mugs, once white but now stained from years of strong coffee. Diego ordered pumpkin pie with coffee and I, after inhaling a big breath of courage, asked for banana cream with hot chocolate.

I fidgeted in my seat, afraid to look around for fear of being recognized. I took in the ambiance, letting the warm café air linger in my lungs, letting this moment stretch. Here I was drinking hot chocolate like a normal person in a café in Elmsville and the world hadn't exploded. Our server delivered pie slices on plates that matched the heavy coffee mugs, then went to stand by the register with the other server.

"How's the pie? Does it live up to your expectations?" I asked as I took my second bite.

He nodded. "Many pumpkins died for this pie. They did not sacrifice in vain."

"Let me try it," I asked. He scooped a bite with whipped cream and held his fork out for me.

Our server walked toward us, and my initial reaction was to cower, but I didn't. Instead, I turned to face her.

"I'm going to take a break," she said. "Can I get you anything?" Diego and I shook our heads. "Okay, Veronica will take care of you, if you need anything."

After she left, I said to Diego, "I should have had coffee. This rain is making me sleepy."

"You're staying up too late working on those papers."

Even if I hadn't been working on papers, I wasn't sleeping well, so it was better to be doing something other than staring at my ceiling for hours on end.

"The world of college application essays needs me," I said. "Last night I saved some poor guy from saying his true abilities were not represented by his scores from standardized testes."

Diego laughed. "Maybe he has non-standard testes."

"I didn't want to ask."

Veronica came over to our table. "Can I bring you any-" Her friendly expression changed to one of disgust as she stared at me with big angry eyes. "What are you-" She turned and stormed away.

I put down my fork. The cream on my pie was sagging in the middle. Even if I hadn't been recognized, I couldn't have eaten anymore of it.

"What was that about?" Diego asked.

Veronica had disappeared into the kitchen, but I could hear her voice clearly. It was high and sharp. "How could you ask me to take that table?"

"What?"

"I'm not waiting on her." There was an exchange of hushed voices.

Diego finally caught up with what was happening. "Come on," he said. "Let's get out of here." He pulled out his wallet and stood. Veronica was already on her way back to the table and she was headed straight for me.

Veronica was probably in her late thirties. Her hair was in a knot on top of her head and the way her eyebrows pushed against each other made deep wrinkles between her eyes.

"How could you even come in here?" she spat at me. "How can you sit here making googly eyes at your boyfriend? Do you know what you did to me?" Her entire body was shaking. "Do you even know?"

Diego was saying something, holding his hand to mine, but all I could take in was Veronica's anger. I shook my head.

"No?" she hissed. "Well, let me tell you. My home burned to the ground. With everything in it. All my children's drawings they made when they were little. The train set my dad spent two months putting together for them. The flag that draped my grandfather's coffin at his funeral!"

I knew I could never leave this booth. My breathing came in ragged gasps as she detailed her losses, each one a knife in my chest.

"We're living with my mother-in-law. Insurance doesn't cover everything, you know. I'm working two jobs now." Her tears spilled down over her cheeks. "I hardly see my kids."

132

"That's enough," Diego said. He reached down and grabbed my arm.

"What I want to know, Tessa Hilliard," she said, her voice breaking, "Is what you are going to do about it?"

Diego pulled me from the booth. "I said that's enough," he said sharply.

The other server put her arm around Veronica, who was fully crying now, and guided her back to the kitchen. "How dare you eat pie?" she said over her shoulder as Diego left a twenty-dollar bill on the table.

By the time we got back to Diego's house, my breathing was under control. I could finally talk without crying; "Now do you see?" I muttered. "Why I don't go to public places?" I jumped out and started walking to my car.

"Tessa, wait," Diego said, following me. "That was awful and I'm sorry, but don't leave."

"You don't know what it's like," I said. As much as I knew none of this was Diego's fault, a part of me resented him for taking me to that stupid café. For making me laugh, for making me feel happy, and then for watching me be humiliated by Veronica. But while I was feeling sorry for myself, I was also thinking about how shitty Veronica's Thanksgiving would be. Not in her own home, none of her own pots and pans, and maybe she'd have to work.

"I know I don't," he said. "But eventually, you're going to have to be out in the world, you know. Let's do it together."

"Together, are you crazy?"

"Why not?"

"Because you aren't the one who fucked everything up! I am, don't you see? I'm the one who has to live with this now, not you!"

"Tessa, calm down," he reached for me. "Let me help you."

"Don't tell me to calm down," I snapped at him. "You can't help me." I knew if I didn't get out of there that very second, I was going

133

to bawl my head off, which would only make things worse. "I can't see you anymore."

"What? Because some lady lost her shit in a restaurant you can't see me anymore?"

"That wasn't just some lady. She lost everything because of me, you heard what she said. And she's not the only one. She's right you know. That's what you don't understand," I said, stomping to my car. "She's right about me." And I didn't deserve him, but I couldn't bring myself to say that.

"Tessa," he started, but I cut him off.

"Don't!" I snarled. "I'm done. I can't pretend like this is going to work. It's never going to work." I got into my car. The rain began falling harder, and within a second Diego was at my window.

"Tessa, don't do this!"

In about five seconds I was going to punch something, and I didn't want it to be Diego. "Get out of my way." I glared through the glass and drove off.

That night, I wrote another letter.

Dear Ms. Martinez,
I can never make up for what I've done. I'm sorry your house burned and all the things you cared about burned with it. I'm sorry that you are living with relatives now and that you must work two jobs and hardly see your kids. I never meant to hurt you. I apologize for my actions, all of them.
Sincerely,
Tessa Hilliard

Yes, I signed my name. Why keep up the ruse of anonymity? My letters had long since overwhelmed the shoebox and I stacked the new ones in a cardboard box I kept in my closet. Whatever I figured out or didn't figure out, this nightmare would be over in 97 letters.

CHAPTER SIXTEEN

The next day, I got fired from Morningstar. The day had started out badly. As I was in the bathroom pulling my hair back into a ponytail, Mom came up behind me, coughing. Her face was pale, her eyes puffy and red. I moved aside, so she had access to the cupboard.

"Are you okay?"

"I've been coughing all night. Got a bug."

"Can I get you something? Some tea?"

She rummaged through the cupboard. "No, I'm taking some NyQuil. Where is it? Oh no, are we out?"

"I haven't seen it."

"I thought we still had some."

"I can get you some," I said.

"No, get to work. You don't have time."

I made her a cup of tea before I left for Morningstar.

When I arrived, Kathy was standing by the front desk. She had put her hair into a bun, but frizzy, rebellious strands were flying out in all directions. Tamara sat primly behind the desk, not even bothering to pretend she was working. I felt the tension as soon as I walked in the door. "What's going on?"

"Come to my office, please," Kathy said. I followed her. In the cramped but tidy office were photos of two kids, a boy and a girl, in a hinged double frame. The office smelled of lavender coming from an essential oils' diffuser humming away on the shelf behind her. My eyes started watering almost instantly.

"I told you when you started, I wasn't putting up with any negative behavior."

I froze. "What did I do?" She must have found out about the eclipse. Oh god, I hoped Regina didn't lose her job.

"I think you know what you did. We're not stupid, you know. I took a chance on you, and you blew it." Kathy leaned toward me, and I waited for it. "We know you're the one who stole that oxy."

"What?" I grabbed the edge of the desk because I felt dizzy. "I didn't steal anything."

"I just hope you're not selling it. That stuff can kill people, you know. Tessa, you did a good job here, and I have appreciated that." Kathy had outlined her lips, but the lipstick had faded or been licked away, leaving just the dark outline. "So, I'm going to do you a favor and not report this. Just go. And get some help."

"I didn't steal it," I protested, but I knew it was pointless. I was a deviant. The girl who set fires. *La pirómana.* No one would believe anything good about me ever again. I shoved the injustice to the back of my throat and swallowed it like a bitter pill. The fact I didn't do it was irrelevant, I could have. I thought of Veronica's face. I was capable of anything.

"Do you want to say goodbye to Effby?" Kathy asked. Her question rattled me. It was one thing to punish me for something I didn't do, but punish Effby? I stared blankly at Kathy as she shoved an errant lock of frizz away from her eye and another one fell into it.

Evidently, there was no medication in Effby's room for me to steal because Kathy allowed me to go inside unsupervised. I hesitated for a moment before going in. My breathing came shallow and fast.

I found Effby sitting in her chair, reading *The Washington Post.* "Those asshats," she grumbled. "What they bother arguing about on the Hill is beyond me. No connection to reality."

I sat across from her and focused on taking deep, calming breaths. The hummingbird feeder was still outside, empty and abandoned.

"You need to ask them to fill the feeder next spring. It's a quarter cup of sugar to one cup of water."

"Why?" She put down the paper. "Why won't you fill it?"

The truth was, Effby had grown on me. She was cranky and obnoxious, but I liked that about her. She had a take no shit policy, and she was great at dishing it back. But she also pointed out the prettiest hummingbirds. She was interested in the world enough to read every newspaper front to back. I liked that her mind was sharp enough to complete a *New York Times* crossword puzzle in a day. That she was now a bigger expert in true crime than me and maybe even *Crime Maven*. I leaned over and put my head in my hands.

"Out with it," she said.

"I can't come back anymore. They fired me."

"Of course, they did, those incompetent morons. What'd they fire you for?"

"They think I stole medication." I paused. "I didn't, by the way."

"I know you didn't." She adjusted the blanket over her lap. "They just think you did because you set the forest on fire. There's no logic to it, but people don't make decisions based on logic. They make them on emotions. Fear, mostly."

I didn't know how to respond. All this time I believed Effby didn't know about my part in starting the fire. But she'd known all along, and yet she'd treated me just as she treated everybody else, maybe even better.

"I didn't know you knew, you know, about -" I struggled to get the words out.

"Of course, I knew about you. I pay attention. Just didn't think it was worth mentioning."

"I'm sorry I can't stay," I thought about my apology letters and the double meaning to my words. I wouldn't be staying at Morningstar, that had been decided for me, but what about the bigger here? Right now, I didn't think I could stay anywhere. "I'm sorry I can't take care of the feeder or, you know, do anything." I slumped further in the chair, picking at loose threads.

Effby smacked the table with *The Washington Post*, and I practically jumped out of my seat.

"There are a lot of things we do in this world to be miserable over. Let's not bother being miserable over things we don't do. Sit up and listen." I did as I was told. Effby's eyes were brighter and more focused than I'd ever seen them. "The truth will make itself known."

"How's that going to happen? I'm not even allowed back here."

Effby rolled her eyes. "We're not talking about the sharpest tools in the shed running this joint."

I had to admit I was a little disappointed Effby wasn't more upset to see me go. She might feel confident in my eventual exoneration, but I didn't. My time was up. Kathy walked me to the front doors as if she were a mall cop, Tamara smirking at me from her tiny domain.

"Hey Tamara," I said. "Mr. Jones needs a linen change. It's bad. You'd better get on that."

"Have a nice life," Tamara said. "Or not."

I sat in my car. It wasn't quite raining, but the air was as damp and cold as if it were. I started the engine, but didn't know which direction to drive in. Since I knew Kathy was probably watching from the window, I drove onto the street and around the block, parking by the curb. I laid the seat back and stared at the endless, grey expanse of sky beyond my window. I had nowhere to go.

I couldn't go to Diego's; I'd made sure of that. I didn't want to go where people would recognise me. And I couldn't go home. I couldn't tell Mom because me being fired meant I wasn't earning community service hours. But more than that disappointment, I was afraid she'd believe, like Kathy, that I'd stolen the oxy.

I put the car in drive and steered out of town. I turned up the heat to try and stop myself from shaking. The highway that followed the edge of the woods was open now, but many of the side roads were still closed. I turned off the main road, following one of the few opened roads that twisted its way into the woods. It was a patchwork of scorched land on either side. Not all the trees had burned, there were some untouched firs standing tall. I wondered how those trees got lucky while so many others were destroyed by flames. Up ahead, barricades and caution tape stretched across the road. I found a spot to pull over and parked. I walked to t'e edge of what was once the forest. Signs read 'Danger' 'Unstable Foundation' 'DO NOT ENTER'.

I stepped over a sagging piece of caution tape. The woods were eerily quiet, no birds, no little slithering movements of underbrush. Mist wet my face. The sharp sound of a charred stick cracking beneath my shoe broke through the silence. I felt like a stranger in someone else's house, tiptoeing through a dark hallway at midnight, trying not to wake the sleeping. I walked on, hoping to lose myself in the trees. But quickly I realized I was kidding myself. With so much of the woods burned to ash, there was no place to hide. I stood in the blackened forest and thought of the envelopes in my drawer, the ash and burned sticks. They could have been taken from this very spot. I remembered Kurt Callahan's testimony about snags, and I looked up, fearful that one could fall and crush my skull. That would be a fitting end, the forest taking its revenge.

I stopped in front of a very large, very old-looking tree. A black mark had seared through the bark nearly the entire length of the trunk, widening midway to a gaping slash. I was sure the tree wasn't going to survive. It was standing now, but for how much longer? I put my hand out, wishing I could repair the damage. Wishing I could fix everything. I stood there for a very long time, shivered in the damp, with my hand on the tree.

Later I drove the long way home, following detours where the road was closed. Eventually I found myself driving into the town of Rogers. I had to pee, so I pulled over at a Dairy Queen across from a Walgreens Drug Store and a Panda Express. I slipped down the hallway unnoticed. When I came out of the bathroom, I put up my hood and headed for Walgreens. The clerk was leaning over the counter, reading *People* magazine.

"Hi, welcome," she said as I entered. A woman scanned greeting cards as she walked along one aisle, while another woman had her eyes on a mascara tube as her young son tried on a leopard mask.

"Mommy look," he said. "I'm a tiger."

I headed down the medication aisle. I couldn't believe NyQuil was $9.99. I picked up a box of Transformer Band Aids, pretending to read the label. I checked over my shoulder for cameras and, confident I was alone, put the band aids back on the shelf while swooping the NyQuil into my purse. Everything went quiet. No one appeared from a back room to arrest me. Feeling brave, I snagged a bag of cough drops and added it to my purse. As I walked the aisle, a voice in my head told me not to leave without buying something, so I picked out a ream of paper from the office supply aisle.

At the counter, the girl was slow to put away her *People*. She dragged my paper across the scanner, careful not to drag her nicely painted acrylic nails along with it. Her makeup was heavy, and I wondered if she had plans after work or if she'd put all that effort into her face just to spend the day at Walgreens reading magazines.

"That's $4.83," she said.

I was careful to open my purse away from her, extracting my wallet so I didn't dump out the NyQuil. But that would be the thief I was, the kind that showed up in security camera footage posted to YouTube titled, "Dumb Chick Criminals" or something like that. Luckily, my clerk seemed intent on only one thing, taking my money. As she gave me change, she mumbled, "Have a good day," then dropped back to reading "Who Wore It Best."

When I got home, the apartment was empty. Mom had obviously rallied enough to go to work. I left the NyQuil and cough drops on the kitchen table where she would see them. Then I opened the ream of paper and turned on my laptop.

The Community Service Log, documenting the hours I'd spent at Morningstar, was due every Friday. Usually, Kathy scanned a copy of the log and emailed it to me, so I could send it on to the court and Tanesha. I pulled up the pdf of last week's log.

Within minutes, I'd recreated the log, which was a simple chart of days with boxes where I wrote in my hours. The Morningstar logo threw me for a minute, but then I found I could cut and paste the image from their website. With a little resizing, it was more than passable. Next, I studied the looping letters of Kathy's signature. It wasn't as hard as I thought it would be to replicate. Maybe I was just a natural.

CHAPTER SEVENTEEN

Over the next week, I developed a routine. A sort of twisted routine full of lies and deception, but a routine none the less. I got up every morning at eight, just like when I was going to Morningstar. I didn't want to risk waking Mom and her seeing me home when I shouldn't be, so I got dressed and made tea. Nothing sweet and fancy, just something to keep me warm. I packed a lunch and left the house. That's when things got weird.

I would often park my car in some random parking lot and sit watching movies on my phone. To keep from being seen, I sometimes drove forty minutes to Delvin, which was a little smaller than Elmsville. I wore my hood up and tried to find places where there weren't many people. I spent a lot of time in the Delvin Public Library. I used their computers and read Anmarie Cross' blog every day. Her blog had stopped two years ago; maybe after she'd taken over the store. I guess she didn't have time to write about her travel adventures anymore, but thankfully they were all archived, and I read them all more than once.

In her last blog post, she wrote about hiking for three weeks along the Appalachian Trail that runs from Maine down into Georgia. It takes most people seven months to hike the whole thing. Anmarie did the section that runs through Vermont, near the Adirondack Mountains where steep climbs and high winds threatened to blow her off the trail's edge. When she put her tent up in the middle of a storm, she had to redo the stakes to prevent the wind from blowing under the tent and capsizing it. When I finished reading her last blog, I felt sad that her adventures had ended. Impulsively, I emailed her. My email address didn't have my first or last name, so I figured there would be no way she'd know who I was, or if she was even still using her blog address.

Dear Ms. Cross,

I really enjoyed your blog and have read every post. Will you be writing any new entries in the future? I think it's awesome you did all that traveling by yourself. Well, thanks for sharing. Bye -

Caitlyn

When I wasn't surfing the internet at the library, I walked the aisles, running my fingers lightly across book spines. I had never had much time for books, outside of required reading for classes. I was too busy with sports, music and doing work for extra credit. Reading for fun was never a priority. But with this strange and sudden time on my hands, and a vast number of books at my fingertips, I wasn't sure where to begin. I landed on *Violin Dreams*. The image of a violin on the cover almost made my knees buckle with longing. I sat in a nearby chair with the book and held it for a long time before opening its cover.

Small town libraries on weekdays are quiet, except for young mothers who bring their toddlers for story time, or just to get out of the house. Toddlers have no voice modulation. They shout with delight over a *Peppa the Pig* book. They pile picture books into cloth bags and drag them across the floor to the checkout counter. The other group who visits the library every day are people with nothing to do but who need a place to go to escape the cold. Somewhat like me.

As I was reading in *Violin Dreams* about an anxiety-filled dream Steinhardt, the violin player, had experienced, the smell of urine overcame me. A woman lugging a reusable grocery bag stuffed to breaking with a blanket had situated herself at the computer station next to my armchair. Her ratted hair poked out from a knit cap, and I watched her pull a wool sweater tightly around her chest. She rubbed her bare hands together before starting to type. I could see the screen as she pulled up Gmail and I wondered who she was emailing. "What are you looking at?" she grumbled at me.

I usually stayed in the library, like the other regulars, until well after lunch. Then I'd find a safe place to stash *Violin Dreams*. I hid it so no other violin enthusiasts would check it out while I was away. Then I'd leave the warmth of the library, with its smells of books and poor hygiene, and find a grocery store or a drugstore to plunder.

Stealing was easier than I expected, and, like a bad habit, it became a regular part of my days. I never stole too much, and often bought something so as not to raise suspicion. And I didn't go to the same place more than once a week. My stealing excursions became the only time I interacted with other people.

I noticed that when you hardly talk, you get better at observing and listening. I began to see people in ways I hadn't before. As I sat in the library's best squashy chair one morning with *Violin Dreams* in my hands, I heard a man at the nearby reading table, fidgeting nervously. His leg bounced as he straightened a stack of books that he'd already straightened moments ago. He glanced at his phone and then walked to the picture book section, scanning the covers before selecting another book and adding it to his stack.

When a woman and a small boy walked in, the man held out his arms. The boy's pudgy face lit up and the ear flaps of his furry hat bounced as he ran toward the man. The woman turned and sat in a nearby chair and began scrolling through her phone.

I watched the father and son read every book in the stack. When the boy giggled, the man giggled too, and it was as if nothing else in the world existed except them and their books. I fumbled the pages in my own book pretending to read until the woman put away her phone and stood. The man hugged his boy goodbye. When the boy left, the man sagged in the middle like part of him had emptied out. I wanted to give him something, a look, or a smile, to fill the void. But he never looked my way.

I also noticed other, more practical, things. Like when the security guard in Walmart was preoccupied with his phone, waiting for a call or text. I noticed the clerk in the CVS drugstore rubbing his eyes and sneezing when he walked down the perfume or hair color aisles. In the grocery store, when deli counter clerks were busy handing out samples, I swiped a couple of packages of meat. I stole food, toiletries, Advil, and hair color. I stole socks, mittens, and earrings. Once, on impulse, I stole a package of oil paints. I was thinking of Diego at the time even though I had no plans to see him.

I left items out on the table for my mother, like small peace offerings. Blush and lipstick, alongside two cans of soup. A set of earrings alongside a package of Fig Newtons. If she asked me how I could afford to buy these things, I planned to tell her I'd been doing extra essay revision work. I woke when she came home sometimes, hearing her open the door, pausing at the kitchen table. I imagined her picking up each item.

Thinking of the old woman's trembling, red hands as they hovered above the keyboard, I left a pair of gloves on the chair of each workstation at each of the libraries I visited. Maybe I was just trying to do penance. I didn't know why I was doing these things and I didn't give myself time to think about it.

At home, while Mom was at work, I dyed my hair. As I rinsed my head under the bathtub faucet, streams of black ran down the drain. I patted my new hair with a towel that instantly turned from green to a dark gray. I surveyed myself in the mirror. The black made my face look paler and my green eyes stand out even more. Where I'd missed some spots and the black streaked my hair, I cut it out with scissors.

Mom was not pleased. The next day would have been my normal day off, so I was in my room when she opened my door to see if I had eaten lunch. I was at the computer, writing another apology letter. I minimized it quickly, although I'm not sure why.

"What did you do?" she gasped.

Where I'd cut my hair with the kitchen scissors, ragged edges grazed my chin. I'd done my best to even them out, but I was hopeless. I'd cut bangs too. I cut them when my hair was wet and when they dried, they were a lot shorter than I'd planned.

"It's just hair," I said.

"Why would you -" Mom came over and I let her run her hand through my hair. "My god, I hope it fades."

I sighed, turning back to my laptop. "Who cares," I said. "It's not like it's permanent."

"Your hair was so pretty," she said. "I don't know why you'd do that. That color makes you look like a ghost."

"Perfect," I said sharply, surprised at my volume. "That's exactly how I feel."

"Tessa," Mom said. "Things are going backwards here. You never even try to do anything anymore. And, Tessa, I mean, your fingers." She gestured to my scabby cuticles. "Look what you're doing to your fingers. Can you please just stop?"

I stood suddenly, nearly knocking over my chair. "Mom," I rounded on her. "Things aren't going back. There is no 'backward' or 'forward' for me, okay? There's just nothing. Things aren't going anywhere." She stepped away looking confused and hurt. But her reaction didn't stop me. "So," I went on, "can you just leave me alone?"

"Okay," she said in a small voice. She walked out and closed the door. I pushed my face into my pillow as hard as I could, trying to suffocate myself. I stayed like that, crying until my pillow was a soggy mess of grey streaks.

That night, I was surprised to see a response from Anmarie Cross.

Hi Caitlyn,

I'm so glad you enjoyed the blog. Those were great memories. I don't know if I'll be writing anymore. Life is really complicated at the moment. But I liked traveling by myself, even though it did get lonely sometimes. What was your favorite blog post?
--Anmarie

I knew what was complicating her life.

The next day was Sunday, and it was snowing. I thought of Effby. No one would bring her copies of the *New York Times* or *The California Chronicle*. Staff would go in and open her blinds, like they did for every resident, but they wouldn't know she hated snow. I wouldn't be there to make sure those blinds stayed closed. I stayed in bed, covering my head with blankets.

When I heard my door open, I pretended to be asleep. I felt Mom's presence by the side of my bed and heard her pull up my desk chair and set something on the nightstand.

"I know you're awake, Tessa," she said. "I brought you hot chocolate and I made breakfast." Suddenly, the smell of bacon reached my nose under the covers. I unburied my head. Mom was standing beside my bed wearing her bathrobe. She'd brushed her hair and removed her makeup from the night before. "Come eat with me," she said, stretching out her hand.

Let me tell you, my mom hardly ever cooks. When I was little, she cooked more often. Things like corned beef and French Dip sandwiches. While Dad worked late, she sometimes made lasagna, thick with Italian sausage crumbles and cheese. But I think by then she'd already decided the kitchen was Dad's domain. She liked to order Hungarian food, Chinese, and Lebanese takeaway that she often reheated, or, if she was feeling especially healthy, vegan salads and muffins that tasted like rocks.

After my brother didn't come home from the hospital, she stopped ordering takeout. Feeding us became my responsibility. I used Mom's credit card to buy things like wonton soup and egg rolls.

I left them on her bedside table, only to take them away hours later because she hadn't eaten any of it. After the divorce, we couldn't afford takeout, so somebody had to start cooking. I had watched my dad cook for years and learned how to make lots of dishes, the easiest being soup. First, I browned onions and garlic, then tossed chopped vegetables into my broth, then cooked to a light boil and simmered until ready. My dad taught me to roast a whole chicken, pick away the meat, and steam the carcass down for broth. It sounds easy, but it takes a time. And that's why, smelling bacon and eggs and knowing how much effort Mom put into making them, this was a momentous thing.

As we walked into the kitchen, I noticed that Mom had fixed the bacon the way I like it, crispy. She'd cut strawberries, peaches, and apples into chunks and drizzled them with honey. Mom poured herself another cup of coffee.

"Wow, Mom."

"I thought we could spend some time together," she said. "Maybe have a pajama day? You don't have to go into Morningstar today, right?"

I didn't have to go into Morningstar, not today or ever again. But a pajama day? We hadn't had a pajama day since I was seven years old. And even then, we'd very occasionally spend a Saturday in our pajamas, playing games, maybe watching a movie. It wasn't something that fit into our busy lives, not then and not now, and I didn't trust it. "A pajama day? Why?"

She sipped her coffee. "Why not?" she said, then pulled her bathrobe a little tighter. "Please, Tessa, let's just try this. Do something different for a change."

It's not like I had any plans. Besides, I was happy Mom was out of her room and that she'd gone to great effort to make this pajama day happen. "Sure," I said. "Sounds great."

After we'd put the dishes in the dishwasher, we dragged blankets out of the bedrooms and climbed onto the couch. "What do you want to watch?" she said.

I had no idea. When I was in school, I usually did homework until late and was always too tired to watch TV afterwards. Kids would talk about different Netflix shows they were watching, a series they found super creepy or funny or whatever, but I never had time to check them out. "You pick." I finally said.

The wind rattled our windows. Snow turned to icy rain that began pelting the glass. I wrapped myself tighter in my blanket and moved away from the cold air blowing through the cracks.

"We've got to weatherize this place," Mom said, tucking her blanket in tight around her legs. "There was a workshop at the library, a 'how-to-put-up-plastic-to-keep-out-the-cold' or some such thing, but I was working at the time." She turned on the TV and selected a show with super beautiful teenagers who were all members of the same drama club and never seemed to do any homework. I wanted to tell my mom that I could have gone to the workshop, but I couldn't have gone because someone might have seen me and then who knows what might have happened. Instead, I promised myself I'd find a video on YouTube and put up the plastic myself.

We watched the show for a while in silence. It was weird sitting on the sofa beside my mom not talking. It wasn't bad, just different. Mom fidgeted with the blankets. "Do you want some tea?" she asked.

"No thanks," I said. I felt her eyes on me.

"What?"

"I'm getting used to your hair."

"Well, that's good. Since you have to look at me every day."

"I think it's sort of cute, actually. In a way. It's a little rough, probably because of the scissors you used." She leaned over and smoothed my choppy bangs. At the touch of her hand on my head

I felt a pinch behind my eyes. "Maybe later I could trim a little? Just even it up?"

I nodded and wiped my eyes with the blanket.

After the show ended, Mom got up to use the bathroom. I scrolled through the options. I let the cursor hover over Dad's show, *Tom's Food Trucks*. My dad's upper torso filled the TV screen as he leaned against his Grilled Cheesy Tom Truck. His muscular arms were crossed, and he grinned into the camera. I let the trailer play and watched my dad show another cook how to drizzle gravy over potatoes in Tom's Tater Truck. He waved to the next scene where he jauntily jogged over to a big stove and poured a small amount of batter into a hot pan in Tom's Crepe Truck. I pretended, like I used to, that his big smile was just for me.

"He sure has personality," Mom said. I jumped and nearly dropped the remote. "No, leave it," she said. "It's okay. We can watch it." Her voice sounded strained, and I worried I'd just undone all the good her hot chocolate and bacon and warm pajama day blankets had created. Wind howled outside.

"I don't want to watch it. Not really. I just, well, I just saw him and . . ." My words seemed to fall away and get lost in the blankets.

"I know you miss him," she said, plopping back down onto the couch. "It's okay to miss him."

"I don't miss him. He's a jerk."

The trailer continued to play and soon Mom and I were watching him drizzle gravy. "He's a big baby," she said. "And kind of a jerk. But we can still miss him, the fun parts anyway. It's hard for me to remember those parts sometimes but look at him." She gestured at the screen. Dad was laughing. I'd seen him laugh like that many times and it wasn't for the camera, it was real. "He had his good parts too." She seemed star struck, like she couldn't take her eyes off him.

"Is that why you just rolled over and let him take everything?" Mom pulled away from me. The sternness of my voice shocked me, but watching my dad dominate the screen, making loads of money with his TV shows and trucks and having fun, made me writhe with anger. Here was my mom and me, freezing our butts off because we didn't have plastic sheeting on our windows, and why? I took a deep breath and tried to soften my voice. "I meant to say, didn't you want to fight for what was fair?" Mom twisted the blanket in her hands as she listened. "Fight for us, fight or me?"

Her lips trembled. "You're right to be angry," she said. "But I just needed it to end. The fighting was too much for me. And I knew, well, I didn't want to get like I've been lately." She paused. "Is that why you did it?" She asked. "Because you were angry at me? At your dad?"

I wish it were that easy to explain. As if I could just name a reason why I set fire to the forest, as if there was any reason for anything, like my brother's death, her divorce, or me being born.

"Mom!" I threw the blanket off and stood. "There was no reason. I didn't think. I just did it! It was an accident. That's all, okay?"

Mom rubbed her hand across her eyes. "I'm sorry, Tess, I thought if I knew the reason, maybe we could get back to where things went wrong and fix them."

It was pointless trying to explain something that made no sense. I was tired of arguing about it. There was no going back to anything, that was certain, and maybe there was no going forward either. There was only now, this day, this hour, this minute. And I was tired of trying to fill this moment with words that meant nothing.

I flopped down and changed the channel to a Christmas movie where the characters lived in manicured homes with trendy decorations and their oversized teeth showed way too much.

My phone pinged. It was April. *Come to a party with me?*

CHAPTER EIGHTEEN

April picked me up just after eight the next night. I left my mom a note. *Going out with friends. Back at midnight.* I figured she'd be happy I had friends.

Of course, I didn't actually have friends. I was going out with four girls I didn't know. Well, I knew one of them, sort of. April flipped her hair as I squeezed in beside two girls in the back.

"Squish in," she said. "Tish, Jackie, Sparrow, this is Essie." Essie was April's nickname name for me. I didn't mind leaving Tessa behind. "Essie," she made a sweeping gesture with her hand. "Tish, Jackie, Sparrow."

I had tried on several outfits in the hours leading up to eight o'clock, hoping to find something that worked with my black, shaggy hair and charcoal eyes. I eventually settled on a tight black crop top I usually wore under a loose shirt and with a jean miniskirt. It was all wrong for the night, because it was cold outside, but judging from what the other girls were wearing I imagined they were just as cold as I was.

I'd been in the car only seconds when Tish, a tiny girl with dark braids, shoved a bottle in my face. "Pre-function?" she asked.

"Pre-function!" April yelled as she sped out of the parking lot.

"Pre-function!" the other three echoed.

"You snooze, you lose," Tish said, and took a swallow. She held the bottle toward me and this time I took it. I tipped it back, feeling a sweet burn down my throat. I coughed and wiped my mouth with the back of my hand.

As we drove out of town and into the darkness, we passed the bottle around and the girls howled, their eyes glinting in the darkness. The car smelled of an intoxicating mix of lotion, perfume, and liquor. These girls were different from any friends I'd had before. They were wild, uncontrollable, and free.

Rain splattered against the windshield as we flew along the highway, shouting at one another over loud, chest pumping music. I flashed a wide smile like the other girls. They clearly didn't know who I was, and I wanted to keep it that way. Tonight, I was one of them.

About twenty minutes later, we turned onto a side road and down a long gravel drive with cars on both sides. We parked behind the last car and climbed out, all of us a little unsteady on our feet. I shivered as we walked up the winding driveway toward a large house with a long wrap-around porch. The path was muddy. One of Sparrow's spiked heels became stuck in a deep tire track, and it took the four of us to pull it free. Laughter, thumping music and the smell of cigarette smoke guided us up the drive. We pushed through the front door.

April raised her arms above her head and shouted, "Hey y'all, the party has started!"

Eight or nine people were lounging across a sectional, red plastic cups in hands. A giant purple bong took center spot on the coffee table, cigarette packs and lighters scattered around it. I recognised Feather Falls, one of the most famous waterfalls near Elmsville, in a photograph hanging above everyone's heads.

One guy pulled himself from the sectional to hug April.

"Hey, you made it." He was tall and attractively scruffy. His unbuttoned flannel shirt hung open wide enough to show off his chest and abs.

"Essie, this is Captain," April said. "This is his place."

"Captain?"

"Yep," Captain said, flashing me a smile. "Ladies, the keg is in the kitchen."

I followed April and the other three trailed behind me as we made our way toward the keg. "He owns this place?" I asked.

"His parents," she replied. "They're only here in summer, so he watches the place for them during winter."

The kitchen was packed with people. April pushed her way through, smiling as each person moved out of her way. I followed her lead, the liquor from the car making me feel warm and confident. When we finally reached the keg, April poured a cup of beer and handed it to me. I took a deep drink. "That's my girl," she smiled. I was already floating and grateful to be out of my drafty apartment. No one here hated me. I looked sexy. I felt strong. I laughed. Maybe this was the life I should have been living all along.

The party got more crowded as the night went on. As I poured another beer, I found myself talking to a group of strangers about superhero movies and laughing along with everyone else. It felt good to be talking to people again, even if it was nonsense.

April grabbed my arm and pulled me toward the back door. "Come on, let's go smoke."

We joined a sizeable crowd on the covered back porch. Smoke hung above our heads as rain lashed down in front of us. "Cigarette?" April asked, holding the pack up to me. I shook a cigarette out, letting it roll between my fingers. "Here," she said. "I'll light you."

I held it to my lips as she leaned in with her lighter. She smiled as I took my first puff and coughed, smoke from my mouth and nose disappearing into the darkness. We propped ourselves against the porch railing.

"You ever wonder what's out there in the dark?" I asked.

"I know what's out there," she said. "Trees."

"Yeah, but what else? It's not like you can see anything."

"You scared of the woods, little girl?" she teased lightly.

"Sort of."

She turned to me, taking a long drag from her cigarette. "Got to face your fears." Her eyes flashed. "Come into the woods with me."

"What? No, it's raining," I protested.

She flipped her cigarette into the rain and, in one smooth motion, climbed over the railing. She turned and held out her arms to me. "Come on, Essie. Face your fears!"

"What are you doing?" I laughed, the alcohol pulsing through me.

"Helping you face your fears!"

Her hair was dripping wet, and rain had soaked through her top. People on the porch started cheering. I jumped over the railing and stood beside her. When she turned and ran toward the woods, I followed. Laughter from the porch faded as we dashed further into darkness. I stumbled, but managed to keep my balance, following the blurry white of April's top.

"Run!" she shouted, then giggled.

"I'm going to hit a tree!" I said, but kept running, my boots sinking deeper into the spongy ground.

April suddenly tripped and flew forward. I tried to stop but stumbled and landed hard on the ground next to her. We rolled around, unable to stop laughing, eventually settling on our backs. All around was nothing but darkness and rain.

"Are you still afraid?" April asked, her face close to mine.

"No."

Back in the house, we washed our faces in the bathroom and tried drying our hair and clothes with hand towels. We were soaked through and muddy, but our insides were warm from all the pre-function liquor and keg beer we'd drunk.

"Come on," April said. "We need more beer."

While we poured another red cup from the keg, a popular song came on and everyone in the living room started dancing. I left April, pushing my way toward the music. I saw Tish and Sparrow dancing, their bodies close. The lights were low, and the music seemed to wrap around me. I let myself move to the rhythm, finding my space in the dancing crowd, loving the anonymity. I could dance and smoke, run and drink in a crowd of people and no one cared.

The spell was broken when the door opened and a group of guys piled in. Several of them lugged cases of beer on their shoulders, which brought cheers from the crowd. Holding one case, shaking his dark hair from his eyes, was Pablo.

I ducked into the crowd. A few other kids I recognized from school had followed Pablo, and I would do whatever it took to avoid being seen by them. On my way to the kitchen, I passed April. A guy had his arm draped over her possessively. She was snuggling up to him in an oversized flannel shirt. She grinned at me.

I'd hoped the group I'd been talking with earlier was still hanging around the kitchen. I tried finding the beer I'd left, but it was gone as well. I poured myself another, unsure where to hide. Eventually I cozied up to a group of strangers and listened for a way into their conversation.

"You warm enough?" a voice close to my ear said. I turned to see Captain. He was standing close enough for me to see his beard stubble and the flecks of brown in his blue eyes.

"Oh sure," I said. "I've been dancing," I added.

"I saw that," Captain smiled.

I wondered how old he was. Out of school, for sure. Until Pablo's gang showed up, I was easily the youngest. "Good party," I said. I glanced around for Pablo.

"Yeah, cool," he said. His eyes fixed on me. "Why haven't I seen you before?"

"Invisibility is my superpower." I waited for a laugh, like I'd gotten from the kitchen crowd earlier, but Captain just kept his eyes on me. Diego would have laughed.

"Want to get some air?" Without waiting for me to answer, Captain grabbed my hand and pulled me to the back porch. We stood facing the same woods where April and I had faced down my fears, what was it, twenty minutes earlier? My head was spinning.

Captain offered me a cigarette and I took it. "Why do they call you Captain?" I asked as he held the flame toward me.

"I run river raft excursions in the summer," he said. "Take families down the Class One sections, all smooth with no action. I take bachelor parties and city kids who want Class Five adventures."

"How long have you been captain of the rivers?"

"Three summers," he said, shifting so his unbuttoned shirt fell open a little further, revealing more abs. "Of course, this past summer doesn't count," he said. I heard the bitterness in his voice. "Shit, to be honest, I don't know how long I can stay here."

"Why?" I asked, gripping the rail to steady myself.

"I save money in the summer so I can get by in the winter doing odd jobs and stuff. Having no rent helps, but I still gotta eat." He raised his cup to me. "And drink. Don't know if I can make it this year."

"I think I need to sit down," I said, stumbling backward onto a patio chair that unfortunately had someone already in it. The girl screamed as I landed in her lap, my beer sloshing on top of us both.

"Whoa," Captain laughed, pulling me up. "Let's find you another chair."

"Dumb bitch," the girl said, wiping beer from her shirt.

"Sorry," I slurred as Captain put his arm around me, ushering me into the house. He was headed toward the staircase and I dimly registered that I didn't want to go with him. I made a grab for the railing.

"No."

"It's okay," he said hotly, his arm tightening around my waist, as he pulled me up the stairs.

A crash came from the living room. "What the fuck?" Captain released me and I fell against the handrail, then slid three steps down the staircase and onto the floor. I pulled myself up and swayed toward the commotion.

The room was full of people with their backs to me. "Cut that shit out," Captain shouted, elbowing his way through the group as there was another loud crash. I pushed forward, smiling flirtatiously at every guy who moved aside until I was at the front of the crowd and could see what was happening.

It was Pablo, fighting a much bigger guy with a crew cut. And it looked like he was losing.

"Come on, Pablo!" I heard myself scream. Crewcut had Pablo on the floor and was punching him in the jaw, knocking his head from side to side. I looked around for someone big enough to stop the fight. I couldn't believe no one was moving to stop it. They seemed to be enjoying themselves. Crewcut socked Pablo again. This time, the blow sent him spinning toward me.

Before I knew what was happening, I was on Crewcut's back. I grabbed hold of his collar and yanked, pulling him up by his neck. I heard choking sounds as Crewcut swung his arms behind, just missing me. It was like a cartoon blur of rage and limbs. I yanked back harder, dragging us both to the floor. But things didn't stop there. While on the floor, I kicked his side hard, relishing the contact my boot made with his ribs. The crowd rushed in, prying my hands from his neck and hoisting Crewcut up and away.

Pablo rolled over, his battered face looking at me. "Tessa, what are you doing here?"

Without saying a word, I rolled away and vomited.

"Get the fuck out of my house!" Captain shouted, yanking Pablo's arm.

Pablo shook him off. "Get your hands off me."

I wiped vomit from my face. Captain had lost his laid-back demeanor. "You too, Bitch!" he barked at me. "Get the fuck out of my house!"

I could see April in the crowd of onlookers, still attached to that guy. Our eyes met and she shook her head and curled her lip. "What the hell?" I heard her say as a hand reached down for me. It was Pablo's.

"Come on," he said. "Let's get out of here." Pablo held my arm just above the elbow. I stumbled out of the house and hauled myself into the passenger side of the truck. Diego's truck. "Try not to throw up," he said.

"I don't think there's anything left."

He reached into the back seat and grabbed a shirt, wiping blood from his face.

"You're a mess," I said. "You need some ice."

"It's fine. See if there's some Kleenex in the glove compartment, will you? If I get blood on the seat, I'm screwed."

As we drove away from Captain's house, I fished through Diego's glove compartment for tissues, handing the package to Pablo. As we made another turn, my head began to spin.

"I think you'd better pull over."

After I finished vomiting on the side of the road, I pulled myself back into the truck. Pablo handed me a tissue. "What were you even doing there?" he said.

"What were you doing there?" I shot back, resting my head against the cold window. The truck smelled like Rippen and Diego and the whole horribleness of the night surged up and I burst into tears.

"Shit," Pablo said. "Just chill out, okay."

We drove along the dark highway, my sniffling the only sound beside the low hum of the truck's engine. I knew it was way past my curfew. I pulled out my phone. There were three texts from my mom. I texted back, *omw*.

As we neared Elmsville, Pablo stopped at a convenience store. "I can't go in there like this," he said. His face was swollen and even through the dim light, I could see his eye was purple and blue.

"Do you need to go to the hospital?"

"I just need something cold." He pulled a twenty-dollar bill from his wallet. "Go in and get me a package of frozen peas and a Gatorade for you. Get two. You'll need one in the morning." He pushed the money into my hand.

159

I tried to avoid eye contact with the store clerk, knowing I smelled of vomit and still had mud in my hair. I bought frozen corn because that's all they had, three Frost flavored Gatorades, a packet of tissues and a bottle of water.

"Having a good night?" the clerk smirked.

"Sssuper," I said.

Back in the truck, Pablo held the corn against his face while the clerk watched us from inside the store. I poured water on a tissue and handed it to Pablo. He used it to clean the dried blood from his nose. I took a sip of the Gatorade, washing the vomit taste from my mouth.

"Hey," Pablo said. "Thanks for helping me out. I mean, that was pretty crazy, but thanks."

"Why'd you get into that fight, anyway? What happened?" I said.

"That guy's an asshole. He disrespected me."

"Do you know Captain?"

"Friend of a friend. I mean, we don't hang out or anything. What were you doing there?"

"I don't know," I said, peeling back the label on my Gatorade. "Trying something different, I guess."

"How'd that work out for you?"

"Not so great." I scratched at the label. My head was hurting. "Can you please not tell Diego?" I asked.

"No worries," he said. "How about we both keep quiet about the whole thing? What he doesn't know won't get him all riled up."

I took small drinks of Gatorade, not wanting to stress my stomach.

"Why'd you call me *pirómana*. I know what it means. Diego told me."

Pablo moved the package of corn to the other side of his face.

"I knew it would piss off Diego. It had nothing to do with you, really. I was just angry. I'm angry a lot."

"Me too," I said. "Sometimes I don't know what to do with it."

"Yeah, me neither."

Pablo set aside the corn and drank from his Gatorade. "Hey, it's none of my business, but you should know Diego misses you. I mean, it's not like we talk about that stuff, but I can tell."

I'd peeled the label off my Gatorade bottle. "I miss him too."

Pablo moved the corn to his forehead. "You guys should figure it out."

"I can't figure anything out right now."

"I hear that."

CHAPTER NINETEEN

As Pablo predicted, by morning, my head was pounding.

I wadded up the clothes I'd worn and shoved them into the washing machine. I thought taking a hot shower would make me feel more human. And it did, sort of. Afterwards, while Mom was still asleep, I gulped a few drinks of water and went back to bed. Sometime later, after a restless sleep, I heard my door open and for a few moments, I felt Mom looking at me. The door closed, and I drifted back to sleep.

Around four, I felt well enough to get out of bed. I found Mom sitting on the couch watching Netflix.

"We need to talk," she said the moment I stepped out of my room.

"I know. I'm sorry." I dumped a can of chicken noodle soup into a pan.

"Where the heck were you? And what, now you're hung over all day?"

"I'm sorry." My head was still aching. "Can we talk about this later?" My brain was in a supersensitive state, and the last thing I wanted to do was force it to answer questions.

"I don't know what to do with you," she barked. "Just when you should be pulling everything together, you're blowing it. Royally." She turned off the television and slammed the remote down on the coffee table. I winced.

"Oh sorry," she quipped, "did that hurt your head?" She stormed into her room, slamming the door.

Tears dropped into the soup as I stirred it. I ate from the pan while standing at the counter. Afterwards I tossed the empty can into the garbage but, because the bin was full, it tumbled out and splashed soup onto the floor.

I lugged the garbage out to the dumpster near the parking lot. I stepped inside the fenced enclosure and hurled the bag up and in. The effort made me wobbly, so I sat on the curb to steady myself. It was just me and the rancid smell of rubbish, which was just what I deserved. The sun was disappearing, and the cool, damp winter air felt good against my skin. I closed my eyes.

"What are you doing in here?"

I jumped at the sound of my mom's voice. She was standing a few feet away. "Why are you sitting out here with the garbage?"

"I don't know." I wondered how long I'd been there.

Mom sat on the curb beside me. "There are less fragrant places to enjoy the outdoors, you know."

"Yeah, but I have the whole place to myself. No crowds."

Mom picked up a piece of gravel and passed it from one hand to the other. "You know I want to help you."

"I know."

She scratched the pavement until the rock left a white streak. I remembered doing the same thing as a little girl, etching my name on the sidewalk of our Portland house, thinking it would always be there. "I just don't know how to help. Maybe you can you tell me how?" She scratched a question mark.

I shook my head. I didn't know how to help her help me. I didn't know how to help myself.

"Well, can we please come inside?" she said. "It's getting cold."

I let her pull me up and lead me back to our apartment.

That night I punished myself by logging into Facebook. A photo memory popped up of last year's volleyball team. We'd just beaten Walton Springs. I was grinning, my arms linked with Tan's, my sweaty blond hair clinging to my face. It felt great to be part of a winning team. To have people in my life. Not that I missed those people with their shallow conversations about movies, makeup, and boys. They seemed so unimportant to me now, but that feeling of belonging – that's what I missed.

I fell into bed without washing my face or brushing my hair, which had become my new routine. Since I didn't have Morningstar anymore, I sometimes didn't shower for days. My library companions didn't seem to mind, and my mom didn't seem to notice. If she did, she never said anything. I laid under the covers and waited for sleep to take some of my loneliness away.

The next morning, I got a call from Kathy. She said they'd made a big mistake. Someone else had been stealing the medication. She asked if I'd please come back.

It turned out Tamara had been skimming medication for weeks. It was easy since they only prescribed opioids to be dispensed as needed. Sure, they were inside metal cabinets under lock and key, but as short staffed as Morningstar was, it was easy for Tamara to slip in when no one was watching and unlock the cabinets. She used a key she'd "borrowed" one day, then ran down to Ace Hardware and had it duplicated. The stealing could have gone on forever if she hadn't gotten overzealous and stolen too much at once. Apparently, that's how Kathy became suspicious. Of me.

When I arrived, I found Kathy in her office sitting at her desk, her hands face up.

"I'm so sorry," she said. "I jumped to conclusions and couldn't see what was right in front of me." Her nail polish was chipped. I might not have noticed, but it was the same bright red as the poinsettia on her desk that had lost most of its leaves. "Will you come back?"

I had to think about it. On one hand, what happened at Morningstar wouldn't be the last time someone falsely accused me. I would always be the first person suspected of causing wrong, whatever it was, because I had a criminal history. I was the girl who started the fire, a *pirómana*. On the other hand, someone needed to close Effby's drapes when it snowed.

"I guess," I said. "I still need the community service hours."

An 8 ½" x 11" headshot of Rudolph the Red-Nosed Reindeer was taped on Effby's door.

"What happened to you?" she asked when I walked in. "Drop a bucket of crude oil on your head?"

"I see you're as pleasant as always." I could tell she was happy to see me because when I gave her a hug, she reached her thin arms around and pulled me close. But only for a second, then she let me go.

"It was Tamara all along," I said.

"Of course, it was. I'd suspected that little nitwit for weeks, I just had to get the evidence."

"Wait, what? You're the one who figured it out?"

Effby rolled her eyes. "Aileen May's prescription shouldn't have run out for weeks because it's only given to her when she asks for it. She hates taking pills. Always trying to manage pain through positive thinking, which is why she's always smiling like an idiot. So, there should be a good supply of pills in her bottle."

Effby straightened up in her wheelchair and I could tell she was excited to share every detail.

"I asked Aileen May when she'd last asked for a pill, and she couldn't remember. And not because she's old and forgetful like everyone assumes, but because it had been so long. But then she had a fall."

"Is she alright?" I realized I hadn't seen Aileen May yet today.

"She'll be okay. She bruised her hip. She's in bed watching *Ellen*. But when she fell, she asked for her medication."

"And there wasn't any left," I volunteered.

"Exactly."

"But how did they find out it was Tamara?"

"I found out," she corrected me. "I asked everyone if they'd seen anyone hanging around the medication room. Asked them to keep their eyes open. William told me Tamara left her desk at least twice a day. Sal said he'd seen Tamara around the kitchen twice the week before. I put Dolores on stakeout."

"Dolores?" I interjected. "The one who mostly sits around drooling all day long?"

"Right. She's got more going on than you'd think and that's what made her so perfect! No one even noticed. So, when she saw Tamara head into the medication room, she wheeled her chair right over to me."

"Wait, she wheeled all the way back to your room?"

"Well, no, that would be too far, obviously. I was in the recreation room playing Scrabble with Sal. So, when Delores alerted me, I got Regina, and we busted down there. Caught Tamara red handed in Aileen May's oxycodone."

"Wow," I said. I couldn't decide what was more surprising, that she'd discovered the real thief or that she'd left her room and was playing games with other residents.

"Welcome back," a voice came from behind. It was Sal, his wafer-thin frame leaning into Effby's doorway.

"Hello Sal. Effby's been catching me up on your Scrabble prowess."

"When are we going to have that rematch?" he asked Effby. "I owe you a butt whooping."

"Ready for more humiliation?" Effby replied. "Always happy to oblige. I'll meet you later."

Sal waved as he shuffled down the hall.

I raised my eyebrows at Effby, and she shrugged.

Regina came, fa-la-la-la-la-ing into Effby's room, leaving a large linen cart in the hallway. She cut off singing "Deck the Halls" to say, "Welcome back. I knew it wasn't you. You aren't the tweaker type."

'Yeah, arson is more my thing', I almost said, but didn't. "How's Shanna?" I asked.

"Counting the days until Santa Claus arrives. Two weeks to go and she can barely sleep." She tossed dirty bathroom towels into the cart and replaced them with fresh ones. "Come help me take this down to the laundry."

As we rolled the cart together, Regina said, "There's been quite a change in Effby."

"Did she stop throwing food at people?"

"Well, not entirely. She'll still wallop you with applesauce if you come in at the wrong time. But not as often. Plus, she's out of her room more."

"Maybe it was good that I left."

"What?" Regina raised her eyebrows at me. "No, girl, you got it started. Then, when you left, she had to get out of that room to find the real culprit, to be the Morningstar detective." She shook her head. "No, that's all because of you."

We parked the linen bin in front of the bank of washing machines.

"Why don't you come over tonight after work? Shanna and I are going to drive around and check out Christmas lights."

"Where? Is there some street where everyone goes crazy or something?"

"No, we just drive around neighborhoods near our house. We vote on the best house with the fanciest lights and then leave them cookies. Plus, I make the best hot chocolate in the whole state."

I hesitated. Making friends wasn't in my plans. My last attempt ended with me getting into a brawl and vomiting all over a strange guy's house. But maybe I wouldn't screw things up this time?

"Sure," I said. "I guess so."

Regina's apartment was much tinier than ours, but it was warm and the Christmas tree on the table sparkled with lights and tinsel as if it was ten feet tall. Shanna must have had a hand in the decorations, which were mainly paper chains and angels made of cotton balls glued on painted cardboard.

Shanna, five years old, took great pleasure in showing me each decoration, one at a time, while Regina stood at the stove making hot chocolate.

"This one is a Christmas train, like in *The Polar Express*," Shanna said, pointing out a cardboard train engine that had been assembled with surprising intricacy for a five-year-old.

"The kid's a master at cardboard and tape," Regina said, adding a shake of spice to the pot. "She's going to be an engineer or something."

Shanna wore her hair in two puff balls on either side of her head. I kneeled to get a closer look at the train.

"Wow," I said. "It's exactly like the Christmas train."

"I had to try three times," Shanna said. "Glue kept getting everywhere."

"I hate when that happens."

"Do you have a Christmas train on your tree?"

I'd been trying to ignore Christmas. We'd left our ornaments at Dad's house. I could probably have asked for them since I'm pretty sure they didn't fit with Tranquility's décor. But maybe a homemade Christmas train would be better? Maybe Mom and I could make our own cardboard ornaments?

"No, I didn't get a tree this year."

Her eyes widened. "Why not?"

"Not everyone gets a Christmas tree," Regina said, dropping plump marshmallows into three steaming travel mugs.

It was snowing as we settled ourselves into Regina's Toyota. I moved aside an empty McDonald's bag.

"Here, let me get that," Regina said, and ran the bag to the trash bin. As soon as she started the engine, an old school hip-hop song blasted out of the radio. "Whoa there," she said, turning it down.

"Mom, I want Christmas songs," Shanna chimed in from the back seat.

"Hold on, baby." She plugged in her phone and selected a Christmas Pandora station.

Shanna provided commentary as we drove at a snail's pace through the neighborhood. They had developed a complex rating system for each house's holiday light display. Houses received zero to ten points for creativity, full coverage, and overall cheer. "Four!" Shanna called out for a house where lights draped over a scraggly tree in the front yard with ornaments dangling from the limbs.

"That's a six, for sure," Regina said. "They had to use a ladder to get to those top branches."

"You're pretty generous," Shanna muttered.

"What will you guys do on Christmas day?" I asked.

"We go over to my mom's," Regina said, one hand on the wheel and the other holding her hot chocolate. "My brother and his kids will be there. I'm working Christmas Eve, though."

Regina seemed to have it so together. She was super smart, and I wondered why she wasn't in college or something.

"How did you decide to do this for a career?" I asked.

"A career?" She laughed, and I thought she was going to spill her hot chocolate. "I don't know if I'd call it that. I mean, not exactly. But it's a good job. I went to technical college and got my certification. I dropped out of high school when I got pregnant. I tried to finish, but I had morning sickness like crazy. I was throwing up in between classes. It was stupid anyway. I couldn't figure out how to go to college with a baby and no money so what was the point? After Shanna was a few months old, I went back for my CNA."

"My mom's a nurse," Shanna said proudly.

"Not exactly," Regina said, "but thanks, Sweetie. I'm actually applying for the LPN program this spring."

"You're good with the residents," I said.

"So are you," she smiled. "They like you. Are you going to get your GED? Or go back to high school?"

I took a sip from my hot chocolate, which wasn't hot anymore. I didn't know what to say, so I took another drink.

"It's not a requirement for life or anything, I'm just asking."

"I don't know what I'm doing," I finally replied. "Honestly, I can't even think beyond one day."

"Well then, just think one day at a time," Regina said. "Sometimes it's all we can do until we can see a little farther."

I recognized the opening of *Carol of the Bells*. There were probably a hundred versions of this song, but the versions with violin lead were always my favorite.

"Can we turn this up?" I asked.

"This is awesome," Shanna said.

"I played this once," I said. "My symphony back in Portland performed this for our Christmas concert. I was the violin soloist."

"You play violin?" Regina asked. "That's amazing. You should play for the residents. They'd go ape."

We passed a lawn with an inflatable Grinch and Shanna called out "seven!" I had stopped trying to critique the displays a while back, but Shanna continued to call out numbers while her mother and I kept talking.

"I don't play much anymore." Or ever, I thought, but didn't say.

"Dang girl, if you have a skill, you should bust it out."

We began singing *Little Drummer Boy* in front of an "eight", with blue and silver twinkling lights draped over shrubs on all sides of the house. My phone pinged with a text from Diego. It was a picture of Rippen, looking annoyed in a Christmas hat. *Merry Christmas. Miss you. Just be friends?*

Maybe it was the Christmas lights or Regina's killer hot chocolate or living this night as if there was nothing else, but suddenly I felt there might be something a little farther out, some possibility waiting for me. Afterall, I was back at Morningstar and everyone there seemed genuinely happy to have me back. Especially Effby. I texted Diego. *Quit torturing your dog.*

On Christmas Eve, I played Scrabble with Effby in the rec room. Most residents had been picked up by family or had gone to bed early after visits from their great grandchildren. Regina, April, and I spent the afternoon putting stockings together for the residents, filling each with lotion, snacks, and a small ornament. April didn't ask me to go do stuff with her anymore, which was fine, but she was still civil. In her world, getting into a drunken brawl at your friend's house was a party foul, but I guess it wasn't grounds for the total silent treatment.

Morningstar's Christmas tree had been put up way too early and now most of its needles were lying on the floor around the stand. We'd lost track of whose turn it was to water the tree.

"Ha!" Effby said, placing six tiles on the board. "Haughty. Seventeen points."

I filled a cup with water from the drinking fountain. "It'll make a great story when I come back from behind and whoop you." I kneeled beside the tree and poured water into the stand then came back and sat with Effby, studying the crappy tiles in my rack.

"Why aren't you home with your mom?" Effby asked.

I shrugged. Mom had said she was turning in early. Last year had been our first Christmas after the divorce and it turned into the weirdest Christmas ever. This one topped last year for weirdness, as in, not even like Christmas. All around me were wreaths and lights and stuff that's supposed to make people feel the Christmas spirit, but I didn't have any and apparently neither did my mom.

"She's probably already asleep. She's tired."

"Well, here we are then," she said. "Two Christmas loners."

I leaned over the table. "Tell me about your family," I said. "I know you used to have someone in your life. I can tell."

Effby grunted and placed several tiles down. "Dollop," she said. "Nine points." She recorded the points on her unofficial score sheet which was just a piece of our drawing paper. "I had children."

"How many?" I asked. "And where are they?"

Effby sighed, then her eyes met mine. *The First Noel* played on the Christmas Pandora channel as rain pattered against the window. "I had a girl Robin and a boy Samuel," she finally blurted out.

"Where are Robin and Samuel?"

Effby ran her fingers over the tiles. "Robin died. When she was a young girl. Car accident. Samuel, well, I don't know," she trailed off. "I guess we just never healed after that. I think it was easier for him to be on his own. He grew up fast. Left fast. We don't keep in touch."

I suspected there had been a tragedy in Effby's life, but I didn't imagine a grown child out there somewhere, choosing not to talk to her. I tried to imagine myself leaving and never talking to my mother again. I could do it with my dad, maybe, but never Mom and I certainly would never think of leaving her in a place like Morningstar with COPD to live her final years alone.

"Where is he?" I asked.

"I don't know for sure," she said. "Last time I knew, he was in Iowa."

"Where you grew up?"

She nodded.

My tiles clicked against the rack as I moved them around vacantly. "Why not try finding him?"

"He doesn't want to be found," she said simply. Then she pushed her wheelchair back "I'd better get to bed before I get told its past curfew."

I rolled Effby back to her room. The nurse's aide on duty helped her into bed.

"I'm sorry if I asked too many questions," I said, as I straightened a pile of crossword puzzle books on her bedside table. A silver ball ornament had fallen from the small tree on her bookshelf. I replaced it and sat down next to her. We both watched the LED lights twinkle for a moment.

"Life is messy," she said. "Sometimes it makes you tired." She closed her eyes.

"It sure does," I whispered. "Merry Christmas," I said and then closed the door softly.

CHAPTER TWENTY

I got up early Christmas morning and cooked waffles and sausages. We ate on the couch, Christmas music playing on my phone. Even though we didn't have a tree, Mom and I exchanged gifts. I gave her a large box of toiletries. Lotions, foot creams and compression socks for her tired feet. At the bottom of the box, I'd hidden Lindt chocolate balls, which I knew she loved, and nail polish. The grand finale was a foot bath.

"For your feet after work," I said. "Until you find a job that involves less running around in heels."

Within minutes, she was soaking her feet.

I'd bought the Christmas gifts with my essay money. My last theft had been from the library. I'd finished *Violin Dreams* long ago but kept it on my nightstand. Steinhardt's playing had gotten him through crippling anxiety, but I wasn't Steinhardt. His nightmares were about not being a good enough violin player. Mine were about not being a good enough human being. I still couldn't pull the bow across the strings. He was forever searching for the perfect interpretation of Bach's *Chaconne*, a piece that both enticed and eluded him. It became a haunting siren that called to him throughout his musical career. I wondered what it would be like to have that kind of passion for something. I was just trying to survive each day. Just that morning I shifted my violin case closer to my growing box of apology letters to remind me of how, once upon a time, I was good at something.

For Christmas, Mom gave me an organizer for next year that said in floral script, "Feels Good to Get Stuff Done." I had to stifle a laugh. I thought of alternative titles more fitting for me. "Feels Good to Not Be a Screw Up Today" was about as positive as I could get. Dad gave me a large box of top-quality pots and pans, along with his latest cookbook, *Food Truck Tom's Gourmet Chow – The Urban Deep Fry*. It was just like Dad to send me a copy of his own book. He signed it, *To my little girl who's not so little anymore. With love, Dad*. I rolled my eyes. Tranquility must have made him watch Hallmark movies. His Christmas card was a photo of him and Tranquility wearing matching Christmas pajamas. I texted him to say thanks.

Send me pics of what you make with the new set, he responded. I found the gift of pots and pans curiously optimistic. In the afternoon, while Mom laid down for a nap, I boiled pasta in my new pan. While cooking, my phone pinged with a text from Diego, *Merry Christmas. Coffee this week?* I texted him back a thumb's up. *Wednesday?*

Mom and I ate my jazzed-up lasagne and lemon custard with raspberries made from recipes I'd found on Pinterest. The entire day an idea had been growing in my mind, bouncing around and gaining strength and momentum and solidity. *It's the Most Wonderful Time of the Year* song came on and I was filled with holiday spirit. I texted Regina. *I have a project I need ur help w.*

The next day at Morningstar, I shared my plans with Regina. "I don't know," she said. "Maybe that son of hers doesn't want to be found." We were standing in the kitchen where I ladled applesauce into cups and she placed them on trays. It was a job for one, but we made it look like work for two.

"Maybe if he knew where she was. I bet the last time she tried contacting him, she was still in California. He might not even know she had a stroke, let alone that she moved to Oregon."

"Well," Regina said, adjusting the bandana holding back her hair. "I can access the files. Kathy keeps her password on a sticky note on her monitor. It's not exactly high security around here."

As I pushed the cart out of the kitchen, I crushed the urge to jump into the air and pump my fist. Reuniting Effby with her son, that would be amazing. I was sure they could find forgiveness, if that was what they needed, or healing from whatever might have happened after Robin's death.

After I'd dispatched the applesauce, I headed to Effby's room.

"Did you get it?" she asked. From my bag, I pulled out a box of hair color, Flame Red #20.

"It's pretty bright," I said. "Are you sure?"

"I don't want to go all emo like you," she said. "But let's shake things up a little around here. I want to see Sal's face."

"Be careful. His heart's not that strong."

I wheeled Effby over to the sink and draped a towel around her frail shoulders. She angled her head over the sink and I wet her hair with cups of water. I lined the bathroom floor with towels, wondering if helping an old lady act like a rebellious teenager would send Kathy into a terminating frenzy.

"I'm not sure about this," I said, squeezing dye into my gloved hand. Flame Red #20 was Christmas red. "What if the dye makes your hair fall out? You have so little to spare, you know."

"Then you'll have to steal me a wig."

My hands paused mid squeeze, "Why did you say I'd have steal?"

"How else do you get things? You don't have any money." She was right, I didn't.

"Well, I quit stealing a while ago, so don't expect a new box of hair color every two weeks."

"Can I sit up? This is breaking my neck."

"Not yet." I massaged the dye through every strand of Effby's hair. Instantly the grey disappeared. Her head, now blazing red, felt light and delicate in my hands. "Okay," I said, peeling off my gloves, "You need to sit here for ten minutes. Don't let your head touch anything." I tried to think of what chemicals would best remove red hair dye from a porcelain sink.

Ten minutes later I rinsed her hair and styled it with the blow dryer. We studied her reflection in the mirror. I didn't have to tell her she looked amazing, I could see by her smile that she knew it.

"Should have done this years ago," she said.

My phone pinged. It was a text from Regina telling me to meet her at Kathy's office. When I got there, Regina directed me to stand guard while she logged into the computer. I tried to be casual, pretending to scroll through messages on my phone. I could hear Regina's fingers tapping the keyboard. Out of the corner of my eye I spotted William making his way toward me, his walker at arm's length and two steps ahead.

"Hi William," I said. I didn't know if he'd find it strange that Regina was on Kathy's computer, but I didn't want to take the risk. This for sure would be a terminating offence.

"Miss Tessa," he said, shuffling slowly closer. "Want to watch *Oprah* with me?"

"Oh, I can't. I'm busy right now." And I was busy, sort of. "You should go see Effby. She's done something to her hair."

"Oh? Well okay, maybe I will." William and his walker made a wide turn like a long ship in a small canal before heading back the direction he came.

"Okay, I got it," Regina stepped from the office. Her face was flushed. "I feel like a regular ol' spy. I think I need a new line of work."

"What'd you find?"

"His full name is Samuel Camdon and I got his address. I'll text you a photo."

I left Morningstar early to start my Google search for Effby's son. I found nearly a hundred Samuel Camdons in the country. It took hours to check each one, but I was able to eliminate those who were the wrong age or whose profile didn't fit and eventually narrowed my search to one guy living at 4201 W. Kearney St. in Bryant, Iowa.

This Samuel Camdon was in his sixties and owned a contracting company specializing in house painting. In an article from a past issue of *The Bryant Daily*, his company was featured for running a

Christmas stuffed animal drive for kids in the hospital. I studied the photo of Samuel carefully, looking for any resemblance to Effby. With thinning hair and deep circles under his eyes, he looked like any tired, old man, and not especially like Effby. But this had to be him. I wondered if he had kids. Effby's grandchildren. She'd love having visits from grandchildren and great grandchildren, if she had any.

I placed my new organizer on the desk. Across the first page of January, where it said, "Goals for This Month," I wrote "Find Samuel Camdon." Even though I'd already found him on the computer, I still needed to find him in person. I texted Regina. *What RU doing? Want to research Mr. C. w me?*

I met Regina and Shanna at Shari's restaurant. They'd already had dinner, but Shanna was excited about a Shari's ice cream sundae. She sat across the table and colored a placemat while I logged into my laptop. I sipped hot chocolate, checking over my shoulder from time to time to see if anyone was talking about me.

"Try finding him on Facebook," Regina said. "Does he have kids?"

"I'm not sure," I replied. "There are other Camdons in Bryant, so, maybe? I'm not sure how big the town is." I logged into Facebook, hoping there wasn't a 'happy' memory from my not-so-distant past to torment me.

"Wow," Regina said. "Seventy-eight notifications?? Don't you ever open those?"

I closed my eyes for a moment. I knew what those notifications were without opening them. I should have deleted my account months ago, but I didn't, thinking that someday I might want to look at it again.

"Not anymore," I said.

I pulled up Samuel Camdon and sorted by location. Finding him was easy. His profile picture was more recent than the newspaper photo from *The Bryant Daily* and his face more wrinkled. He had his arm around a girl wearing a bright pink tutu and tights, her hair pulled into a tidy bun at the top of her head. This must be Effby's great granddaughter.

"Is that him?" Regina asked.

"Yep, that's him."

"I want to see," Shanna licked chocolate syrup from her spoon as I turned the laptop to face her. "She's pretty," Shanna said, then focused on her sundae.

"What are you going to do?" Regina asked, taking a slurp of chocolate milkshake.

"I don't know yet."

After I'd packed up my computer, we stood at the register while Regina negotiated with Shanna about whether she could have a free sucker after she'd just eaten a whole sundae. I heard someone moan and turned to see Cammie. Geri and Tan were not far behind. I hadn't seen Cammie in months, but nothing about her had changed. Her eyes passed over Regina and Shanna, then focused on me.

I suddenly hated everything about her, her perfectly arched eyebrows and platinum blond hair, the short plaid skirt she was wearing under a tight-fitting sweater. I hated that she could stroll into a place like Shari's anytime she wanted and not worry that someone might recognize her and what ugly things they might scream in her face. Sure, it was me who threw the firecracker that set the forest on fire. But none of that would have happened if Cammie hadn't dragged me into the woods. If she hadn't started flirting with Brent and I hadn't been so needy, following her around hoping for a little of her golden girl attention, then things would have turned out differently.

"Tessa," she said, a look of disdain on her face. "I thought you moved. Or died. Or something."

I felt Regina step closer and pull Shanna in.

"No," I said, moving past Cammie. "Still here."

"Yeah," she said. "I guess you are. Sadly." Her eyes flickered over Regina and Shanna.

Regina pushed forward, pulling me by my sleeve. "You've got a little something on you," she said to Cammie as she passed. "Oh wait, that's just your face. Sorry."

"This town is overrun with low-lifes," Cammie said over her shoulder to Tan and Geri.

"This town has been full of low-lifes for a long time," I said lightly. "I'm just glad I'm not hanging out with them anymore."

"Come on, Tessa," Regina grabbed my sleeve, "Let's go."

I held eye contact with Cammie until she turned away, muttering, "Freak."

As we crossed the parking lot, Regina said, "Girl, that was some laser eyes you just got. What's her story?"

That story was too long to tell. "Just someone I used to think I was friends with."

Later that night I wrote to Cammie:

> *Dear Cammie,*
> *I'm sorry that I threw that firecracker, but I'm sorrier that I followed you into the woods and everywhere else because I helped you feel you were better than me, and better than anyone else. I'm sorry that I wasn't strong enough to know who you really were. Or who I was. But, thinking about this now, I guess I'm sorry I didn't help you be a better person.*
> *Sincerely,*
> *Tessa*

Cammie hadn't been on the apology list, but I added her name and after I'd written this letter, I crossed her off. I had 28 letters to go. Instead of writing another letter, I sent a Facebook message to Samuel Camdon.

Diego and I had agreed to meet at a frozen yogurt shop in Rogers near the Walgreens where, a couple weeks earlier, I'd stolen a hat and scarf for my mom. I didn't want to risk another run in like at Shari's or the cafe, and thankfully he didn't seem to mind driving twenty minutes out of his way to meet me.

I saw him through the glass doors. As he waited in line, he turned periodically to look over his shoulder. He'd changed out of his work clothes and was wearing clean jeans and a flannel shirt. He was more attractive than I remembered, more attractive than I wanted him to be, standing in line clumsily passing his sketchbook from hand to hand. When I opened the door, he swung around and smiled, and I was immediately at ease. Like it hadn't been over two months since we'd last seen each other, like we were just two friends meeting for a catch-up, like being out together was the most normal thing in the world.

"Hi," I said.

"You look great."

"So do you," I said, then laughed.

We got yogurt and found a table. He pulled the chair out for me and as I sat, my cheek brushed against the soft flannel of his sleeve. He smelled like grease and aftershave and a little like dog. I missed his smell.

"How have you been?" I asked.

"Okay. Busy at the shop. Rain always brings extra work. Oregon's a great state for running an auto body business. Fender benders all day long."

"How's Pablo?" I hoped Pablo had kept his part of the bargain and not mentioned the last time we'd seen each other.

"He's doing good. Keeping up in school. He's working at the shop one day a week now."

"Christmas was okay?"

"Yeah, it was good. You know, never as good as you think it should be. What about you?"

"Kind of weird," I said. "Like the Hallmark Channel hired writers from *South Park*."

Diego laughed, choking on his yogurt. He was someone who got me, or at least got my sense of humor.

"How's Effby?" It was just like Diego to remember Effby's name and to ask about her, as if it wasn't weird that my best friend was an old lady in an assisted living center.

"I missed you," I said, staring at my pistachio yogurt, "but I can't, you know, I…"

Diego reached out, touching my hand. "Hey," he said. "I'm not going to ask for more than this. I just want you in my life, as a friend."

"I don't deserve you as a friend."

"Yes, you do." He sat back. "And if I can't convince you of that, then just pretend. For me because I need a friend." He smiled and I nodded.

"How's the drawing?" I asked, gesturing to his sketchbook. He must have noticed by now that his sketch of me had been torn out, but I was grateful he never brought it up. I still had it, folded up in my desk drawer.

"Good," he said. "Want to see one from yesterday?"

He opened the book to a sketch of Rippen jumping up to catch a tennis ball. The lines were solid and confident, the expression on Rippen's face was one I'd seen many times.

I reached for the book and set it on the table beside my yogurt. "It's really good," I said. "Wow." I flipped through the pages. Birds, the shop, cars, and then a girl. It was me, but I hardly recognized myself. I was shooting a basket in Diego's driveway. I recognized the rhododendrons and garbage bin in the background. I pulled at the short ends of my black hair as I examined the drawing more closely. He'd captured the ball as it was leaving my hands and the amazing thing was, I was smiling. "It's me," I said. "But not me."

"It's you," said Diego. "At least the way I saw you on that day."

After he drove away, I sat in the parking lot and checked Facebook for the twentieth time that day. Still nothing from Samuel Camdon.

When I got home, there was another mystery envelope in the mailbox. This one contained a map of the forest printed from some random website. Someone had used red Sharpie to draw a bold circle around the acreage that burned in the Horseback Falls fire. I added it to my drawer with the others and started writing letters.

"Maybe it's the wrong Samuel," Regina said the next day as we started our shifts at Morningstar.

"Why wouldn't he tell me he was the wrong Samuel? I know my message has been read, I can see the notification."

"Sometimes people don't want to be found," she said. "Families are complicated. Maybe you shouldn't be getting in the middle of this one."

"I know I can make this happen," I said. "Effby deserves another chance."

The next day was my birthday. I tried to ignore this fact, but when I got home from Morningstar, the smell of Chinese food greeted me at the door.

"Hi, Mom? Aren't you working tonight?"

"I asked for the day off," she said. "Happy Birthday. Come on, let's eat."

Mom scooped pork fried rice and sweet and sour chicken onto two plates. She'd cleared the living room of the high heeled shoes she was forever kicking off the second she got home from work. Her hair was curled and makeup beautifully applied and she looked relaxed in jeans and a sweater.

"The house looks nice," I said, a little confused. I hung my coat on a hook rather than tossing it on the couch like usual. "You seem, different."

She sat down. "Do I?"

I sat across the table from her as she fiddled with her chopsticks. "I know I haven't been very accessible. I know I've been, well, how I get sometimes." Her hands shook a little as she talked. "But I made an appointment today to talk with someone."

"Mom, that's great!"

"I can't promise every day is going to be a good day, but I want you to know I'm trying. It's my hope that if I try, and if you see me trying, then you'll try too. And what better time for us to start trying together than today, your seventeenth birthday."

I picked up a fork instead of chopsticks. I knew what she wanted. She wanted me back in school and playing volleyball and for our life to return to how it was before. I didn't have the heart to tell her it wasn't going to happen. But seeing her out of her pajamas and eating with a smile, I couldn't say no.

"Okay, Mom."

That night I stalked Samuel Camdon online. I searched for other Camdons in Iowa. The ballerina in the picture, if it was his granddaughter, meant there must be other relatives, but every search I tried turned up nothing. I finally went old school and wrote a letter.

Dear Mr. Camdon,

I am reaching out because I feel sure that I know your mother, Frances Belinda Hartson. She is living in an assisted living facility where I work. She and I have become friends, but she's lonely. I don't know what happened in the past, but I know she would love to connect with you. She can be cranky, but she's also very kind and funny. I hope you will contact me so we can talk about this. I don't normally stick my nose into other people's business, but she really loves you.

Please call, email or Facebook message me. Thanks!

--Tesseract (Tessa) Hilliard

I only had five apology letters left to write. In the days that followed, I waited for a message from Samuel Camdon. Every day, I ran to the mailbox, in case he was an old person technophobe. I kept my phone charged and turned on.

Anmarie Cross helped distract me. I'd responded to her questions about which blog post I liked the most and from there we'd begun exchanging emails a couple times a week. I asked her questions about the places she'd travelled to, and she described them to me. I also asked about her store. She told me how heartbroken she was that it had closed. Insurance money didn't cover her losses, leaving her to figure out what was next in her life.

I knew I should come clean and tell her who I was, or quit emailing, but I admired her strength. And something inside told me she was going to come out of this situation on top and I wanted to see her do it.

I began clearing out my Facebook notifications, but first I read them.

You're a spoiled brat with no appreciation for your surroundings.
I thought you were a good person. Boy was I wrong.
This is the last you'll hear from me. I'm unfriending you.
My cousin has asthma and can't breathe in this smoke.

The messages were old, mostly from the first weeks of the fire. The smoke was long gone, trails were being rebuilt and jobs had returned. But every message drug me back to that day I threw the firecracker as if it were yesterday.

I was down to the last few Facebook messages when Regina texted to tell me Effby was in the hospital. She'd had a "heart incident." Without hesitation I changed out of my pajamas and drove to the hospital.

Effby looked weaker than ever with tubes in her arm and an oxygen mask covering most of her face. I pulled a chair as close to the bed as I could and sat in it. Her eyes fluttered opened. I was relieved they were sharp and alert. She moved her hand to the oxygen mask, tearing it away from her mouth.

"No," I said, but she interrupted me.

"You look like shit," she croaked, "I hope you weren't out on a hot date dressed like that." She replaced the mask and took a deep breath.

I spent a restless night sleeping on a pull-out couch meant for immediate family.

"Are you her granddaughter?" A nurse had asked me.

"No," I said, "just her friend."

She smiled. "Good friend."

The next morning, she was stable enough to go back to Morningstar. Regina shared the directions they'd been given for Effby's care and recovery: monitor oxygen levels; encourage her to eat.

The COPD had weakened her heart. Of course, the cardiac incident weakened her overall, and it was a horrible cycle I didn't want to see repeated. Despite Effby's newfound interpersonal skills, no one except me wanted one-on-one duty with Effby.

I made her comfortable with an extra pillow and then left her to rest. It had snowed earlier in the day, so I pulled the curtains closed. I replaced the water in the bouquet I'd bought for her and arranged the seven get well cards residents had made. Then I went home.

I checked Facebook and email. Nothing. Why wasn't Samuel responding? It couldn't be because he recognized my name. I pulled up a map to see how long the drive to Bryant, Iowa would be. Twenty-five hours. Probably longer now because it was winter. But this couldn't wait for Spring. Effby didn't have time to wait.

CHAPTER TWENTY-ONE

I'd saved a couple hundred dollars and decided it would be enough to get me to Bryant, Iowa. I couldn't sleep in my car, since it would be in the low twenties at night, so I'd have to pay for cheap hotels. My plan was to drive to Pocatello, Idaho the first night, then cross Wyoming and western Nebraska for the second leg. Both days would involve around nine hours of driving. The third seven-hour day would bring me to Bryant and Samuel Camdon. I had no idea what to do once I got there.

The night before I left, I emptied my drawer of the envelopes with ash and burnt sticks and maps of the fire. The creases of my cuticles, which I hadn't scratched for days, became blackened by soot. I took out Diego's drawing of me and placed it on my desk, then ran my sooty hands over it, dipping my fingers in the ash and drawing shapes of mountains across my cheekbones. I used one of the sticks to make a tree. It was still a drawing of me, but across my face were the mountains and trees of the woods I'd destroyed. I drew streaks of ash down my face, these were my tears. Then I wrote an apology letter.

Dear Mr. Callahan,
I know how much you love the woods. I didn't understand them, and I didn't respect them. But that's no excuse for what I did. I'm trying to learn from my mistake. I get now that these woods and I and you are all part of the same thing. By hurting the forest, I hurt you and myself. I hope you can forgive me.
Sincerely,
Tessa Hilliard

This was my second apology letter to the firefighter who'd testified at my hearing. The first had checked a name off the list, but it was hollow. Stupid and lame. Tanesha and the court didn't care, but I did. And I'm pretty sure Kurt Callahan cared too. I decided not to send this letter to Tanesha but instead placed it and my drawing into a large envelope and addressed it to Mr. Kurt Callahan at the local fire station.

The next day, I pulled Regina aside while we were in the rec room organizing games.

"It's a terrible idea," she said, jamming Battleship onto the shelf between Sorry and Scrabble.

"I know, but I'm going to do it." At my trial, Tanesha had said my brain wasn't fully developed, and maybe it still wasn't developed enough to know this was a terrible idea, to drive halfway across the country in the middle of winter. Alone. But it was all I could think about, like an unsolved episode of *Crime Maven*. "I'm going to find Samuel Camdon, and when I do, I'm going to convince him to forgive his mother."

"I'm just worried about you."

"Regina, you're a badass single mom working fulltime and raising your daughter and you, of all people, should know badass girls like us can do what seems impossible."

She regarded me with a raised eyebrow. "Fine," she said. "If you're gonna put it like that. What can I do to help?"

"Cover for me. I'm telling Kathy I've got the flu – can you back me up? I don't want her calling my mom."

"What are you telling your mom?"

"That I'm apartment sitting for you."

"Oh really," she said. "Where am I going?"

"On vacation to visit your grandma in Bend."

"I don't have a grandma."

"You do now." I gave her a light punch.

"Fine." She sighed. "You better text me each night."

I knew my conversation with Diego was going to be harder, but I didn't want to just disappear. I stopped by Kip's after work. We sat on the smudged plastic seats in the waiting area which was, thankfully, empty.

"Tomorrow? Are you crazy?"

"Probably," I said. "But I can't help it. I've got to do this."

"She hasn't spoken to him in thirty years. Why can't this wait until spring? That's only two months away." He ran a hand through his rumpled hair, smudging a curl with blue paint.

"I don't know . . ." All my words became stuck in my throat. "I don't know if she's going to make it two more months." I swallowed. "I'll be fine. I'm a big girl." If Anmarie Cross could hike through India by herself, I could drive three days to Iowa.

"I know. I just don't want anything to happen to you."

I knew if I met his eyes right now, I'd either throw myself at him or implode trying not to. My cheeks flushed. He leaned in close. The door opened, jangling the bell, and I pushed him away.

He stood to help the customer who had just entered.

"Hold on," Diego whispered to me. "Don't go yet." To the man he said, "Be right with you," and then he disappeared into the back. He emerged a couple minutes later with a set of tire chains which he handed to me. "Your order came in. And just in time. You're gonna need them."

I stopped by Woods Hole on the way home. On my way inside, I misjudged the depth of a puddle and drowned my foot completely. I knew Mom would be working until at least ten and I hoped to be packed up and in bed by then. My plan was to take off early in the morning, leaving her a note. I'd be practically at the Oregon border by the time she read it, and hopefully she'd buy my story of apartment sitting at Regina's.

I pushed through the heavy doors. I didn't see anybody behind the counter, but there was a middle-aged couple at the bar, half-finished pints of beer in front of them. Since I wasn't twenty-one, I couldn't go into the bar, but I could sit in one of the booths in the restaurant a few feet away. Mom emerged from the kitchen holding plates of cheeseburgers and fries.

"Tessa," she said, halting momentarily.

"Hi Mom." I stepped toward her, my foot sloshing around inside my wet shoe.

She placed the food in front of the couple. "Another pint?" she asked the woman, who had just emptied her glass. After Mom poured another beer, she came over to me.

"What are you doing here? Is everything okay?"

"Yeah, Mom. It's okay. I just wanted to stop by and see you."

Her face relaxed a little and she seemed genuinely pleased. I'd never visited Mom at work before, and as I stood there thinking of what to say, I wondered why. Woods Hole was a pretty nice place.

"Well, great," she said. "Are you hungry?"

"Sure." I wasn't particularly hungry, but thought I'd better eat something in case there wasn't much to eat along the road. I sat in a booth at the back. There was a family with two small kids at one table and a couple teenagers at another, but otherwise, the place was empty. Mom brought over a grilled cheese with pickles, the way I liked it, and a bowl of beef barley soup. She set the food on the table and then sat across from me.

"How was Morningstar today?" she asked. She hardly ever asked about Morningstar these days.

"Good," I said. "Well, Effby's back from the hospital, but she doesn't look too great."

"Old folks' homes give me the chills," she said. "And they smell funny."

I ate a pickle that had fallen out of my sandwich. "They do smell funny," I said. "But you get used to it."

"I think care centers scare me because I'm afraid that's where I'm going to be someday."

"It happens to a lot of us," I said.

"Hey," Mom leaned forward. "Can I tell you something?"

"Yeah, sure, what?"

"I'm going back to school."

I dropped my spoon, which bounced from the bowl to the table. "What?"

"Timberline Community College has a business program. Classes start this spring."

"Mom, that's great," I said.

"Really? Are you okay with it?"

"Of course," I said. "You know I think you'd rock a business degree. You should totally do it."

"Good," she patted my hand. "Now we can be in college together."

My fingers pressed into the bread until cheese was pushing out of both sides. It was my fault we were in this situation. It was my fault I couldn't be who she wanted me to be. But listening to her talk about college made my anger boil up. "Why do I have to go to college? Why can't you just do it by yourself?" I watched as the smile drained from her face. But crushing her optimism wasn't enough to stop me, "Can you just, for once in your life, do something that doesn't involve me?"

"Hush," Mom whispered, "Don't make a scene."

I stood, "I don't want to hush," I said. My wet shoe squeaked along the floor as I walked away. I left my mom sitting at the table.

By the time I got home, my plan was clear. I was leaving early in the morning. I threw some things into a bag and scavenged the kitchen junk drawer for Mom's emergency credit card. I could forge her signature if I needed to and, if no one asked for ID, I'd be okay. I got into bed with my computer, hoping for a message from Samuel. Instead, I had another email from Anmarie Cross.

> Caitlyn,
>
> *I love that you've read my posts with so much attentiveness. I sense that you are a super independent person with a lot of adventurous spirit. You should know that I always had lots of help behind the scenes. People who encouraged me, people who checked on me and helped me along the way. So don't think you always have to go it alone.*
>
> *This year, I've had to remind myself again and again that sometimes we just need help. I'm making changes right now in my life that involve relying on other people, and that's okay.*
>
> *Take care and keep in touch.*
>
> *Anmarie Cross*

The next morning, I got in my car and drove away. I plugged in my phone and blasted rocker chic violin music, trying not to freak out when the trucks on the highway splashed torrents of dirty water onto my windshield, blinding me each time. As I put miles between me and Elmsville, I felt a sense of lightness. The view of the long and open road provided a glimpse of the world's limitless possibilities, and I could pretend like I was free, at least until I got to Bryant, to explore them. I wondered what Effby was thinking. I'd left a note with Regina to give to her.

> Hi Effby,
>
> *I hope you're feeling better. Even though I'm not there, you'd better be nice to Sal. He's been cranky ever since you went to the hospital. I'm going to be gone for a few days and if all goes according to plan, I'll return with good news. I didn't tell you before because I knew you'd yell at me, and you know how my delicate ears can't take your foul mouth, but I'm going to find your son. You're probably cursing me right now, but he's your son. I know he loves*

you and I think you have to try to fix things with him. Give him a chance.
Don't worry - I won't tell him what an asshole you can be.

See you soon,

Tessa

My plan was to drive all the way to Pocatello, Idaho, but the rain had turned to snow and it was really slowing me down. I snacked on beef jerky as the road curved up the mountain pass. When snow began falling fast and thick, I pulled over to put on the chains Diego had given me. It took several tries and by the time I crawled back into my seat, my jeans were soaked through at the knees. My fingers were frozen and numb, even with gloves on. I rubbed my bare hands together in front of the heater vent to warm them before driving back onto the highway

I crawled along the slick I-84, peering through a white wall of snow. The hours passed slowly, with me driving in a line of cars all plodding forward in the same track. I had left at seven in the morning, hoping to arrive in Pocatello around five, but I was hours behind schedule. My tired eyes strained to follow the car ahead of me, with nothing but a blanket of white on either side of the road. I felt a headache coming on. Without warning, the car I was following swerved. I knew not to slam the brakes, so I tapped them and turned the steering wheel. My car was suddenly out of the track, loose and sliding toward another car stranded in the road. It happened so fast, but in slow motion, and I thought for sure I was headed for an accident until I felt the chains grab. I managed to steer clear of the stranded vehicle. After that I slowed way down and pulled off at the first motel I came to. Travelodge.

"You by yourself?" The woman checking me in was around sixty, with thick jowly cheeks.

"Yes," I said.

"Bad night for driving."

I handed her seventy-five dollars in cash for the room while she gave my driver's license a quick glance. The motel didn't say you had to be eighteen, but I knew if she went there, I was screwed. She handed back my ID. "If you need anything, just let me know," she said.

"Is there anything to eat within walking distance?"

"Not in this weather. But we have some food over there." She pointed at a case with Lean Cuisine and microwave pizzas. I picked out a pizza and paid cash for it.

I never thought I'd be happy in a crappy hotel room with frozen pizza, but I was. I plopped my purse down on the nightstand beside a 'Getting some Zzzz's' door hanger and immediately changed into sweatpants. I curled up under the thin comforter and turned on the TV. Next, I checked my phone.

There were three messages from my mom.

Where are you staying?

How long are you apartment sitting?

Why didn't you tell me last night?

I hesitated, then texted back. *I'm going tb a few days. I shld have told u last night, but was afraid u'd say no. Don't worry, I'm fine.*

There was also a text from Regina. *U better text me. Effby's doing better. She read your note, tho. Hasn't opened her door since.*

I texted her back, letting her know I was in La Grande for the night. *Keep an eye on Effby for me.*

Diego sent a message too, *Call me!* I dialed his number. He picked up on the first ring. "Tessa?"

"Hi," I said. "Quit worrying. I'm fine."

"I saw the weather. Did you use the chains?" I loved the sound of his voice.

"Yes, and guess what, they didn't fall off. Thanks for those. I wouldn't have made it without them."

"Where are you?"

"La Grande. At the spacious and grandiose Travelodge where I'm indulging in room service, otherwise known as a microwave pizza."

He laughed. "Sounds luxurious. Wish I was there."

I paused. "I wish you were too."

"How far are you going tomorrow?"

"As far as I can," I said. "I just spent nearly half my money, so I have to make good time tomorrow."

"Don't push it," he said. "You need to come back in one piece. Or Rippen will be pissed."

After my call with Diego, I turned off my phone and fell asleep to reruns of *The Office*. I dreamed of crows landing in snow. There were so many of them, they came in groups, cackling and cawing until all the white had disappeared and there was nothing but a sea of black.

A knock on the door woke me from my dream. The digital clock beside the bed blinked 7:00. I'd slept for twelve hours. I staggered to the door, passing the 'Getting Some Zzzzs' sign I'd forgotten to hang outside before going to bed. I opened the door and Diego was standing there, flakes of snow clinging to his curly hair.

CHAPTER TWENTY-TWO

"Can we come in?"

"We?" My half-opened eyes peered into the parking lot. I don't know who I expected to see standing there, but it wasn't Diego.

"Of course," I said, wondering how bad my bedhead was as Rippen came into the room. After a good shake, Rippen made himself comfortable on the bed. I brewed coffee with a machine that should have been put out of its misery long ago, while Diego propped the pillows and got comfortable on the bed beside Rippen.

"Creamer?" I asked, holding up the small packet.

"No, those are awful. Just black."

"You look exhausted," I said as I handed him coffee in a paper cup. "What are you even doing here? Wait, are you trying to get me to come back? Because I'm not coming back until I talk with Samuel Camdon."

He leaned forward. "No, I just wanted to come with you. We can leave one of our cars here and do the rest of the trip together."

I scratched my head. "I can do this by myself, you know, I'm quite capable." I said, a bit more harshly than intended.

"I knew you would be totally fine, but I also knew you had little time or money. Am I right? And I thought with two of us, we could share the driving."

I took a sip from the hot chocolate I'd made. It was weak on chocolate and pretty disgusting, but I took another sip. "But this isn't your deal," I protested. "It's not your situation."

"You're my friend, right? And this is what friends do. Your situation is my situation because we're friends. So, let's do this together."

It would be way easier with two people, quicker and cheaper too. "Okay, we'll go together." I thought of Anmarie Cross' email. Maybe this is what she had in mind when she talked about getting support. Having Diego along wouldn't make me any less determined. I was still going to do this whether or not he came with me.

"Good," he said, relaxing back into the pile of pillows and taking a sip from his cup. "But you get the first driving shift because I'm wiped."

We took my car, since I had newer chains and my Subaru was better in this weather than his pickup. The snow had tapered off overnight, leaving around seven inches on the hood of my car. It sparkled in the morning sun, like Regina's princess make-up, and I took that as a good sign.

We left at nine, taking with us a few individually wrapped muffins from the breakfast bar in the lobby. They looked okay in the package but tasted like cardboard. Even Rippen wouldn't eat one.

The highway had been cleared, thankfully, so it was easy to see the road between fields of white spreading out in the distance on either side. Rippen curled up on the backseat and fell instantly asleep as if he'd been the one driving all night. Diego made a pillow from his wadded-up jacket and fell asleep against the window. His hair was still damp from the shower he'd had just before we left. When I knew he was asleep, I reached over and twisted one of his curls between my fingers.

I pulled off the road in Boise, Idaho for gas and snacks. Diego roused for about five minutes. I put a bag of Nutter Butters between our seats in case he wanted some when he woke up. Rippen was awake now and chewing on a bone I'd given him from Diego's bag. Even though there was a long road ahead, and many miles still to cover, I felt hopeful. If Effby and her son could reunite after all these years, maybe there was hope for me.

Clouds had overcome the bright morning sun by the time I pulled into a rest area just outside Pocatello. I leashed Rippen and Diego ran with him through the snow while I stretched my legs. I did a long plank followed by several burpees, just to wake myself up. I might have done sprints too, if the terrain had been more inviting. Temperatures had dropped and the sky had turned the color of steel.

"We'd better get going," I said as Diego and Rippen ran past the car. "Stay ahead of this weather."

"I'm worried this weather is in front of us," Diego said. He gave Rippen some water from a special bowl and then ushered the wet dog into the backseat.

I wondered if Mom would notice my car smelled of dog. She wouldn't be happy about that. I'd sent her a text before we left the hotel. *Everything good here. Soup in freezer. Luv U.* I knew she thought I left because of our argument, but I couldn't clear that up until I got home. I felt pretty awake after our pit stop, so I insisted on driving. "Sleep some more," I said. "You'll have to drive later." I turned at the Highway 15 exit and we headed south.

By the time Diego woke an hour later, we were passing Soda Springs. He was surprised when I told him we were about an hour from Wyoming and not so happy to see snowflakes falling again.

"Nutter Butter?" he asked, holding up the bag.

"Nutter Butters remind me of *The Magic School Bus*," I said.

"Did Ms. Frizzle eat them?"

The snow was on the verge of becoming rain, so I flipped on the wipers. "No, I did. My mom always gave me four Nutter Butters while I watched *The Magic School Bus*."

"Just four?" Diego reached for another.

"Just four and never more. Although, on the day Ms. Frizzle drove the school bus through Ralphie's intestinal tract, I didn't eat any."

"I remember that episode. I drew pictures of the intestinal track for days after that. My mom hung them on the fridge."

"Lovely," I laughed. "Just what you want to see when you're going for a sandwich."

"Right? Perfect weight loss method." He reached into the backpack at his feet to retrieve his sketchbook.

"Inspired to draw an intestinal tract?" I asked, eating another cookie.

"Just going to draw what I see out the window, I guess," he responded. Endless fields of snow stretched out on either side with dry grasses and rough looking sage poking out of the whiteness. In the far distance I could just make out some hills.

"Have you ever driven through here before?" I asked.

"No, this is all new. Before I lived in Portland, we were in California for a little while, and I've been to Mexico, to visit my grandparents. I haven't had too many chances to travel, I guess."

"Me either," I said. "My dad flies all over the place, but I've hardly ever been out of Oregon. I'd like to see this part of the country when it's not snowing."

"Look at that road," Diego said. There was a spur in the road and a narrow track meandered off and disappeared into the horizon. "Doesn't it just breathe adventure?"

"Yah, maybe with a supped-up 4-wheel drive with monster tires." I wanted to let myself breathe possibility, to see the road as Diego did, leading to some place worth discovering, but my focus was on the man I hoped to find at the end of the road we were on.

When Diego offered to drive, I let him. My eyes burned, and I was thankful to be in the passenger seat where I could lower the back and put my feet up. The snowflakes were big and fluffy now and the occasional wind gust brought whiteouts and pushed the car across the lane.

"I didn't mean for you to get the hardest part of the drive," I said.

"We got this."

I flipped through his sketchbook. With a few quick strokes of his pencil, he'd captured the Idaho hills just as I'd seen them. There was a sketch I hadn't seen before of an old truck, and another of a woman, maybe in her mid-thirties. Her dark hair wrapped around her head in a thick braid and her eyes were fixed on something in the distance. "Wow," I said, "this one is amazing."

"Drawing keeps me busy," Diego remarked.

"You could do this for a living."

"Maybe I will someday," he said. I envied his optimism.

I dozed off but woke suddenly when the car jerked to one side. The sun was long gone and the only light on the road came from our headlights. The windshield wipers were whipping furiously as the snow seemed to blow past us sideways. Diego's hands were tight on the wheel.

"Whoa," I said. "It got bad. What time is it?"

"About six," Diego said, leaning forward and straining to see. We were moving slowly, maybe thirty-five miles an hour. "This wind is really shoving us around."

I checked my phone for the weather. "There's a major storm warning for most of southern Wyoming," I said. "It doesn't seem like it's going to let up anytime soon." The car veered into the other lane as another gust of wind hit.

"This is crazy," Diego said, slowing down even further. "I know we're supposed to be driving all night, but-" he trailed off.

"I know," I sighed. It was the last thing I wanted, but I couldn't deny that it was the most sensible. "Let's find a motel to ride out the storm, then maybe we can make up the time tomorrow."

We pulled over at the next exit, following signs for Rawlings. We were down to twenty-five miles an hour as we crept into the Motel 6 parking lot. We weren't the only ones getting off the road. The parking lot was full of trucks. I handed over another seventy dollars, unsure what we'd do for money after this. Mom's credit card would be a last resort. Bryant was still a twelve-hour drive away.

Regina texted me a picture of Effby playing Scrabble with Sal. It made me happy to know she was out of her room, although Regina said it was the first time since she'd come back from the hospital.

Diego and I braved the blizzard and walked two blocks to a burger place. We had Rippen with us. We'd tried leaving him in the hotel room, but he started barking the instant we closed the door. So, here we were, the three of us exploring the snow-covered streets of Rawlings at night.

"Hey, you wanted to come," Diego reminded Rippen when he whined. I didn't blame him; the icy wind stung my face too. When a powerful gust shoved me backward, Diego grabbed my arm. I laughed, holding onto him as we struggled forward.

"Do you think we're going to freeze to death on the way to the restaurant?" I yelled over the sound of the wind. "That would be a dumb way to die."

"We might die from eating their burgers," he responded. Rippen whined.

In the warmth of the restaurant, we took our time ordering double cheeseburgers and fries. The clerk said we couldn't stay in the restaurant with Rippen, so we carried our food back to the hotel. The room, covered in wallpaper that matched the dirty carpet, was probably older than me, but I was glad to be in it. We pulled off our snowy shoes at the door and I brewed tea with water from the coffeemaker. We sat on our separate double beds, eating burgers while Rippen jumped from one bed to the other depending on who was waving a French fry.

"That's cheating," I said, when Diego fed him a hunk of burger patty and he settled in at Diego's feet.

"All's fair in dog love and war."

We ate in silence for a while and sipped hotel room tea that tasted like overripe oranges. "The woman in your sketchbook," I said. "Who is she?"

"That's my mom," Diego said.

"I thought so. Her eyes are like yours."

"People always said I looked like her and Pablo like my dad."

201

"When did she pass away?" I asked. I knew it hurt him to talk about her, but I knew nothing other than she'd died from cancer. He was pretty closed off about it, which was unusual because he was open about almost everything else.

"Four years ago," he said. He wadded up the burger wrapper and tossed it into the garbage can across the room. Rippen ran after it then came back to the bed.

"What was she like?"

Diego was quiet for a while. I wiped the last bit of grease from my hands and jumped over to his bed. He moved to give me some room.

"She was like the dirt we were all planted in, you know. Like she was the foundation, the thing that gave us strength. Kept us all moving forward as a family. I realized without her we were all just spinning crazy."

I heard Rippen snoring while Diego rubbed his foot against his dog's ribs. "In California, we had these grapes that grew wild in our yard, and she always canned them. She refused to buy any jelly because she said we had plenty. I used to complain and beg for some other flavor because I was so sick of grape jelly, and we had like entire shelves of it. Then one day, sometime after she'd died, I went into the pantry for another jar and there weren't any. I couldn't move. I had to sit on the floor. I didn't know how to keep going after that. The sun kept coming up every day and I couldn't believe the sun could rise and days could keep coming when we were all frozen, paralyzed, like a big part of us was dead along with our mom. You know?"

"Yeah," I said. "I mean, I know what it feels like when you've lost the ground you used to stand on. How did you get moving again?"

"I don't know," he said. "I just kept getting out of bed every morning. Most days I picked up a pencil or pen and I drew. I noticed Pablo was around less and less and pretty soon he went off the rails.

And then I knew I had to get my ass in gear. If my mom wasn't there to keep things together, someone had to do it."

I leaned into him, and he stretched an arm around my shoulders. I rested my head on his chest, feeling it rise and fall in gentle waves as the beating of his heart slowed to an even rhythm. The wind howled outside, but we were warm as we curled into each other. We fell asleep like that, in our clothes, with my head against his chest and his arm wrapped around me.

CHAPTER TWENTY-THREE

The storm had passed by morning. Diego drove first, since his shift was cut short the day before. I sipped more hotel hot chocolate as we headed east on Highway 80. My phone pinged twice.

The first text was from Regina. *U there yet? Kathy keeps asking about u. Thinks u must be dying of the flu.*

The second was from my mother and there were also two missed calls from her. *I'm worried about you. I need you to visit me at work or come by the house.* Well, that wasn't going to happen anytime soon. We were still fifteen hours from Bryant, then we had the entire trip back home.

Diego and I shared stories and listened to music as we drove past the outskirts of the Medicine Bow-Routt National Forest. I never thought Wyoming could be so beautiful and I wanted to take it all in, but the texts had me bothered.

"What's up?" Diego. "You're distracted today."

"My mom knows something's up. She wants me to stop by."

"What are you going to tell her?"

"I don't know." I'd texted her the night before, letting her know I was okay, but I wondered how long she'd let this go on before she alerted the police or Tanesha. Maybe even my dad.

"Maybe you could tell her the truth?"

"She wouldn't understand," I said. "She'd just tell me to get home right away because I'm violating my probation by crossing state lines in addition to not getting my community service hours done and I'll never get into college if I continue this way."

"Do you want to go to college?"

"No," I said sharply, and immediately regretted my tone. "I'm sorry. I just don't want to think about college or the future or whatever."

"Why not? I mean, it's no big deal either way, but what do you want to do?"

I rested my head against the window and closed my eyes. "Nothing," I said. "I just don't want to do anything."

Diego wanted to stop for the night, but I was having none of it. The roads were clear, and I was awake, and time was running out. Besides, I figured we'd end up in the same bed again, and frankly, I loved that just a little too much. We stopped for sodas and I took over driving, taking us through the entire state of Nebraska.

We rolled into Bryant around eight in the morning. As I pulled up to a gas station, Diego roused himself and rubbed his eyes blearily. "Where are we?"

"Bryant," I said.

"Whoa, are you okay? I didn't mean to sleep so long."

We had arrived. I couldn't have slept if I wanted to. "I'm good."

Diego gassed up the car while I splashed water on my face in the restroom. I put on some deodorant and brushed my teeth. Diego had paid for the gas and was in the driver's seat when I got back. He handed me a hot chocolate. "All right," he said. "Where to?"

I pulled up the address on my phone of Samuel Camdon's contracting company and plugged it into the GPS. We drove down Bryant's Main Street, which was a strange collection of car dealerships, coffee shops, a Home Depot, and a Krispy Kreme. It was a gray day, drizzling with rain. We pulled up to the All Paint and Repair, a small building sandwiched between a nail salon and a bank. I stepped out and took a deep breath.

Thankfully Diego came with me. I didn't know what I was going to say when I saw Samuel. I hoped he'd at least talk with me when he found out I'd just driven three days to see him.

The shop smelled of paint like Kip's, but it was tidier. A young man in his twenties was behind the counter. "Can I help you?" he asked.

I smiled. "I'm looking for Samuel Camdon. Is he here?"

The man raised his eyebrows. "No, not anymore. He retired a few weeks ago."

"Oh," I said, fighting my own panic. It hadn't occurred to me he wouldn't be working anymore.

Diego stepped forward. "Do you know if he's still in town?"

"Oh yeah, he's still around. He didn't move away or anything."

Back in the car, I plugged the address into my phone. It felt a little weird to just go knock on the man's door, but obviously, that was what was going to happen. I hoped he wouldn't freak out when he heard what I had to say. I hadn't really thought of his reaction. Like if he might cry or have to sit down or something. What if he had a heart attack? In my imagination, I'd sort of skipped ahead to the good stuff, the reunion.

His house was in a neighborhood where houses were all pretty much the same, with small, tidy lawns and two-car driveways. Samuel Camdon's house was robin's egg blue. The lights were on inside. A snow shovel rested on the porch. We parked on the street.

"Let me do this one by myself," I said. I walked to the front door, took a breath, then rang the doorbell. After a moment, Samuel Camdon opened the door. I knew it was him right away, although he seemed smaller than in his profile picture. His shoulders dipped forward as if he had a backache and the hand grasping the door was calloused and rough. I caught a flash of Effby in his eyes.

"Samuel Camdon?" I asked.

"Yes?" he said. He stepped back like he was about to close the door. "I'm not buying anything."

"No," I interjected quickly. "I'm not selling anything. I'm Tessa. I'm a friend of your mother's. Frances Belinda."

He stared at me. "The one from Oregon?" He looked confused.

"Yes. I drove here from Oregon. Effby, your mom, she was in the hospital. She's out now, but I'm not sure she's doing very well. I wanted to talk to you because she misses you. I know she misses you and I thought if you could just talk with her, everything would be okay, you know?" I rambled on and on even though Samuel Camdon's face was shutting down and I could feel him pulling away from me. "Because I know she loves you and I know she might not have much time, but you're her son, and she doesn't have anyone else." I stopped. "Please."

"Does she know you're here?"

"Yes," I said. "I mean, she didn't send me or anything. I didn't tell her what I was doing before I left. She's afraid, well, I think she's afraid of you rejecting her or something."

He leaned against the doorway; his eyes were so sad they were exactly like Effby's. "I'm sorry," he said. "I'm sorry you drove all this way. But I can't. My mother has been dead to me for a long time."

"But it doesn't have to be that way," I pleaded. "Whatever happened, it can be fixed, right? We can make it better."

"No," he said, and I heard a steel edge in his voice. "Some things can't be made better." He shut the door in my face.

I stood on the porch, staring at the closed door, until I felt Diego's arm around me. He guided me back to the car. I stumbled, feeling the full exhaustion of having been at the wheel of my car all night. I let my head drop against the dashboard. "He wouldn't even talk to me."

Diego put his hand on my back. "Maybe it was too much to take in. Maybe he needs some time."

"No," I said. "You didn't see his face. He's not changing his mind." What was I going to tell Effby now? I'd just made things a hundred times worse. Like I always did.

"What do you want to do?" Diego asked.

"I have no idea."

As I tried to get my brain to work, tried to accept that I was going home without Samuel, a car pulled into the driveway. A woman wearing a puffy coat got out, holding a purse over her head to protect it from the rain. The back door opened, and a little girl jumped out wearing a raincoat and boots. She ran straight for a large puddle and stomped it hard, sending muddy water splashing all around her. She pushed her hood back and laughed, her braids swinging from side to side. It was the ballerina from the photograph. It was Effby's great granddaughter. I leaned forward and watched the little girl push open her grandfather's door. Mother and daughter disappeared into the house.

"Let's wait," I said. It wasn't long, maybe fifteen minutes, until the mother came out of the house, got into her car, and drove away. "Come on," I said. "Let's follow her."

She drove through the old downtown and then along a series of residential streets. Eventually she pulled into a parking spot in front of a large apartment building and Diego found an open spot a few spaces away. She got out and I jumped from the car.

"Ma'am, excuse me, Ma'am" I called. She waited, her eyes passing over first me and then Diego. "I think I know your grandmother," I said. "Please, will you just talk to me?"

Effby's granddaughter, Rene, poured two tall glasses of orange juice and put a pot of coffee on as we sat at her kitchen table. Light came through the window above the sink. A hummingbird hung from the ceiling. If the sun had been out, it would have sent light flooding through its glass wings. From my vantage point, I could see a large, comfy couch in the living room and a computer and monitor on a desk piled high with papers. "It's lucky you caught me," Rene said as she poured three cups of coffee. "Milk or cream?"

"Either," I said. I hoped some caffeine would give me whatever I needed to get through the rest of this day.

"Usually Emily's at school, but they had an in-service day today and I'm on a deadline with an article. So, she went to her grandpa's." She handed Diego and I coffee and sat down at the table. "So, how do you know my," she paused, "grandmother?"

I told her how I'd met Effby, leaving out the part about how I came to receive mandated community service. "She's a good person," I said. "But she's really lonely. I thought if I came to Bryant and talked with Samuel, your dad, in person, I could get them talking with each other again." I paused. "You know, before it's too late or something."

Rene sighed. "My dad's a stubborn man," she said. "And there's a lot of water under that bridge."

"What happened between them?" I asked. "I mean, why can't it be fixed?"

She stirred sugar into her coffee. "There's a lot of anger there," she said. "I'll try to talk with him, but I can't make any promises," Rene said gently. "I'll have a conversation with him when I pick up Emily tonight. But for now, how about something to eat? I bet you're tired too. You're welcome to lie down in Emily's room."

I skipped the sandwich Rene offered and laid down on Emily's bed, pulling her *Frozen* themed bedcover up around my neck. Diego stayed in the living room, sipping coffee, with Rippen at his heels. I felt empty inside. There was nothing left to do, so I closed my eyes and let sleep take me.

I woke sometime later to a small person's face peeking through the door at me. Seeing my eyes open, Emily pushed the door open and came in. I sat up. "Hello," I said.

"That's my new bedspread."

"It's very comfortable," I said. "Thank you for letting me use it."

"Who do you like more?" she said. "Elsa or Anna?"

"I like the snowman best," I replied.

"Me too," she smiled.

Entering the living room, I smelled food and realized how ravenous I was. Rene stood at the sink washing dishes while Diego sat at the table scrolling through his phone. He got up when he saw me.

"Feel better?" he said. "I thought you might sleep through the night."

I sat at the table, feeling a bit discombobulated. Emily climbed into the chair beside me. "My mom said you drove from Oregon," she said. "Where's that?"

"It's next to the Pacific Ocean," I replied.

"I've never been to the ocean," Emily said longingly. "Did you know I'm a ballerina?"

I searched Rene's face for any sign of how the conversation with her dad had gone. She gave a nod in Emily's direction. "We'll talk after dinner."

We ate lasagna and bread. It felt good to be warm and fed after the ordeal of the past few days. In fact, it felt good to have someone taking care of me for a change. But through every bite, my mind was on Samuel Camdon. After dinner, I convinced Emily to watch *Frozen*, while Rene, Diego and I sat at the kitchen table.

Rene shook her head. "I'm sorry. I tried to persuade him, but he wouldn't budge."

"But why?" I asked. "It's been so long. And it's his mother." I felt guilt uttering the word 'mother', thinking of my own mother who I'd kept in the dark about what I was doing, who sometimes made me so angry I couldn't stand to be in the same room with her. But that anger never stayed with me for long. "What happened?"

Rene glanced at Emily, who was happily eating a Red Vine, jumping up periodically to twirl around with her hands above her head.

"I don't know if it's for me to say. It's not my story."

"But I can't understand it," I said. "I can't believe there's not a way to fix this. I know that Effby's daughter died, and all she has is her son, so why didn't her death bring them together?"

"How did she die?" Diego asked.

"It was a car accident or something, right?" I said.

"Yes," she paused. "And Samuel's mom was driving."

"What? Effby didn't tell me that."

Rene shook her head. "Well, that's the key, isn't it? My dad told me the story once. Only once. He asked me not to bring it up again."

"Tell me please," I said. "I have to understand."

"Frances was driving my dad and his sister to a Christmas performance. Robin was eight years old and she was playing an angel." Rene smiled briefly. "My dad said her wings kept poking him in the face. He was ten years old and remembers he could hardly see anything that night through the snow." She paused. "He said his mom had been drinking. I guess she drank most nights. Then there was the accident. My dad was okay, but Robin -" She trailed off. "I don't know who he blames more, his mom, or himself for surviving. But maybe you can see why it's no simple thing to fix."

I stared at the surface of the kitchen table until it became blurry through my tears. No wonder Effby never told me. I leaned on my elbows, covering my face with my hands.

"My dad loved his sister. But it was more than that," she said. "His mom, she just shut down. She didn't talk, she wouldn't come out of her room."

I imagined Samuel Camdon as a ten-year-old boy. I knew what it was like to be a child alone in the house when your mom wouldn't come out of her room, couldn't come out because she was paralyzed by grief and guilt. I felt Samuel's anger. Both Effby and my mom had quit on their children. Not that it excused anything, not my mistakes nor Samuel's decisions, but maybe there were reasons I hadn't considered before for why I was who I was. Painful wounds, and maybe they weren't too distant from Samuel Camdon's.

"I think," Rene said, "if she'd mothered him, if she'd shifted her focus to him, then it might have been okay. But she wouldn't. Or couldn't. Eventually he wrote to his father who came to get him and moved him back up here." Rene reached out to touch my arm. "I know people change and evolve and I'm sure the woman you know has some good in her. I can tell she does because you have so much

211

good in you. But my dad is permanently damaged, and he will never forgive her. It's too late for that."

I knew Rene was right. It was too late for Samuel Camdon to forgive his mother, and too late for Effby to forgive herself. I guess some things were too broken to fix.

CHAPTER TWENTY-FOUR

Rene's daughter's ceiling was purple with a sky full of mesmerizing, glow-in-the-dark stars. I laid awake most of the night counting them. My plan had been to do something good for Effy, but maybe what I'd hoped for all along was to do something good for myself. To make myself feel like I deserved friendship and happiness and possibilities for the future. Like I deserved to have my problems fixed. As I counted the stars again and again, I wondered which star Emily most liked to pin her wishes on and envied her for having a star. I envied her for having wishes.

In the morning, Rene packed sandwiches, chips and sodas for our road trip. I think she felt bad we'd driven halfway across the country only to be disappointed by her dad. Or maybe she was just that thoughtful of person.

"Thank you," I said, as she packed a cooler for us. "You've been really kind."

"I'm sorry. I mean, that things didn't work out as you were hoping."

The clouds outside were slate gray again. I almost hated leaving the cozy comfort of her apartment and the warmth Rene brought to it. "It's okay. I shouldn't have gotten involved."

Rene reached across the cooler and gently grabbed my arm. "Hey," she said. "You were trying to do a good thing."

Diego took the first leg of our three-day journey home. He tried starting conversations and making jokes, but it wasn't working for me. I laid back and closed my eyes and pretended to be somewhere else. Like on another planet. When we stopped at a rest area a few hours later, Diego leashed Rippen and they ran around. I got out to use the bathroom and went straight back in the car, staring vacantly out the window. My mind was on getting home. After a few minutes, Diego knocked on the window. "Come on," he said, "Come walk with us."

"It's too cold," I said. While Diego walked Rippen, I picked up his sketchbook and began flipping through it. I paused at a sketch of the hummingbird dangling in Rene's kitchen window. I ran my finger across its delicate wings, then closed the book.

Diego drove for a few more hours, his eyes red and squinting against the sun. "Maybe we should stop for the night," he said. "Get some rest."

The weather had improved, and I'd already dozed for a couple of hours. "Let's keep going," I said. "I can take the night shift."

"Are you sure?" he said. I could hear the disappointment in his voice.

"Yeah, I slept. Besides, my mom is freaking out." Which was true. I'd texted her that I was fine and would be home in a couple of days, but she kept calling. I'd had to turn off the ringer. I couldn't answer her questions right now.

I drove through the night, back across Nebraska and into Wyoming, drinking soda after soda to keep me awake. If I felt the least bit sleepy, I rolled the window down to let frigid air blow over me. Diego stirred occasionally.

"Want me to take a shift?" he mumbled.

"No, I got it." I kept on until Rippen whined for a pee. We were on a barren stretch of I-80, about an hour past Laramie, so I eased over to the roadside. Diego was fast asleep, slumped against the passenger door.

I hooked Rippen's leash on and we headed into the tall, dry grass. It was dark and the ground was flat. I stumbled over some sagebrush but quickly found my footing. The weather was cold and above me was a vast network of stars, much more enchanting than Emily's ceiling. I searched for the grandest of them all, one worthy of a wish.

Here, in eastern Wyoming, constellations spread across the sky as if they'd been painted by an especially wide brush. I looked behind me. The car, a dark spot against the horizon, seemed far away. Rippen pulled me further into the vast nothingness as he happily sniffed every bush. It felt like I could just keep going, the car behind me getting smaller and smaller until it disappeared. Or I disappeared.

Something shot out from a bush ahead of us and Rippen jerked toward it, yanking the leash from my hands. He disappeared into the darkness, barking madly.

"Rippen!" I called. "Get back here!" I ran a few steps, following his bark. Despite all the star light, I hit something with my foot, stumbled and went down. Something popped and a searing pain ripped through my knee. Rippen's bark became more distant.

"Tessa?!" Diego's voice was a long way off. "Where are you?"

"Here!" I called, gripping my knee. "Get Rippen." I took quick breaths as fire coursed through my leg.

"Keep talking, so I can find you." I heard Diego curse.

"I think my leg is broken," I cried out.

"Hold on, I'm coming." I could see a dark silhouette moving toward me, but I couldn't hear Rippen anymore.

"What happened?" Diego dropped down beside me.

I tried to speak; to tell him how I'd lost Rippen because I'd stupidly driven to Iowa for nothing. But my words were swallowed by gasps and sobs of pain.

"Come on," he said. "Let's get you back to the car. Can you stand on your other leg?" He put his arm around my back and under my arms, pulling up while I shifted my weight to my good foot. An unbearable pain shot through me, and I collapsed into him. Diego caught me and lifted me off the ground. He carried me back to the car and tucked me into the back seat, doing his best not to move my bad leg.

Diego left the engine running so I'd stay warm and went off to find Rippen. I tried to catch my breath, but between thoughts of

Rippen being lost in the cold Wyoming wilderness forever and the searing pain in my leg, all I could do was bawl. Amazingly, Diego returned after a few minutes with Rippen, who pressed his dirty paws onto the window.

"You found him," I cried. Rippen settled into the front seat as if that had been his place all along.

"He's better at coming when he's called than he used to be," Diego said, strapping on his seat belt. "I mean, not great, but better. How's the leg?"

"Hurts."

"We're getting you to a doctor."

"I just want to go home."

"We can't wait that long." He pulled onto the freeway. "At least it's almost morning and Laramie's close."

"I'm going to be so screwed."

We hobbled into a Laramie hospital emergency room an hour later. Thankfully it was nearly empty. A man in scrubs pushed a wheelchair over and I dropped into it. He wheeled me and my throbbing leg to the intake station where a woman peered over her glasses at me.

"I can see you're in pain. You'll be seen right away. Just a couple quick questions." She turned to her monitor. "What your name?"

"Tesseract Hilliard." I felt like throwing up. I knew what she would ask next.

"And your birthday?" When I told her, she acted surprised. "Since you're under eighteen, I'll need to speak with your parent or guardian." I clutched my stomach with one hand and squeezed the thigh of my bad leg with the other. My mom was about to get a very unpleasant phone call.

"Okay," I whimpered, and mumbled my mom's phone number.

"We'll get you taken care of, don't you worry."

"Thank you," I muttered. I was thankful for anything to lessen the pain but, if I could have gotten up from that wheelchair and walked out of the emergency room, I would have, just to avoid the confrontation with my mom.

The doctor moved briskly and efficiently. "Okay," she said. "Let's check you out." She gingerly stroked my shin, which made me scream. I squeezed Diego's hand and bit the inside of my cheek. "We'll need x-rays, but I'd say that's broken. I'm going to get you something for the pain."

There was a knock on the door, and the intake nurse stepped in holding a cell phone. "It's your mother," she said, pushing the phone toward me. I reluctantly let go of Diego's hand and took the phone.

"Hi Mom," I tried not to cry.

Her questions came out as one long breath. "What are you doing in Wyoming? Are you okay? What happened? Why didn't you tell me?" She broke into tears and, between the pain I heard in her voice and my own, I couldn't hold back. I started crying too.

"I'm fine," I said through my sobs.

"No, you're not." Her voice had become gentler, and she appeared calmer. "Tell me what's happening."

"I'm okay," I snuffled. "I just, fell on a rock."

There was a pause. "I'm coming to get you." I knew there was no point in arguing. Besides, more than anything right now, aside from that pain medication I'd been promised, I wanted my mom here holding my hand.

Diego sat with me as they cleaned out the scrapes on my leg with antiseptic and surgical sponges. They'd hooked me up to an IV, which delivered an immediate, calming numbness throughout my body. "Feel better?" Diego asked.

I nodded. "Doesn't hurt so much," I said. "What about Rippen?"

"He's fine. I'll go check on him in a few minutes."

The pain medication made my thinking cloudy, but I was alert enough to remember one thing: my mom was coming.

"I wann my mom." I heard the slurring of my own voice.

"I know," Diego said. "That's why she's coming."

I blinked at him. "I'm sorry your mom isn't here."

He leaned down and stroked my forehead. "Don't think about that right now."

I slipped into soothing blackness. Nothing seemed real, not the sensations in my body, not the thoughts in my mind, not the hand on my head. "I just want to tell you in case we run out of time."

"What do you mean, run out of time? We have lots of time."

I watched the ceiling tiles skip around like tiles on Effby's Scrabble rack. My mind skipped to Wyoming's night sky. And Emily's room of wishing stars. So pretty. "I only hhhave a fffew letters to rrrite."

"What?" Diego's voice sounded distant, like Rippen's barking as he disappeared into the night.

"Just a fffew-" My voice bounced around like the morning sunlight though Rene's stained-glass hummingbird. "to figure sssomething out."

"Figure what out?"

I suddenly had great clarity in my mind and my words came out fully formed. I raised my head, "I didn't figure out shit and now my time's up."

"What are you talking about?" I could hear concern in Diego's voice, but I wasn't worried about anything. I was being pulled into a fluffy feather bed. I slipped under the heavy comforter of medication and went to sleep.

Hours later, when I finally opened my eyes again, the first thing I saw was Mom texting on her phone from a chair beside my bed. She'd taken a plane to the Laramie airport and a taxi to the hospital. She was wearing no makeup, and her hair was in a sloppy bun. "Mom?" At first, I wasn't sure she was real. But then she reached for me and kissed my forehead. I felt like everything was going to be okay and fell asleep again.

I left the hospital with Mom, Diego, Rippen and a cast on my lower right leg. Mom drove my car, with Diego in the passenger seat, and Rippen and me in the back. There was tense silence coming from the front seats, except for the drumming of Mom's fingers on the steering wheel. The gentle rocking of the car and the pain medication lulled me to sleep.

Sometime later, I woke to voices. "I just don't understand what you two were even thinking. You know she's on probation. She's not supposed to even leave the state."

Diego said. "Maybe you can talk to her about why she felt she needed to go. I just didn't want her to go alone."

There was a long silence. "That's just it. She doesn't talk to me. About anything." Mom's fingers were no longer drumming but were holding firm to the wheel. We pulled into a Motel 6 somewhere outside of Boise, Idaho, just before 10 pm. Mom charged two rooms on her credit card. Diego carried my backpack from the car and Rippen followed at his heels.

"Rippen, down," Diego ordered after Rippen jumped on Mom while she set her overnight bag on the chair.

"It's okay," she said, scratching Rippen behind the ears. "He's been a good car dog all day." Mom was pretty chill for someone who hated pets.

Diego sat down on the bed beside me. "Are you hungry?" he asked.

I shook my head. I felt Mom's eyes on us.

"Well, I'm hungry," she said. "I'm running over to the Denny's across the street before it closes. I'll bring you something."

After she left and Rippen was busy sniffing around the motel room, Diego said, "Your mom's pretty cool."

"Yeah," I said. But it bothered me to hear him say this.

"She invited me over for dinner at your place when we get back."

"That's weird."

Diego shifted slightly away from me. "Why? Would it be weird for me to be at your house?"

"It just would," I felt there was this huge thing standing between Diego and me, and I knew it was all coming from me.

"What do you mean," he asked.

"You've been a great friend," I said. He winced but I continued, "especially this week, with this stupid trip and all."

"It wasn't stupid. I had a great time with you. I mean, even with all the chaos. Tessa, I just want to be with you."

I couldn't deny that hearing those words softened something inside me, but I shoved it down until I felt my hard, steely edges return. "I can't do that," I said.

"Why? I don't believe you don't care about me."

"Well, too bad," I snapped, shifting the position of my cast. "It doesn't matter what you believe."

"Don't do this."

"I don't want to be with you." I said, but of course I was lying.

"Tessa, we can get through whatever this is together."

"That's where you're wrong. Not together. I don't want to be together with you." I hoped the tone of my voice was convincing.

He reached for my hand. "I don't think you mean it."

"Why do you think you can tell me what I feel?" I shouted. If my leg wasn't throbbing, I would have jumped up and stomped toward the door.

Diego stood up. "Okay, fine. You want your space; you can have it." He opened the door. "Come on, Rippen."

Rippen jumped to his feet and followed Diego out the door. I turned away and, when I heard the door close, I dropped my head and it hit hard against the headboard.

The next day, Mom and I dropped Diego at his truck. It had been the quietest five hours of my life, the drive from Boise to La Grande. Diego sketched in his book almost the entire time, while I alternated between staring at vacant hillsides that we never seemed to pass and sleeping with my head against the seatback. I pretended I was still asleep when Diego and Rippen climbed out of the car. Mom stepped out and they spoke for a few minutes, then I heard his truck engine start and he drove away.

We arrived back at our apartment after dark. Mom tried to help me with my crutches, but I waved her off. I hobbled unassisted to my room. I'd left for Bryant in a rush, leaving my bed unmade and a sweater that didn't fit lying on the floor. The sweater was now hanging in my closet, and someone had made my bed. I noticed a new pillowcase too. My desk was tidy, and a small, unlit candle made the room smell of pine trees. I felt a wave of guilt for leaving Mom like I did and all the worry I'd caused. When would I start getting things right? Mom knocked on my door and, without waiting for a response, she walked in. "We need to talk," she said.

"Mom, it doesn't matter."

She sat down in my desk chair. "Everything you are doing matters. Are you kidding me? Everything you just did matters."

"Mom, I'm exhausted."

"We're both tired." She reached over and clasped my arm gently. "I won't go back to school if you're not ready for that."

"Oh my god, Mom, my leaving had nothing to do with that."

"But you left right after we talked about me going to college."

"Yeah, I know, but I'd already planned this trip. Mom, I want you to go back to school. Haven't I always said you were smarter than what you're doing? Jeez, Mom, do something for yourself once in a while. Quit rolling over and letting the world screw you."

She froze. I saw the hurt my words had caused, but there was no stopping them from tumbling out of my mouth. I had to let them out because they'd been with me too long and were ripping me apart inside.

"Why?" she seemed to struggle for words or maybe she was struggling to believe that I was her daughter. "Why are you so angry?"

"Because I have to be angry for the both of us!"

She took hold of my arms. "Tessa, we can get past this and get back on track. Refocus on your future."

I yanked my arms away. "My future? You still don't get it. Your focus on my future is just an excuse for you to avoid dealing with yours."

A look of confusion passed across her face. She reached for my hand again, but I pulled it away.

"What do you mean?" she asked.

"Did you ever ask me what I wanted? Maybe I don't want to finish high school."

"Why wouldn't you want-" she began, but I cut her off.

"Maybe I don't want to go to college!"

Mom's eyes filled with tears. "Well, what do you want then?"

"I don't know! I just...I just wanted a minute to figure it out. For myself. It's like you only feel you're a good mother if I'm living the life you have chosen for me." I scraped at my cuticles and choked out the rest of my words. "What if what you want for me isn't what I need? And what if when I really needed you, you weren't there for me. What kind of mothering is that?" I buried my face in my hands.

There was silence in the room, the kind of silence that threatens to swallow everything. I felt my mom's hands and I let them pull mine away from my face. I rested my head on her sleeve.

"I'm sorry," she said. "After your brother -" there was a catch in her voice, "after that, I just couldn't find a way forward. It felt like it was my fault. I couldn't stop thinking about what I could have done differently. If I could have saved him."

"Mom, those things just happen," I said. "It wasn't your fault."

"I knew that in my head, but my heart refused to believe it. The only way I could get myself out of that dark place was you. Yes, I let you do the work for us both and that wasn't fair to you." I felt warm as she held my hands in her lap. "I can do better. Tessa, if you'll give me another chance."

That night, I wrote the last of my apology letters, including one I didn't have to send to court.

Dear Mom,

I'm sorry we couldn't find our way together, and that, like Effby and Samuel, it might be too late for us. You know that dark place you talked about? It's where I am right now and where I've been since the day of the fire. It's too big for me to see through. I thought I might figure things out, but the opposite has happened. Maybe this is how you felt after you came home from the hospital. You asked me to give you another chance, but I don't know if I can give myself another chance.

I love you Mom.

Tessa

I placed this letter with the others. The box was so full now, letters spilled out onto the floor.

The next day, I knew I had to see Effby. Regina picked me up since I couldn't drive. She peppered me with questions all the way to Morningstar, but I gave her only short, curt responses until she said, "Well alright then," and stopped asking questions.

"Why are you acting weird?" She asked as she helped me out of the car. I didn't have an answer.

Effby was sitting by the window when I hobbled in, doing a crossword puzzle. It was cold outside, but clear, and a patch of sunlight blazed straight onto her red hair. As I sat down across from her, I felt the sun's warmth coming through the glass.

Effby eyed my leg. "Did my son kick you in the shins?"

"I fell chasing a dumb dog."

"Maybe you shouldn't chase after stupid things."

I'm sorry, Effby." I said, "I shouldn't have gone."

She folded the newspaper and let it drop into her lap. Outside the window, a squirrel chased another squirrel up the old tree where I'd hung Effby's hummingbird feeder.

"How did he look?" she asked quietly.

She seemed older than when I'd left, less feisty. "Good," I said, "he looked good."

"I knew he wouldn't talk to me. Some things can't be forgiven."

"I know," I said. And I felt the weight of that knowing in my whole being.

"No, you don't," she said simply. "You think you do, because you lit that fire, but you don't know. He would have forgiven me for the car crash. But I pushed him away after that." She wiped her eyes with a trembling hand. "Poor little guy. He tried, but I had so much shame. I couldn't forgive myself. I couldn't let him close. And that," she shook her head slowly, "was my failure. He could forgive me for causing his sister's death, but he couldn't forgive me for pushing him away. For giving up on him when he had so much to live for. And I don't blame him."

"I thought I could fix it," I said.

"Not this. Sometimes you can't go back. Can't fix things. You can't undo what's been done."

"Exactly."

She smacked my arm with the folded newspaper. "No, you thick-headed girl, listen to me. I've spent the entire rest of my life punishing myself for that mistake. I pushed my son away. I pushed away all my friends. All I did was work. I existed, but I didn't live. That was my punishment."

"Would it have been better to give up?"

"No, it would have been better to live. Really live, not just exist."

My eyes filled with tears and my chest began to heave. "I thought if I could fix this one thing with your son, it would make up for all the other stuff."

I felt Effby's hands as she placed them gingerly on both sides of my head. "You already did a good thing. You took a miserable old woman who pushed everyone and everything away, a miserable, cranky, nasty woman who was just waiting to die, and you brought her back to life. You, Tessa Hilliard, showed me how to live. Now it's your turn to forgive."

"My mom?"

"Yes," she said. "And yourself." She pulled me closer. "Cut this shit out and be the person you want to be."

I let Effby hold me until my tears stopped soaking her shoulder.

"Shit, I don't even want to die anymore." She laughed. "Ironically, I'm probably about to, but for the first time since that accident, I want to live."

"I'm so lonely," I snuffled.

"I know," she said. "And I know you're just waiting for all this miserableness to end. But stop waiting to die and start living. You can't fix everything. So what? Live the way you want. And what's this about being lonely, you have me. That's at least one cranky old bitch to hang out with."

I laid my head on Effby's chest. Her heartbeat was steady. I let her hold me in the warm sunlight until I didn't want to be among the unliving any longer.

THE EMBERS

CHAPTER TWENTY-FIVE

My healing began that day with Effby. Or maybe it started back with Kurt Callahan's testimony or Anmarie Cross' blog. All I know is that the apology letters were written and even though I didn't have every answer to life's problems, I was pretty sure I deserved to live, and I had enough desire to get out of bed each day.

Kurt Callahan never wrote back, but I received no more mystery packages. For that, I was grateful. I did, however, write to Anmarie Cross to let her know there was no Caitlyn. I figured I'd never hear from her again, but her response was swift.

> *Dear Tessa,*
>
> *I am trying to be angry with you. But I was 17 once too, and I wasn't perfect. You were right. If I'd known your identity, I probably wouldn't have answered your emails. So, if I'm honest, I'm glad you did.*
>
> *What's done is done, and our lives (yours, mine, and so many others), are different now. But they're not over. Just different. One incident, as horrible as it was, doesn't define you, just like my divorce didn't define me. So, let's move on, shall we? I'm leaving soon for a trip—going hiking through the Everglades in Florida. Time to get this body into shape again—lol. In the meantime, if you'd like to get together for a cup of tea or something, let me know.*
>
> *Anmarie Cross*

Mom started seeing a therapist once a week. Then she found me a therapist, so I went once a week as well. At first, I thought it was stupid, but after a few visits I began to look forward to it. Not to the session specifically, but to the end when I walked out of the office feeling a little less weight on my shoulders. Eventually, that little embroidered duck didn't hurt so bad. And the apology box in my closet felt a little less daunting and my wounded cuticles were no longer scabby.

One day, as I was heating olive oil in a pan to sauté garlic and onions, my phone rang and I saw Dad's number. I'd been avoiding his calls, but decided the time was right to pick it up.

"Hello?" His voice sounded surprised that I'd answered.

"Hi, Dad."

"What's up? How are you?"

"Dad, I'm glad you called, we need to talk."

There was a pause. "Okay."

"I need to ask you," I fumbled for words, but then took a breath as my therapist had suggested I do. "Why did you screw Mom so badly in the divorce?" I held the phone with one hand and pushed olive oil around in the pan with a spatula in the other. I turned the heat down.

When he finally spoke, his voice was not the Tom's Food Truck voice. It was small and a little strangled. "Maybe we should talk about this in person."

"No, Dad, I need to know now."

"Hey, there are two sides to every story," he said. "Your mom had totally shut down on me. I was hurting too, and I needed her."

"You didn't need her. You just needed work. And you left us both and then took everything."

"Your mom agreed to the terms."

"Because she was broken, Dad!" I said, feeling years of anger rising to a boil. "Because her heart was broken! And what about me? I mean, you've made it clear I don't fit with your perfect little TV world."

I let him fumble for a reply, but, in my mind, there was no good explanation. He finally choked out, "I know I made mistakes. I'm trying to make up for them."

"I'm not seeing it," I replied. "But you'd better figure it out because I don't want to talk with you until you do."

When I hung up the phone, I turned the heat back up and released a long breath. I knew Dad loved me, but he was as big a mess as anyone. He needed to make things right with Mom, and he needed to make things right with me.

Turns out, Mom wasn't waiting for him to figure anything out. After one of my therapy sessions, I came home to find Mom watching Netflix. My dad was judging a food truck competition, taking small bites of a fried crepe while three workers waited pensively in the background for his judgment.

"What are you doing?" I asked, tossing my jacket on the couch. "Why are you watching this?"

Mom paused the show. "When's the last time you talked with your dad?" she asked.

"I don't know. A couple weeks, I guess."

"You were right," she said.

I sat beside her. "Right about what?"

"To be angry. I let you take that on for me. Maybe I couldn't take it on myself. Not then." She shut off the TV. "But I can now. I have an appointment with Tanesha next week. I'm going after increased alimony and child support." She squeezed my arm. "I just wanted you to know."

"Good for you, Mom," I hugged her, "that's great."

It was a small shift, like a quiet breeze blowing through the early hours of the morning and bringing a whiff of the approaching season. Change was coming, even if I couldn't see it yet, and I felt like it was taking me with it. Things from the past could never be undone, and some could never be fixed, but Mom and I could make changes and find a new way of moving into the future together.

I volunteered at Morningstar every day, and Mom stopped by at least once every few days. As winter stretched into spring and after my cast was removed, she and I walked Effby around the grounds, watching green shoots and soft pussy willow buds emerging from their cold sleep. Effby and I passed the afternoons playing Scrabble and listening to *Crime Maven* podcasts. Mom quit talking about how I needed to get back on track. She still refused to cook and instead brought home Chinese food or Thai or pizza to give me a break from the kitchen. We brought Effby home for dinner once a week, setting her up on the couch with her oxygen tank to watch old episodes of *Criminal Minds*. Mom didn't ask me about my goals anymore, and to be honest I didn't have any; but it didn't seem to be a problem. At least not right now.

Mom did something that surprised me, probably more than any other changes she made, she came home with a dog. Luna was a medium-sized mutt with dark curly hair that clung to the carpet and sofa and especially Mom's white pants. She was timid at first, hiding when Diego or Effby came to visit, but eventually she settled. She was Mom's dog, no question about it, and every morning through the crack in Mom's bedroom door I'd see Luna sprawled on the bed next to Mom.

Over time, Effby became less mobile, played less Scrabble, and spent more time in bed watching for signs the hummingbirds had returned. When Rene and Emily came for a visit, Emily pulled out all the stops. She pirouetted around Effby's room and demonstrated her favorite dance routines. I framed photos of those visits, Effby, Rene and Emily together, and placed them on Effby's bookshelves beside the paintings we'd made on one of our first Morningstar outings together.

I had coffee with Anmarie Cross one day and it wasn't even that weird.

"I'm not one of those people who believe that everything happens for a reason," she'd said to me. "But I do think that when some doors close, others open. It's time for me to travel again. And," she tapped her finger on the table between us, "it's time for you to see what doors are open for you."

Bit by bit, piece by piece, I started creating a life that wasn't anything like what it had been, but also wasn't the dead-end I made the apology box out to be. One day, I felt strong enough to remove my violin from its case. I held it to my chin. The strings under my fingertips felt familiar, although my calluses had softened.

Once I'd tuned the pegs to their proper positions, I drew the bow across the strings. It made a dull sound, but one full of strength and promise. I played for an hour until my arm ached and my fingers were red and raw. I didn't follow any of my old music but instead played wild, chaotic melodies. They made no sense, but they were free and wonderful, and they inspired me to get rid of the apology box.

By late May, the hummingbirds had returned. Two hovered outside Effby's window, drinking from her feeder and seeming to warm themselves in the sunshine. "Welcome back, you little buggers," Effby said from her bed, reaching a frail hand out as if to invite them inside. They took no notice of her, but I could tell this was a big moment for Effby.

She died not long after that, on a day when the sun streamed through the windows of Morningstar and in the forest fresh growth thirsted for rain. My mom, Regina, Sal, and I were with her when she passed. I wondered what hell she'd be raising in the afterlife. It was just over a year since my fire had changed hundreds of lives, including my own, but meeting Effby had changed me too, in ways I was just beginning to understand.

I went back to school for my G.E.D. I enrolled in the same community college where Mom was taking accounting classes, but in the certified nursing assistance program. Between classes, I'd run into Pablo, who was taking his prerequisites for a transfer degree.

After achieving my certification, I went to work at Morningstar, no longer a volunteer but making an actual income. Kathy insisted on giving me the new hire orientation, but I didn't care. That was her job, and I was just happy to have mine. I paid rent and worked down the fines I'd resolved to be paying for the rest of my life, but I tried not to think about that. The judge had already dismissed all remaining community service hours and lowered my fees to a couple hundred dollars a month. It was a lot to pay from my meager paycheck, but it wasn't impossible. Plus, I was no longer on probation.

After a year of work, and a month after we'd helped Pablo move into an apartment in Portland where he was attending university, Diego and I said goodbye to my mom. We'd packed my Subaru to the ceiling with our clothes, a few blankets, Diego's sketchbooks, and my violin. Regina's daughter had given me a Christmas train that dangled from the rear-view mirror.

Rippen turned in excited circles in the backseat, evidently feeling the same eager anticipation for the journey Diego and I shared. We were going south to find work and adventure. Anmarie Cross had suggested I write a blog about it. We hugged Mom and, with packages of Nutter Butters and Oreos between us, Diego drove us out of Elmsville.

We followed the road through the forest until we reached the highway. As I rested my head half out the window, sunshine bathed my face. I could smell the woods, the same woods my fire devastated, and they smelled of possibility. Seedlings were growing taller, and underbrush had become thicker. Nature was doing its job, and I knew it would take many years before these scorched woods would recover, but life was moving on.

"Take this turn," I shouted, pointing at an upcoming side road.

"Okay," he glanced at me sideways. I guided him further up the mountain, following narrow roads deeper into the forests.

"Pull over here," I said, pointing to a wide spot along the roadside.

"What's up?" Diego asked, shifting the car into park.

"Just something I need to do." I reached over, cupping his cheek in my hand. "I'll just be a minute, ok?"

He squeezed my hand lightly. "Sure."

I walked for about fifteen minutes, passing an older couple with walking sticks, then left the trail and pushed my way through the underbrush. Dry needles and sticks snapped under my shoes. I reached my hand out and brushed the tops of bright green fern fronds until I found the tree I was looking for.

I'm not sure why I wanted to visit this tree. I'd already dealt with my apology box. Diego and I together. Last April. We'd driven into the woods and stopped at a small picnic area with a fire pit. We had the place to ourselves. Diego lit a fire, and I hauled the shoebox of letters from the back of my car. I fed the fire one letter at a time and wondered if the recipients felt any better for having received them. I hoped so. Some of my earlier letters were meaningless, just me apologizing because I had to. But I'd rewritten those. Sitting beside the fire, I thought of the ravaged forest and homes, the suffering of alpacas, horses, and countless woodland creatures. I thought of restaurants and sports gear stores forced to close. I thought of Veronica from the diner and the others whose lives I changed forever. Then I took a deep breath and decided I would forgive that girl who'd thrown the firecracker. I would forgive myself.

For a long while we sat together, Diego, the forest and me, not saying anything. When the flames had burned through the last letter, I crushed the box and shoved it into the flames. It folded in on itself, turning from orange to red, like Effby's moon, and then blue before joining the pile of grey ash. The rain that had been falling all day turned from a slow drizzle to a torrential downpour and put the fire out. Even with the rain, I didn't want to leave. I pushed my hood back and let the heavy drops wash over me.

Now, standing in the shadow of this old tree, I felt humbled. Its scar reached nearly its entire height, wrapping part way around the thick trunk. Partially covered in soft moss, I knew the scar would never disappear. New leaves fluttered from branches high above my head as dappled sunlight found its way through. I spotted a beetle plodding along the trunk. A nearby bird whistled a sweet tune and a sharp 'rat-a-tat-tat,' let me know there was a woodpecker close by.

I placed one hand on the burned gash and ran my fingertips across the blackened bark. The thing about colossal screw ups is not one thing or another. Like someone isn't just a deviant. They're one tree standing in a vast forest, like there's lots of factors behind one bad decision. My colossal screw up, the one that wounded this tree and scarred an entire community, that was my fault. I accept that. But it wasn't the end for this tree, and it's not the end for me.

Listening to the sounds of the burgeoning forest rising around me felt a little like Steinhardt finding the miracle of Bach's *Chaconne*. I didn't understand how this tree was healing, but it was. So was the rest of the forest, and the people of my town, and my mother. And so was I.

I placed one hand on my heart and made a promise to myself in the presence of that unshakable tree: no matter how many mistakes I made in life, I would never again give up trying to live up to the name my mother gave me, Possibility.

ACKNOWLEDGEMENTS

When I first started writing in earnest, with the hope to publish, writing was a very solitary endeavor. What I've learned over the years is that writing continues to be a solitary endeavor and creating something really good involves a small community. Finding a path to publication involves an even broader community. I am grateful to so many for helping this book come to life.

First, a huge thank you to Cynthia Huijgens at Idle Time Press for taking a chance on this book and for her ongoing support and encouragement during the writing and revision process. Thanks to Diane Zinna for helping me build my writing community through AWP's Writer to Writer Mentor program. Gratitude to my Writer to Writer colleagues for their friendship and support.

Thanks also to Shanna McNair and Scott Wolven from The Writers Hotel for their thorough reading and recommendations and all my Writers Hotel colleagues for their friendship, encouragement and sometimes, commiseration. Julie Carpenter, Scott Branks, Lyndsie Clark and Diane Oatley. You rock!

Appreciation and gratitude to my writing mentor and friend, John Domini, and my AWP mentor, Ken Waldman. J.R. Estes, without our writing vacations this book wouldn't have come to be. Thanks also to Nancy Pyburn, with whom I first shared this story when it was just a tiny seed of an idea.

Finally, eternal love and gratitude to my husband, Heath, and my boys, Logan and Elijah for their never-ending support and understanding.

AUTHOR'S NOTE ON MENTAL HEALTH

The Apology Box is a story of a young woman who struggles with self-harm issues. Even though it is a work of fiction, self-harm is a real issue, and it affects teenagers and adults. It can be a one-time event, or ongoing. For many, like Tessa, it's a way of coping with intense emotional pain, anger and frustration. Although self-harm is not necessarily connected to suicidal ideation, in this story, Tessa's depression does push her to the brink.

Our society faces a huge challenge when it comes to suicide. According to the National Institute of Mental Health, in 2019, death by suicide was the 2nd ranking cause of death for young people between the ages of 15 and 24. Just like Tessa, it's not always easy to tell when someone is struggling. However, there are signs and symptoms. Some of those include withdrawing from friends or family, using drugs or alcohol more frequently, eating or sleeping more frequently, or taking dangerous risks.

If you are concerned about someone who shows any of these signs, you can be a friend to them by listening without judgement and being there for them, but also by connecting them with professionals who can help. Two quick ways to connect are the National Suicide Prevention hotline at 1-800-273-TALK (8255), or text the Crisis Text Line at 741741.

Many of the symptoms Tessa and her mother exhibit in *The Apology Box*, such as sleeping more than usual, isolating themselves, and not keeping up with personal hygiene, are common symptoms for depression. If you are concerned you may be experiencing depression, talk with an adult you trust. Therapy can be a healing experience that guides you through difficult times. I spent two years in therapy while in graduate school and have become healthier and stronger for it. Together, let's keep ourselves and each other safe and healthy so we can live our lives to the fullest and achieve our possibilities.

ABOUT THE AUTHOR

Naomi Ulsted writes young adult fiction and memoir. Her work has been published in *Narratively*, *The Forge*, and *Mud Season Review*, among others. She was the recipient of an Oregon Literary Arts fellowship in 2017 and has been awarded scholarships to attend The Writers Hotel and Martha's Vineyard Institute of Creative Writing. She's a member of SCBWI, Willamette Writers and AWP. Naomi lives on the Oregon coast with her husband and two boys.

ABOUT THE PUBLISHER

We love books, you love books!

The book industry uses a lot of energy and generates an incredible amount of waste. To help reduce waste, Idle Time Press is using print-on-demand. If five books are ordered, then five books are printed, if one book is ordered, one book is printed. This means a delay between the day you place your order and the day you receive your book – but maybe that's okay. You can still order Idle Time Press books through your local bookstore, and we encourage you to do so.

As our books spend more time in your hands and their pages become dog eared and smeared with jam, we hope you'll continue to love them as if they were new. And please, when you're ready to close our covers for the last time, we hope you'll pass them along to someone who loves books as much as we do.

Idle Time Press is a small independent publisher of books for young readers. Its 2020 debut collection included rhyming picture book *Polar Bear and the UFO* and middle grade action-thriller *Boy Between Worlds: The Cabinet of Curiosities*. For more titles, visit us at www.idletimepres.com.

We love book reviews too!

Thanks for picking up this copy of *The Apology Box* by Naomi Ulsted. Please leave a review at Goodreads, Amazon, LibraryThing, BookBub or wherever you share book news.

Lightning Source UK Ltd.
Milton Keynes UK
UKHW022256051121
393429UK00007B/154

9 781737 262992